River River

Friend of the wild and lonely

Jean Louise Allen

This is a work of fiction. The idea for this book had its origin in the tiny fragments of oral history told me by the old people of my younger years. The characters are fictitious and are not intended to represent any persons. Some politicians or historical figures of the period are referred to but are not quoted. Kotare Creek and the town of Sedgely are also figments of my imagination. If the topography were suitable, they would be somewhere between Ruawai and the Otamatea River on the banks of Northern Wairoa River, New Zealand.

To purchase please email pakiti@xtra.co.nz
Telephone +64 9 473 5910

First published in New Zealand in 2012 by AM Publishing New Zealand, www.ampublishingnz.com, for Flatty Publishing
Cover painting: Lillian Fromont
Cover design: Bev Robitai
Author photo: Angela van Vliet Photography, Auckland, NZ

ISBN 978-0-473-20748-9

Other works by Jean Louise Allen:
Bitty by the River
River at War
The Little Person children's series

Dedication

For my husband Jim and my children – Sharon, Rosalie, Kathy and Terry – and to my late mother and father, Roy Forrester and Bessie (née Roberts), who kept my feet on the ground while giving me the wings to fly.

River river raupo rye
I see the sun
I see the sky
I see kotare
flying by.

Acknowledgements

My manuscript received a Creative New Zealand/ New Zealand Society of Authors appraisal by Elizabeth Smithers, for which I am most grateful.

Special thanks go to all my teachers, especially my sixth form teacher, the late Sister Mary Veronica. Thanks also to Adrienne Morris for her work on the first edition, and Bev Robitai for her work on the second.

Rae McGregor, NZSA member, critiqued the manuscript as it neared its last stages.

I also wish to thank my husband Jim for his constant support in the writing of this book, the New Zealand Society of Authors (PEN NZ Inc.), my Mairangi Writers friends, John Watson for doing the initial edit, friend Julie Nilson, 'speller extraordinaire', and many others who also encouraged me.

Kaipara Waters, you will ever hold that special piece of my heart.

Northern Wairoa River – I salute you!

Prologue

The memory of that day would come alive in him at odd moments like a recurring dream.

1912

In the week of his fifteenth birthday in January 1912 his father sent him upriver from Helensville to do a small job for a builder at Kotare Creek, a little north of Sedgely. He went by steamer. His father needed to use their work launch that day or Caleb would have reached the place an hour earlier.

The road from the wharf was dry and dusty, and being overhot he looked for a shortcut.

He climbed a fence and walked a narrow cattle track that wandered through a paddock of high summer grass. Had he been walking any faster he would have stood on the girl.

Head bent, intent on what she was doing, she didn't move when he jerked to a stop – a fair child, with her long, summer-bleached hair lifting in the breeze and shining white in the sun. The wild grasses swam tall around her – their stemmed heads bending, arching, enfolding – while she sat crossed-legged peeling a Scotch thistle.

"Hello," he said. "Is there a building shed near here?" She looked up. Her eyes were a deep, purple-blue – almost the shade of the silk thistle hair she was removing so delicately so as not to prick her fingers – and they searched his face, then withdrew. She nodded the direction.

Only then did he hear the faint sound of a man at work with wood. He stood up on an old log and saw above the shimmering rye grasses the roof of a shed not far down the slope on the river's edge. He also saw a house gate further up the paddock and thought, *Had I walked further along the road and come in that way I would have found the shed for myself and missed the phantom child.* The idea of a phantom child shocked him, and he jumped down from the log ready to mutter his thanks and move on, when ... he stilled.

At the same time as he wanted to leave, something new in him wanted to stay. He became a bit impatient. He considered he had moved ahead of children, away from childish things. He knew what she was doing with the thistle. He had done the same thing many times. Saliva flowed into his mouth. He could almost taste the nut to which the girl was making her way through those prickly green leaves.

And again that something new in him made him conscious of the picture before him – conscious of a beauty he'd not encountered before. Children, in his vast experience, moved in groups. They were noisy, sulky, cheeky – sometimes frightened. This girl looked as if she had grown there, alone.

"Are you Uriah's daughter?"

She nodded but did not look up. White lashes rested on childish cheeks, like half-winged moths. Ripe lips pursed in unaffected concentration. It all seemed so natural, yet unnatural – hauntingly unnatural.

He was a little annoyed. No child had a right to seem so regal in the middle of paspalum and rye. No child had the right to ignore an adult – even a rather young adult such as himself. Nevertheless a new gentleness stopped him from intruding too harshly ... and he wanted to see her eyes once more.

"How old are you?" his question soft.

"Twelve."

She sighed the word, stood with a long-grass movement and held the precious nut out to him – a lazy gift to bridge the years. A gift that spoke of unutterable, never to be regained pleasures.

"What's your name?" he asked as he opened his hand. At last her eyes lifted, held his and he felt drawn into innocence and knowledge, into the timelessness of summer skies.

"Iona," she told him, her fingers warm as she placed the thistle core into his overboned, not-quite-man hand.

"Iona Annabel Anderson-Keyes," fingers caressing, arms back-trailing the high grasses into which she disappeared.

All he could hear was the rhyme she chanted over and over ...

River river raupo rye
I see the sun
I see the sky
I see the silvereye flying by ...

... until he could no longer hear her; until he saw only the faint aura of her hair above the grass-tops shiver as she moved, within her own secluded freedom, towards a stand of manuka and ponga and flax that grew beside her river.

Chapter One

1913

Iona crept onto the porch and waited. The silence of the house settled on her like the night. She inched through the front door and, muttering under her breath, glided down the hall and into the kitchen where she made straight for the pantry. "Where can mother be? I usually hear her breathing even if she's upstairs."

"Where have you been, Iona?" her mother shouted down.

"Blow, she *is* home."

"Iona! I know you're in the kitchen. You leave those plums alone. It's nearly dinner time."

"It is not. It's two hours away. Why does she pick, pick, pick all the time?"

"Iona!?"

In a flash Iona ripped off her cardigan, jammed the plums and a crust of bread into the sleeves, tied them together and tiptoed outside. "Rotten! She's rotten to the core ... like a rotten plum ... But plums don't have cores; their hearts are made of stone. Like hers."

Thoughts racing, she hurried on the balls of her feet down the front drive and out across the dusty road to the hay paddock. At a gap in the fence she dropped to the ground. Wriggling, squirming and pushing, she soon lay inside the fence. "Here is not safe."

She began to crawl along the inside of the fence. At the corner of the paddock she relaxed her body and rolled into the dry floodwater drain. Immediately she sat up, bent over and gorged on the fruit. Not a red drop fell on her clothing. A crack ran right up the side of the drain, and she crammed the plum stones well into the earth. "Got rid of the evidence, Mother!" she jested.

One hand lifted above the edge of the ditch, yanked out a handful of buttercup grass then disappeared again. She cleaned her hands and face. Is it safe to get out? Listen. She turned into a statue, just like their cat Crooner. She had learnt to copy the clever little hunter.

No human sounds. Good!

She climbed out, bent low and began to move through the ripe hay towards the hill. A patch of wild cape gooseberries grew near a deserted shack up there. They should be ripe now, and mushed up they made a dry crust worth eating. There, also, dribbled a freshwater spring. It would give enough water, even in summer, to quench her thirst. Of course, she'd be in trouble. Her mother could make trouble out of a saint's smile. She'd be sent to bed without any dinner, but at least she wouldn't be too hungry through the night.

"'Trouble, trouble, you're nothing but trouble.' That's what my mother says to me," she sang in a whispery voice, then stopped.

A kereru swished heavily above her into the old puriri tree. She loved these big native pigeon. Their white tummies made the dark green and copper feathers of their cloak shimmer and shine.

She became as still as the lizard beside her foot while she watched the handsome pair eat their fill of the red berries.

"Ona?"

Such a tiny whisper Teddy had.

"Iona! I got some cold spud and a lamb chop."

"Thanks, Teddy. Now go back to bed. If Mother wakes, you'll be in trouble too."

"Don't care, Ona. Ma's nasty to you. Dad told her you were on time but she said no."

"I'm all right, Teddy, but thank you. I am a bit hungry."

"Sorry I only had my hanky to wrap it in."

"You're a good kid, little brother. Now get back to your bedroom, quietly."

The boy bent and gave her a cuddle. She patted his bony back, letting him stay resting on her shoulder for a few seconds, then gently pushed him away. Things would be so much worse if their mother caught him giving her food from his own plate.

God knows what's been on this handkerchief. Never mind. I'm too hungry to care.

The cold, greasy food went down a treat. When she'd finished she wiped her mouth with the disgusting lump of rag and stuffed it under her mattress.

"I'll have to chuck that in the river tomorrow without Her Highness seeing."

All the same, she smiled at the March moon and fell asleep now that her belly didn't complain.

Her father had completed a furniture order, and today it would go down to Batley to the owners. Iona had already drawn the pieces: a large dining table with six chairs and a tall hutch dresser to match, all handcrafted in golden kauri. They stood, crated and ready on the concrete apron in front of the work shed waiting for the tide to come far enough up the ramp to make their loading easy.

Uncle Toi Tira and Ani – who was the same age as Iona – had come down to catch a ride with 'Baldy' Craig, the launch owner.

The girls were splashing around the shallows in the dinghy when Uncle Toi called, "Hoihoi!"

So they quietly rowed the boat ashore. Iona tied it to a post while Ani got out and tiptoed over to her father. Iona could not hear what her uncle whispered to his daughter, but she knew he would be telling her the Maori name for a bird he could see.

By the time Iona crept over, Uncle Toi had seen a second bird. "Kotare," he whispered.

"Kotare," murmured Ani.

"Kotare," imitated Iona. She knew the Maori name for the kingfisher bird. She practised with Ani because she wanted to learn the correct pronunciation. Many kingfisher came to Kotare Creek and sat on the tops of cabbage trees or posts to watch for tiny fish for their dinner. Iona loved the sound of the Maori language and had been gradually learning birds' names through the skipping rhyme she and Ani had made up.

Once there were no more birds about, Uncle Toi nodded to them to go off and play. The girls ran to the shed to get Iona's skipping rope. On the hard clay by the apron landing, Iona tied one end of the rope to an iron ring on the wall of the shed, and the girls took turns turning the other end so that one of them could skip and do the actions to their song.

Ani skipped first, singing the rhyme Iona had made up.

"River river raupo rye
I see the sun
I see the sky
I see kotare
Sitting up high
River river raupo rye."

And when she had finished she took the turning end and Iona had her skip. They knew many birds' names now and were about to start sing the tauhou verse when Uriah called, "Time to stop now, girls. Barge coming in!"

The girls ran to put the rope away and sat on the edge of the ramp where they dangled their legs and waited.

They knew not to get in the men's way when work like this took place. Both of them knew Sybil never came here. She considered it 'not a place for ladies' and had little knowledge of the amount of time Iona spent with her father. Ani liked it too. She had been once to the house and would not go again. Sybil had been rude about her dress, which was too long, being a hand-me-down from her older sister.

"That lady doesn't like me, and I don't like that lady," she told Iona that first day. At just five years old and the youngest of Toi's large family, she knew the sound of prejudice.

"Good day, Baldy!" Uriah called as the launch approached.

The riverman nodded. Every part of him honed in on the manoeuvre he was about to begin. The engines revved, the launch turned, the barge swung, and Baldy put both boat and barge through a series of acrobatic turns that neatly placed the barge up the ramp in the exact position needed for loading the crates.

Baldy's son took over the wheel. The engine held the boat in place. Her father and Uncle Toi had already levered the crates onto Uriah's special trolleys, and now they helped Baldy put heavy planks from the barge to the front of the first crate. The rolling, the pushing and the heaving began. This time it didn't take long. Everything seemed to go in the right place, and Baldy, with his huge, powerful muscles, made the loading easier.

Uncle Toi lifted Ani on the barge. She scrambled up to the other end and then onto the stern of the launch. The men shook hands. Uncle Toi climbed aboard, and off went the furniture to its new home.

"Lucky thing," said Iona, thinking of the lovely trip Ani would have.

"You've had plenty of furniture trips, girl," Uriah remarked, a little sternly.

"Sorry, Father." She knew he was right but she still wished she could be there with Ani, riding the river and feeling the wind in her face.

It had been an icy day at school, and Iona felt relieved she didn't have to walk the river road again for a couple of weeks. Staying inside with Mother for the holidays didn't appeal either. She whipped round the front door and started up the staircase, eager to have another look at her prize.

"What's that you're trying to hide, my girl?"

"It's just schoolwork," she threw over her shoulder and kept climbing.

When a long shadow fell on her she knew it was her father. Even though she would be thirteen in four months her dad still towered over her – and most other people.

"Let me have a look, Iona."

There was no dodging him, so she handed over the package that wouldn't fit in her case and watched him unwrap the parcel, feeling her mother's eyes drilling into her back. At last he finished reading the card.

"You've done very well, my dear, to attain such high marks in arithmetic. Do you enjoy the subject?"

"Yes, Father, I do."

"Why do you enjoy it?"

"I think because numbers are predictable."

"What's she done now?"

"Our daughter, Sybil, has brought home a special certificate in arithmetic from her teacher. It seems Iona is so far ahead of the other pupils Miss Taylor wants to start teaching her mathematics in the new school session."

"Well, that's very fine, Uriah," Sybil's voice slid towards them like a woman's hand over satin, "but really, I thought she would leave school at the end of this year. I mean, what good will mathematics be to the girl when she's a wife and mother?"

"We discussed that. She is to continue her education for two more years, Sybil."

Father and daughter looked at each other. With a hint of a bow, Uriah moved sideways to let the girl pass, and as she did, he whispered, "And a very nice compass set in that leather pouch. Good work."

Iona's cheeks turned pink with pleasure. Her father's praises were few and far between. Her mother, though, had not finished with the subject.

"Have you finished drawing that spray of pansies for me, Iona? I'm ready to embroider the new tray cloth. She's much better at drawing, you know, Uriah. Such an asset in a young lady, sketching, don't you think?"

Iona, listening from the top of the stairs, thought she saw her father smile as he made for the back door. Was he thinking of her box of sketches in his work shed? The drawings of his furniture before it went away; sketches of the river birds she had been doing since before she went to school. Drawings her mother didn't approve of then and wouldn't now. One day she would get away from her mother. One day she'd be free.

Chapter Two

1914

Three months after his seventeenth birthday, Caleb McKay boarded a train out of Helensville. He found a seat by the window, swung his leather Gladstone bag up into the luggage rack and settled down. He was glad to get this seat. In the aisle seats, people bumped against your shoulders or knocked your elbows as they moved up and down the carriage.

No one saw him off. That was the way he wanted it, so he left the window closed. He felt shut away behind the dirt-stained glass and welcomed that. He began to unwind, pleased he'd booked first class. These new padded seats were comfortable – not like the old wooden benches. Stretching his legs out, he loosened his tie and undid the top button of his shirt.

He slipped his fob watch out of his waistcoat pocket and flicked the lid. Five minutes to go. The carriage was filling up but no one had sat next to him yet, and he hoped no one would. *Hot damn!* he thought, *I'm out of here at last!* He reached for his tobacco tin and got out one of the roll-your-owns he'd fixed up the night before.

One quick strike of the wax match and it was alight. He inhaled, leant back and relaxed.

"Caleb – Caleb come back!" He sat up. Surely not mother! She wouldn't. Not when he'd asked her not to come? Last night's scene flashed at him from the glass. Then he laughed.

Outside, on the now near-empty platform, a young mother ran after her small son. The boy was streaming towards the engine, his face alive with excitement. Bright red curls bounced and shone, turning his head into a miniature sun. Then the arm of a uniformed figure swooped down, and the child swam in mid-air, held by his braces.

"Billy's got you safe, boy!" Caleb grinned to himself as he slumped back into his seat.

Old Bill Basely, guard on this line for more years than people wanted to remember, had an easy smile. Caleb watched him set the boy down, put the small hand into the mother's and in one flowing movement walk away. Billy was to be admired, even envied, for his complete acceptance of his life and for his unfailing good humour.

"I should be more like that, I guess. Oh, what the heck!" His cigarette had gone out. He'd squashed it almost flat when he'd heard his name called. No one used his full name any more – except his mother. Even his father used the shortened 'Cal' though it didn't sit right on his lips. "Caleb," his mother had often told him, "was bold and brave and entered the Promised Land."

But it had made him feel different from the Jacks and the Johns and the Toms – the boys he had played and fought and laughed with when he was a lad. He

10

hoped that little fellow would have more luck than he over his moniker.

He watched the child, now subdued from having his breeches dusted by his mother. As the pair moved out of sight the train's noises changed. The iron beast began to inch forward, steam hissing at the windows. Couplings jerked, chains clanged and rattled. The carriage moved in creaks and judders – then jumps and jolts – until a heavy rhythm was born from all the battling. The township that rested so snugly at the top of the Kaipara River, the sights of his childhood – the busy wharves, the dairy factory and the winding mud creeks – were gone.

By the time they reached the plains the train had quietened to a smoother motion, and Caleb became drowsy from the vibrating drone. He opened the window a little and breathed in the cool air. Off at last. Heading for Auckland – a modern man in a modern machine, fast putting the miles between him and his father – giving him the separation he needed. He had rights to his own life.

He was grateful for the years of apprenticeship worked out in his father's engineering shop. It had been a privileged learning. Though in this last year he had found it harder and harder to have patience with the older man's dominance, which pushed and pressed about him. The old man would never listen to him. He was a first-class engineer, his father, but he lacked the business head needed for today's world. His father would do fine without him. He'd get another young apprentice – the workshop would be a happier place. It was done.

But his mother would have to bear the brunt of all this. She'd been pretty good really. Tight-lipped, trying to understand, her eyes swivelling from one to the other, doing her best to be the peacemaker. She'd been upset last night, he knew. He remembered her firm words – the words that let him leave.

"You were young once, Henry. You had your chance. Now it's the boy's turn. Let him go," and the quiet, "My dear," hardly heard by Caleb but certainly heard by his father. Funny, he couldn't imagine his father ever being young. Strong, yes – but young?

" 'Day, Cal!"

The voice woke him from his brooding. Billy was beside him, swaying slightly in the passage, grinning.

" 'Day, Billy."

Caleb fished out his ticket and handed it over. "Off for a time, are ya, boy?"

"Yep! Making for Rotorua, Bill."

"Ro-to-rua!" He drew the name out like a soft bar of music and ended with a whistle.

"What would you be goin' way down there for, Cal lad?"

Caleb had prepared himself for this. He leaned back, looked up at the old guard and gave out the prepared titbit.

"Well, Billy – there's a chap offering me a foreman's job down that way. Thought I might give it a go. Good experience."

"Yeah, well now. Never thought there was anything much down there but those steamy geezers and sulphur in the breezes."

Caleb gave a short laugh.

12

"Seems they've been putting more launches on the lakes down there. Tourist trips, fishing trips. They're making a fair whack out of rich Americans and such. They need their engines looked after."

Billy was not yet satisfied. "My word, Cal, I didn't know you'd got enough of your papers for that sort of job."

"I haven't – not yet. But this chap's willing to take me on and train me at the same time."

Billy's head, with its black serge cap, nodded. He digested and considered – he wanted another go.

"Must be some bigwig, Cal. He musta took a shine to you, boy, you hardly out of short pants and all."

Caleb felt his neck redden. He lit another smoke and turned to his inquisitor with as easy a smile as Billy himself might produce. "You're right there, Billy. This Mr Randall came up to me at the last regatta. You were there."

"By golly, that were a great day, Cal. You and your lot nearly went and won that big cup. And now you've gone and got a good start down the island, eh? My congratulations to you, boy."

Caleb accepted the coin-greasy hand and had his own pumped up and down. "Thanks, Billy – lot of luck really," though he knew it wasn't. The *Muritai* was a grand little boat, and they had sailed a good race that day, he and his mates.

"Folks keen for ya, were they?"

"Oh, yes, Billy. Good folks my people – real proud."

Billy stared hard into Caleb's eyes and saw only innocence. He'd have thought old Henry McKay would have wanted to hold this boy to him – and to the business. He'd even had 'AND SON' painted above the engineering shop doors. Still, the lad seemed happy, and there'd been no whisper of trouble. He lifted his cap with one hand, pushed back some of the nonexistent hair with the other, and thumped Caleb's shoulder.

"Besta luck, young Cal. Yes, sir – besta luck!"

The guard wove his way down the aisle nodding, smiling, leaving his words 'Besta luck – besta luck', droning on and on in rhythm with the iron wheels, hands bouncing up and down with the pistons while the steam sang 'shu-sha-da … shu-sha-da …' and left rivulets of water gently running down the windows – to drop like a mother's tears.

Chapter Three

1915

Iona would finish school in two days' time – the day of her fifteenth birthday. Her mother, having given in over her further education, insisted that she now required her daughter to help her in the running of the home.

"She has had no training in home management at all. I could do with her help, and she needs to know how to run a house and how to be a gracious hostess."

Uriah felt he had no option but to agree. However, he made one condition, and Iona could hardly believe her luck. "The girl needs a break before she starts labouring away here, Sybil. I will be going off for seven days on a buying trip. There are bedside cabinets to deliver and timber to be bought, if it is good quality. I then need to go on to Auckland to have meetings with two new clients."

Once Sybil realised he would not be moved on the subject she gave in sooner than Iona expected. At least this lull made the house easier to live in for their last two days.

They left before breakfast on the sixteenth. By chance they were out of the house before Sybil had finished her toiletries. Uriah wanted to sail on the top of the tide and have the ebb tide to help the boat move along faster. His old working launch, *The Bell*, had been built on wide lines in the stern, which made it excellent for delivering small furniture to his river customers and carrying timber back on the return trip.

At first Iona sat in the stern with her father where it was warm from the engine. *The Bell*'s motor made a low-pitched harmony, most pleasant for travelling, and the boat smelt of stale water from the bilge, oil fumes, wood resins and many other familiar whiffs and wafts similar to his workshop. An early morning wind played over the water making it choppy, but once the outgoing tide got underway *The Bell* rolled happily along, running down the waves like a child let out to play. Later in the day they crossed the entrance to the Otamatea River and began chugging along a narrower waterway.

Iona went for'ard and lay on her stomach on the warm cabin top. The light of the day had mellowed into soft colours that turned the river into a painting. Each bend appeared before them as an entrance to yet another magic place; each stand of trees took on a softer look than the last, and each unexpected display of sparkling sunlight on the now muddy water seemed to take her further and further into another country altogether.

It seemed no time at all before the engine changed tempo. Iona had trouble getting her wits about her and sat up, blinking, as *The Bell* began her swoop towards a sturdy little jetty. She moved back to the stern to hold the wheel while her father roped the boat to the jetty.

When he came back and turned off the motor her ears were hurting from the sudden stillness.

"Where are we?"

"In the Oruawaru River."

She had never been here before.

"I'll go up and get the buyer while you tidy yourself up." He walked off up a wide track while she stood gaping after him. He had never told her to tidy herself up before.

It took a minute or two before his words sank in. This was business.

In the cabin she straightened out her blouse and tucked it into her skirt. The rusty mirror showed her hair sticking out in all directions. Grabbing her brush she dealt with her wild locks, wiped her face with a dampened facecloth and put on her sandshoes. Voices drifted down the road. When the sound of trolley wheels told her they had reached the wooden platform she went out and stood in the cockpit.

"Iona, this is Mr and Mrs Stanley."

They were a young couple and by their self-conscious smiles probably not long married.

"I'm pleased to meet you, Mr and Mrs Stanley."

She and her father were invited up to the house where he unwrapped the cabinets. The Stanleys were obviously delighted with the one-drawer rimu cupboards.

Once they were back on board and underway Iona remarked on how much the young woman liked his small furniture.

"It's a sprat to catch a mackerel, my dear. That is all they could afford at the moment, but if they like their first pieces, in time they will buy more."

A few minutes later he pulled in to an old landing post. "We need to wait on the tide, Iona. This post makes a good mooring."

Iona held the wheel again while he took a coir line and, lashing it around the pole, tied it to the central cleat of the boat, tethering *The Bell* by her ample waist.

The next day they made a comfortable trip down the Wairoa River, over the heads and up the Kaipara River.

Rain set in as they left Helensville by train for Auckland. Iona felt tired.

Last night the tide had dropped to a shallow draught and the boat, in settling on the mud, had leaned. The coir rope had stretched, but held. Her bunk, however, was on such a slant that every time she drifted off to sleep she rolled into the boat's frame and woke up. Luckily the tide rose enough in the early hours to right the launch, and she had slept soundly for a few hours before dawn. Her father had thought it a great joke. He had made himself comfortable on the cockpit floor and jammed himself in position with extra blankets.

"You get used to it after a few years," he grinned.

The rain continued for the whole of their journey south. It streamed down the windows and blocked any views of the countryside. Once or twice, when she lifted her head, she caught glimpses of movement on the land: a dripping dog working a dripping herd of cows for his master; a saturated horse patiently waiting for the skies to clear. She took the horses' example and became a stoic body in a rollicking train.

In Auckland they stayed in a boarding house. Her bedroom had a grubby, grey view of the backyard of a shop. Her father disappeared for a day – 'meeting with clients'– whom she wondered about when he came back early to 'have a lie down and read a book'. The next few days proved happy. He took her with him when he met some of his varnish and paint suppliers, and they walked the waterfront eating hot fish and chips out of newspaper and chatting with labourers, skippers and anyone who cared to pass the time of day. He also took her on her first visit to the art gallery and made her wander the place while he went off somewhere else. Iona had never had such freedom in the city before. She looked at so many paintings and statues she felt dizzy and realised she was hungry. At that point Uriah turned up again.

"Did you enjoy that?" he gruffed.

"Oh, yes, it is the most wonderful place."

"Good, you should see this sort of art more often. Now let's get a meal."

The next day, they tramped downtown Auckland, called in on business contacts at Freeman's Bay, and climbed a gangway onto a ship tied at the Auckland wharves, where the captain fed her on cheese and pickled onion sandwiches from his private cache while the two men talked. Then they caught the ferry to Devonport. She liked this day the most.

"When I was a boy the Auckland waterfront was quite different, and the boats … well. I loved the old ferry. The *Takapuna*. It had giant paddle wheels and a deck on top of the cabin," he told her as they embarked.

"My father, your grandfather," he reminisced as they left the ferry at Devonport, "would buy me a curly stick of brown toffee from the sweetie pedlar on the wharf."

He always called lollies 'sweeties' – a relic of his own childhood, which he rarely talked about except to say he was brought up in an orphanage after his father was killed in a dray accident. He bought Iona a bag of aniseed balls from 'a wee shop' near the wharf and then proceeded to eat most of them himself, sucking and chomping noisily like an overgrown boy.

They stood at the rails for most of the return trip, watching the ships and tugs plying the harbour. Her father talked animatedly with a fellow passenger about a new invention – the Walsh Brothers' flying boat machine that had been tested over the harbour. In a sudden buzz of excitement they caught a glimpse of the flimsy looking craft.

Iona, surprised by the unexpected shape in the sky, forgot where she was and exclaimed in loud voice, "It looks like a canoe with wings," at which her father laughed wholeheartedly, and she laughed because his laughter was so catching.

On the train trip back to the Kaipara she saw a pair of purple pukeko birds stalking on a creek bank, their red, stilt-like legs high-stepping along in the grass and their heads going up and down, up and down, in awkward grace. Then a long line of toetoe flags, south of the town, fluttered with excitement as the train roared past, and then they were at the station.

The boat trip going home seemed long. The holiday over, she had nothing to anticipate but housework until her father spoke as they came into their own landing. "Your mother has agreed that you have one and a half days a week working on my accounts in the shed. It will save me time and put your number skills to good use. "

Iona could think of nothing to say.

Chapter Four

In the last week of November 1917 two women confronted each other across a kauri table. Maude Kelly, still in her outdoor coat, stood taut, trying hard to control her anger. In her mid-thirties and still attractive, her gentle goodness shone on all who knew her, and all who knew her appreciated her qualities – all, that is, except her elder sister Sybil.

Self-discipline normally sat easily on Maude's shoulders, but not today.

"You can't do this, Sybil."

"What are you referring to, my dear?"

"You know what I mean. The child is too young to enter into this ... this ... union."

"Oh, come now, Maude. Iona is no longer a child. She is a young woman."

"She is not yet seventeen, Sybil!"

"Ah, but she will be on her wedding day. Now, compose yourself, and we will share afternoon tea. How is our dear mother?"

Maude stiffened. "Mother is well cared for as you know, Sybil."

"And have you managed to do something about her rheumatism?"

Caution went to the winds. "For goodness' sake, Sybil, Mother is old, and she has come through a cold winter. Of course she has been rheumatic of late."

"I am merely concerned about her care, Maude."

"I have cared for Mother's every need meticulously – so meticulously that you find no need to visit her except once or twice a year. Don't ask me about our mother, Sybil. Ask yourself about Iona."

"Iona is my responsibility."

"Then why have you pushed her into this marriage? Oh, don't deny it. I know you are behind this. What on earth made you do such a thing? And with Albert Hammond, of all people! Twenty years her senior – and it is said he drinks too much! A skinflint, he is, giving himself airs as if he owned the Bank of New Zealand. You know what he's like, Sybil. You must know. Call it off, for God's sake!"

"Be quiet, Maude! Don't you dare talk to me of goodness' and God's sake – you with your pious airs …"

"What are you talking about, Sybil …?"

"Ah, yes, that's stopped all your fine words, hasn't it, Maude Kelly? Miss Kelly – the town's little saint. Well, you can just get on with your sainthood and keep out of my affairs. This has got nothing whatsoever to do with you. The girl is headstrong …"

"She is not …"

"She is. She's headstrong and sly. YES – and she'll be seventeen in a few days and well legal to marry, and it'll be the best thing for her. She's very lucky to have such a match. Albert will curb her lack of self-control and provide for her at the same time. If you make trouble, Maude, be assured it will be Iona who suffers. So be quiet. Your responsibilities are with our mother. Mine are with my husband and children. You have no say in this matter. Now, pull yourself together and have afternoon tea in a civilised manner."

There was silence. Maude heard the ticking of the clock, the quarter hour chime and knew she had mishandled her visit. Yet she tried once more. "Uriah cannot be in agreement with this."

"Do not underestimate me, my dear. Uriah relinquished his rights to speak years ago – and a rumour can start very easily. Women of my age who have been put upon for years have been known to go into a decline. Weak health, a delicate fever, loosens a woman's tongue. The good ladies who would come to nurse me in my time of trouble are not as close-mouthed as the priests would have them."

"How can you sit there and say such things?"

"I am doing my duty to my daughter as I see fit. Not all marriages are set on romantic nonsense. As Hammond's wife, she will be well housed and have some standing in the town. The other way – well, you know how cruel people can be. I don't think she would remain here long if you caused rumours about her impending marriage."

"Sybil …"

"I will not discuss this any longer, Maude. It is none of your business. You have no right to intervene in my family."

"You could never bring yourself to love her, could you, Sybil?"

"Don't you dare talk to me of love!"

Just for a moment Maude saw her sister's façade begin to slip. The square, plain face hardened ... with what? Anger? Hate? No, surely? Then as the eyes veiled again Maude thought she knew what this planning of Iona's future was all about. Sybil wanted revenge. Poor Iona – and poor Uriah. The past might have been buried but it hadn't been forgotten. Sybil had ever wanted everyone to suffer for her own mistakes.

Love ... she doubted whether this woman had ever known love. Or had she once, long ago, begun to taste its sweetness and found it unreturned? For a fleeting moment Maude pitied her elder sister. Uriah had paid. Sybil had seen to that. Were the facts known, Iona would be called 'a tainted thing'. Things like that had to die out with the generations. Maybe the girl would suffer less away from this house.

"Very well, Sybil. I will not talk to you of love, or duty, or goodness; but ..."

"No more, Maude. Sit down. We have not had afternoon tea."

Maude sat in silence while Sybil went through her lady-of-the-manor procedures. Sandwiches cut in perfect triangles, lemon cake knifed with a first slice – waiting. It was the ordeal Sybil meant it to be. Being the elder, she had always had the power to silence the younger. When she smiled and asked, "More tea, Maude?" Sybil enjoyed twisting the knife a little more.

And Maude Kelly suffered it because she knew no other way.

Sybil had a signal that ended all these skirmishes, so that when Maude saw her sister touch her mouth with the serviette, place it back on the table and twist her wedding ring, Maude rose and moved towards the door. She was shaking from the effort this visit had cost. She felt bewildered and lonely – but most of all she felt a failure. She had not helped the situation.

"You will be at the wedding, of course? People will expect her aunt …"

"Yes, Sybil. I will be there. As you pointed out so clearly – I have no rights."

Chapter Five

Tomorrow she would be seventeen. Tomorrow she would be married. Tomorrow she would belong to someone else. Tomorrow, tomorrow ...

The words flowed on and on like the waters of the river by which she stood. The river bank grass was deep green, summer a million years away, and the spring earth bulged with moisture. Trees hung water-heavy, while the river rushed and roared in sheets of dirty brown. Last week's rains, forced between banks too narrow to contain their volume, were doing their relentless damage. Within an hour it would not be safe here, and she had still to squelch back along the creek to get home.

Iona climbed up on to the flood bank to where the trees would screen her from the house. She was wet and cold, and soon she would have to go home or they would come looking. She had come for the peace of the singing waters. Instead, the battle inside her had succumbed to the night storm, and the last three months darted and licked inside her mind in flames of insight.

Her mother had been relentless in her training. Housework, cooking, washing, flower gardening, shopping for supplies, jam making, preserving – Sybil drilled and criticised and never gave up. Iona fell into bed most nights, asleep on her feet. Only the alarm clock woke her. In the work shed she often fell asleep over her father's accounts, and he did not disturb her rest. Her time 'roaming the countryside', as her mother put it, became limited. Occasionally she rebelled and went missing for a morning or did not appear for a meal on time, and although she was never again sent to bed without dinner, she did not put on weight for over a year.

In the winter of this year, at sixteen and a half, she adjusted to the long hours and heavy work. She filled out a little and developed slightly. Her 'curse', as her mother put it, arrived in June, and things began to change. It had been easy to hide her body's transition into womanhood in the winter. Fewer daylight hours and bulkier clothing were an effective camouflage, and fortunately her mother – brooding in her weather-bound sitting room – had ignored everyone.

Her father had glanced at her differently sometimes and then withdrawn even further from her, not meaning to be unpleasant. He simply meant it as silent respect, his mute way of telling her she had reached a woman's standing in his eyes, even if her slightness hid it well. The only tangible action to accompany his changed behaviour was the extra money she had been given. Twice, he had taken out his worn leather wallet and handed her some notes, saying, "You'll be needing more clothing, Iona," quickly remarking on the fine lunch she had brought to his workplace, or commenting on her work with the accounts; and then, shutting her out, he had resumed his endless planing in slow, rhythmic movements – steel on wood – lift – steel on wood. She could see in her mind the thin wood shavings curling, toppling, falling to the shed floor.

Iona understood. He was a kind man, a quiet man – and he now looked on his daughter as a woman. Nature had taken over and grown a wall between them. The years of unspoken warmth, when he had considered her a child, were gone. Her body had lost her the only easy companionship she had ever known. Uriah Anderson-Keyes was a good father. *But women*, thought Iona, *he curtains off in his mind.*

He had a patterned procedure – the tipping of his hat, the setting of a chair and, most important of all, the walking out on a scene. She had watched his unspoken words make the barrier between him and her mother. Iona wondered if he shut himself off from other things in his life as well. Like the furniture she knew he wanted to make – but didn't.

He called himself a 'jack of all trades'. "I build what people need," he told her the odd times she had questioned him; he said it with a smile and thought his daughter wouldn't know the desires of his heart. Iona felt that when he was near her, he had always been a little softer around the mouth – a step closer; a breath warmer – until this winter when he alone had noticed her changing shape.

But then someone else did notice. As spring began to warm the Northland earth back to life, the potent mind of Sybil Anderson-Keyes had moved out of its grey dreams – and fixed itself on this new creature now living in her home. Each day she watched Iona's beauty unfold, and each day her resentment grew until, as Maude had suspected, it turned into hatred.

The spindly girl, who had only ever been half-biddable and never what she wanted in a daughter, had now become a radiant reminder of what Sybil would never be. For a few weeks the young woman was a festering sore. Then she became the weapon to be used against an indifferent husband – and a plan took shape. Iona could now be removed cleverly, according to the rules of society. An English tradition, employed by the aristocracy to secure family lands and wealth, gave Sybil her opportunity.

Albert Hammond, twenty years Iona's senior, was a business friend of Uriah. Reasonably well off by most people's standards and openly eager to improve himself, Hammond's drive had left him a lonely bachelor who needed little encouragement to visit for a meal once a week instead of infrequently as in the past. Sybil laid the foundations thoroughly. Iona had always been present at the meal table but now she had to help earlier and was delayed later into the lengthening evenings.

Sybil rearranged the dinner table seating. Iona now sat opposite Albert, where the lamps made the most of her fairy hair and glistening skin. Sybil also made the girl serve at table and, watching the effects on him of Iona's nearness – the small breasts, the warm scent of the young body – saw her plan was working. Iona appeared unaware and uninterested.

"She's too thin, of course," Sybil's calculating mind muttered. "It's because she roams all over the countryside like a wild creature. She's odd. I don't know what he sees in the silly girl. I must instruct Mrs James to do a little bit of padding in the wedding dress."

But Albert knew the promise of beauty when he saw it. He pictured her in two years' time, and he wanted a future with that loveliness beside him – and now, for that matter. Three weeks, and the older man's emotions were well aroused.

Sybil's suggestions encouraged Hammond's hope in the possibility of a marriage. She became a scrupulous chaperone. It would do her own reputation no good to have a pregnant daughter led to the altar. Within six weeks of Sybil's plan being put into action, she set the wedding date – 12th December.

"Do you not think Iona is too young for this?" Uriah had queried one night after Sybil had informed him of the Christmas nuptials.

"No, I don't, my dear. Iona is mature for her age and seems more than willing. Had you not noticed?"

The lie was sweetly couched. Uriah could not contradict her because he had noticed her maturity but not any sign of willingness, but feeling the whole set-up was wrong he tried again. "The engagement is very short, surely?"

"You would not want any scandal to touch your daughter, would you, Uriah?"

And Uriah was lost. Was Iona pregnant? Was that what Sybil meant? He could not stand it if Hammond had done such a thing to his girl. Could Iona be wayward? How could he even think that? Surely Sybil would know about such things. His heart, though, was heavy. Who could tell what Sybil meant? If he pushed her she would be sure to start one of her screaming matches, and Iona would hear and everyone would be upset.

"Surely you have seen the way things have been going? Are you blind where that girl is concerned?"

A small pause – a tired sigh.

"I have tried to keep them apart for weeks. Albert would have things under way long before this. As it is I have had to let it be known that this marriage was privately arranged a year ago, but out of consideration Mr Hammond had kindly insisted on waiting until Iona turned seventeen. Really, Uriah, you might take some thought for me, your wife, instead of living in your own little world and seeing nothing of what goes on around you?"

Uriah said no more ...

Iona started to walk back to the house but a picture of her mother's triumphant face flashed before her eyes. She staggered, stopped and relived that day.

"Albert Hammond has asked for your hand in marriage, Iona. Your wedding is set for mid-December. We shall have to get some suitable clothes and have Mrs James make you a dress for the ceremony."

"What?"

"Do not say 'what' to me, girl. If you did not hear me then say 'I beg your pardon, Mother'."

"I'm not marrying anyone, least of all that old man!"

"Yes you are. The marriage is set. Your father and I have already begun the necessary arrangements."

Her father had left that morning for a two-week timber buying trip.

She tried to speak but found she could not breathe, and by the time she had herself under control her mother had left the room. She saw her being picked up at the gate by her awful friend Lily Grantham. By the time Iona ran outside the carriage had gone.

Over the next few days Iona tried to fight the older woman. Shocked into action, she'd refused the marriage, threatened to run away and cried in front of Albert when he came with smiles and flowers. She even resorted to trying to cajole Sybil. Nothing worked. Each day the postman brought cards and letters of congratulations from her mother's friends. One day when she went walking up the road towards town, three people stopped her, their smiles bearing down on her, their eyes greedy for information. She hurried back to the house and stayed in her room hoping that when her father returned he would save her from the nightmare. That hadn't happened, of course. Her father came back exhausted, looking ten years older, and went straight to bed.

"Your father has bronchitis and must not be disturbed. What are you trying to do? Send him into pneumonia and kill him?"

With an air of righteous caring Sybil had left Iona completely on her own to squirm and to go into her own decline until the role she had been forced into became an inescapable reality.

Now, as the light melted in the evening sky, Iona began to sob. She had known loneliness, and even as a small child had learned to embrace indifference; but this was the first time in her life she had known the powerlessness of fear, the hopelessness of defeat. There, beside her river, she cried out against the injustice of her position. Young, unmarried girls had no standing. Their parents were supposed to know what was good for them. Did they consider Albert Hammond to be good for her? She shivered. There was something about Albert. What was it? He was old, yes – but... his eyes. His eyes never looked true.

She thought of her brother Edward, whom everyone – except Mother – called Teddy. He would arrive by train from boarding school to see her married the next day. Only one year younger, he had a sense of fun and a freedom she would never possess. He would never be sold, as her mother was selling her. His self-assurance, his inner knowledge that he could do anything he liked with his life, gave him a lightheartedness others found entrancing, while she would exist merely through another person.

The dark beginnings of night slipped around her like a cloak. Time, now, to return for the last time to the home she would leave tomorrow. For a few more moments she watched the rushing river. Something had been taken from her – the last of her childhood had been thrown away. Well, if it was to be then she would see that last bit of childhood right now. She would see it strewn on the waters in front of her, see it racing away on the river floods.

Nothing would be taken from her tomorrow by that man to whom she would never belong.

"I wanted to get away, but not like this."

Her head swam with plans which all seemed impossible.

Perhaps this was the only way to leave. Perhaps she was going mad!

"I give my heart to you, river," she cried. "I leave it with your waters, in these rushes, on this air. I cannot give it to that man." Her last cry whispered on the wind. She had done it.

Her unformed dreams of future years had been ripped away by the very people who should have stood beside her – her mother by what she had done, and her father by what he had not done. But she would reform. She had seen her father forge red, molten metal, seen him reform it into some other shape. She determined her inner core would never again be vulnerable. Somehow she would learn to protect herself. Any small dreams of warmth and honesty, sincerity and trust, she left here, in this child space. Only to the elements – the trees, the rivers and seas – would she show herself.

"God ..." she shouted out, above the noises of her place. "God, I love your land, your growing things, your moon and stars, your wind and rains. But in your people I see no love ... not even in myself."

She turned and walked stiff-spined to sleep her last night beside her river.

Chapter Six

The train from Helensville was fifteen minutes late getting into Auckland, and Albert, who had been in quite a good mood for most of the journey, had become irritable.

"You wait here by this pillar while I go and see to the luggage. Just stay there, and don't move until I come back."

Iona watched him stride out along the station. She felt angry herself. "Does he think I'm seven years old?"

A woman passing by stopped, opened her mouth and then moved on. Iona began to giggle. Had she spoken out loud? She clapped her hand over her mouth. She felt so tired and so nervous she … Oh no!

Now she'd dribbled on her new blue gloves, and she'd got a cinder in her eye about half an hour before they'd arrived, and Albert's attempts to remove it with the corner of his handkerchief had made it worse. It itched and burnt, and she dared not rub it. She hadn't wanted a honeymoon, let alone this elaborate train trip Albert had insisted on 'giving her', and he was nagging.

"We'll have to hurry to make the dining room at the Central before seven," he'd grumbled at least ten times in the last ten minutes.

In November she'd suggested they leave the wedding until after Christmas. That had not gone down well. 'Dear Albert', as her mother called him, wouldn't agree to that. Now she would be stuck in Auckland for a week and then dragged back on a train again to go to Rotorua. There would be no time this Christmas with Teddy. He was only home for Christmas Day then off to a friend's farm for a month. They would have no sailing or tramping together over the holidays.

If all brides had to put up with this why did women ever get married? How many girls were shunted into marriage by their parents? How did anyone know? She sighed.

It had been a morning wedding, and her mother had made her get up at six o'clock to make sure she was dressed. From then on she'd been pushed and poked and prodded and crammed into stupid clothes and new shoes when all she wanted was to be wandering the hills of her creek. Now she felt hungry. She'd been unable to eat much at the hot luncheon after the ceremony. That had been hours ago. Where had the day gone? She sighed again. I'll have to stop that, she thought, or Albert will glare again. And where's he got to? Ah, there! He's coming back.

Oh Lord, he was waving his arms and shouting into the ear of the luggage boy. Why did he have to do that? The lad seemed to be steering the cart expertly. He dodged heels and missed pillars without any trouble. Her old case and Albert's flash portmanteau were wobbling and jumping about a bit. They looked like two funny old people in an argument. Iona couldn't help laughing. She turned away so Albert couldn't see, but the young porter noticed, and he gave her a knowing grin.

"Follow us to the Central Hotel," Albert ordered the boy.

All of a sudden he grabbed her and swung her into a river of hustling people that carried them out of the station and into the city street. She felt like a naughty child being towed along by the hand. Etiquette had been rammed down her throat for the last three months by her mother and Albert – yet it wasn't even the end of their first day of marriage and she felt embarrassed by her husband's lack of manners.

When some of the crowd peeled off in a different direction and Albert pointed out the small distance to the hotel, Iona managed to disengage her hand and started walking briskly. An older man, stinking of stale beer, staggered in front of them, nearly tipping her off her feet.

"Get off, man!" shouted Albert and shoved the drunken fellow back against the wall of a building. The man seemed to have no bones. He swayed about, his tongue lolling out of his slack mouth, and the push Albert gave him in the stomach made him burp loudly.

"Disgusting fellow! Absolutely disgusting! Shouldn't be allowed." Albert grabbed Iona by the arm this time and forced her along the footpath continuing a descriptive spiel as they did a jerky quick-march together. A tram rattled past drowning his words. Then three soldiers, singing with gusto and trying to prop each other up, came rolling towards them. Iona felt a little frightened. She had not seen anyone behave like this.

Now in an extremely agitated state, Albert hauled Iona off the footpath, onto the road and back again to avoid the drunken men.

"Albert ..." she started to snap.

But Albert presumed she was pointing out the entrance to the Central Hotel and carried on over the top of her.

"Yes, that's it. That's the Central. At least this is a decent place. God knows where that riffraff have been drinking."

"Albert will you ..." Iona began again.

"It's this six o'clock closing time," he went on. "Ridiculous! They chuck them out on the streets like this, then the stupid temperance women see them and they jump up and down. A man's entitled to a drink or two. He just needs to keep it under control."

Then, in a split second, his voice changed, and he turned to the luggage boy waiting patiently to be paid. "There, my lad, sixpence as agreed."

The lad scampered off, his cart clattering on the uneven footpath while Albert saw their luggage safely into the hands of the hotel staff.

They were shown to their room, tidied themselves up and made the dining room by seven, where the head waiter told them they had until nine if they wished. *So why the rush?* thought Iona, but said nothing. She'd lost her appetite again and pushed the meal around her plate while Albert grizzled about her 'not eating his money's worth'. But he couldn't fault her table manners, and he became more expansive as he drank his wine.

Iona felt grateful for her hot cup of tea, and also to the waiter who suggested she might like to get some eyewash from the matron in residence, when Albert went to the men's room.

"We are well used to travellers requiring eye lotion. Grit in one's eye is most painful, is it not, madam?"

Iona, who had never been called 'madam' in her life before, immediately reacted to the title with a poise she did not know she possessed. She stood and gracefully thanked the waiter, following his instructions. The matron in residence proved to be a fund of knowledge, and the soothing effect of the eyewash started easing the pain within minutes. Iona took the lotion with her to their room.

Albert walked in not long after and busied himself checking his luggage had been unpacked, then said, "Well, I'll leave you for an hour or two to recover from the train trip. There's some great conversation going on downstairs. I'll get back and let you rest up."

Iona undressed and put on the fine white cotton nightdress her mother had instructed her to wear for her first night. In truth, she was pleased to be on her own for a while. She looked out of the window above Queen Street. Although the early summer sky looked pretty she didn't think she liked this city any more now than she had as a child. Tonight, though, she felt like a frightened child.

Certainly she had seen animals coupling and knew that, somehow, people did too. Nobody had ever explained how, and she had never known anyone she might have trusted enough to ask. If her aunt had been a married woman she could have asked her – but she was not. She was a very well-respected maiden aunt. *I suppose I should have asked Mother.*

"No, never Mother!"

She pushed the fancy bedroom chair in front of the dressing table and began brushing her long fair hair. One, two, three, four – slowly the thought of Albert Hammond getting into that big bed with her floated out of her mind.

When her husband did come back to their room he was almost as drunk as the men she had seen earlier on the street. The smell of him lying all over her and slobbering at her mouth repulsed her but she remembered her mother's words – 'A husband is entitled to do what he likes with you, so behave.' She tried to calm her nerves and keep still but she needn't have worried. In all the strange fumblings that went on, Albert seemed as incapable as she was inexperienced. Suddenly he began to snore. Iona gently pushed his body off her chest, moved away to the very edge of the bed and began to pray that he would stay asleep. She was so exhausted she fell asleep herself before she finished the prayer.

Each day he urged her to 'do the town'. She was not all that interested in fashion, but on their first morning in Auckland Albert had become so incensed by her lack of enthusiasm, he'd insisted on going with her to buy a new outfit.

A saleswoman with an angelic smile and an older woman's wisdom covered for Iona's lack of fashion sense so well that Iona could have kissed her. Albert, puffed up with pride by the shop assistant's praise of his wife's trim figure, insisted on buying her a chocolate brown silk evening skirt and matching jacket. Iona gave in without a murmur. She had fallen in love with the tiny shell-like buttons which reminded her of the beaches of the lower river.

They attended a theatrical evening that night. Iona had never heard of a minstrel show. She sat entranced by the songs and spectacular dance routines while her husband hooted through the jokes. It ended up being the one interesting night of their Auckland stay.

The smells and sights of Rotorua, that strange geothermal town in the middle of the North Island, captivated Iona. Floating steam from hot, sulphur pools whispered around her on her early morning walks in the town's park, making it seem like another world. All the unusual activity kept her so engrossed she forgot everything that had been and everything that might be and got caught up in the mystery of the place.

Two days before Christmas they joined a tour group. They followed a smiling Maori guide who didn't look much older than herself and who tucked Iona in beside her for most of the informative wanderings. They watched one geyser play for several minutes and were mesmerised by the boiling water rising, falling, shooting high – again and again.

"It must have known you were coming," the guide whispered to Iona, a little-girl grin lighting her face.

At Whakarewarewa laughing Maori children dived from a bridge to claim the coins visitors threw in the river, and Albert obligingly gave her plenty of coins. When a breeze caught one man's hat and took it over the rail three boys dived after it. They brought it back, smiling hugely, and got half a crown from its owner for their trouble.

Iona felt so homesick today. Christmas Day had always been special. It was the one day in the year the family spent in peace together at Grandma Kelly's. Her mother would cause a little scene – but once that passed, the rest of the day became cheerful. Her aunt would cook a big, hot roast of lamb and dish up her steamed Christmas pudding, bulging with hidden threepences and capped with yellow brandy sauce. Her grandma spent the day with a rosy face from her dandelion wine, and her father seemed more alive. She'd not thought about it while they were visiting the sights, but when she woke up beside Albert on Christmas morning, she yearned to be at home. He smelt bad and she felt awful.

All through the hotel festivities she had the miseries, and when the manager asked everyone to be quiet for two minutes in memory of the New Zealand soldiers killed at Passchendaele in October, she felt guilty she knew nothing about it. She had spent that time either hiding herself away from her mother's eyes or lying exhausted in her room, squirming like a bug on a pin as she tried to find a way out of her own dilemma. Fortunately, Albert and the couple next to him were too absorbed with the rich foods and free drinks to notice her dismay so she was at least spared another reprimand. Some of the other guests had got the impression Albert was a big businessman, which made him happy. Iona listened without shame to the man next to her and the man across the table discussing the war and the mounting number of New Zealand men killed on the other side of the world and vowed she would find out as much as she could about what had been happening.

Boxing Day was boring, which disappointed Albert. He didn't realise Iona's lack of enthusiasm was the reason. They spent the last day floating in the famous hot sulphur waters of the Bath House, luckily in the segregated pools. The weather was a bit too warm for her liking, but Albert refused to allow her to swim in the lake.

"It's too chilly," he said, and she did not like to say, "Well I'm a lot younger than you and I like it chilly."

On the train journey back to Auckland two days before New Year's Eve, Albert again fell asleep and Iona felt baffled. They had been away for nigh on eighteen days, and she still did not understand why her husband had been so insistent on this honeymoon. He had spent every evening in the hotel's Private Bar, with his 'great fellows' of little acquaintance – and got himself drunk, so drunk he came to bed incapable of doing anything to her. Not that she minded. She didn't want him to do anything. It was not right, though, she knew, from her mother's warnings. Still, maybe if it had to be like this it wouldn't be so bad after all.

The last train trip north out of Auckland had them both overtired. On the Helensville to Dargaville steamer Albert went straight to the saloon again, instructing Iona to go to their cabin for the night – but Iona remained on deck. She found a seat in the deserted stern. She supposed he'd be mad with her for not obeying him. *Why should I worry? He'll be there for hours,* she decided, and choosing a seat alone at the stern she wrapped her evening cloak around her and relaxed.

The summer sun was mellow in the season and the river calm. She leant her head against the post behind her and felt the ship's engine vibrating through her body like a kindly, giant pulse. As it lulled her towards that warm drowsiness in which she loved to drift, the voices of the people in the open cabin softened to a faint murmur that droned faintly on and on below the music of the engines.

Her eyes opened long enough to catch a glimpse of a heron poking around on a sandbank – then closed. She breathed in the northern air, smelt those familiar whiffs of mud, mangrove, raupo and rye. Home – she was going home.

She dozed.

She had forgotten that her home was now in Hammond's house. She did not know – how could she? – that the slightly irritable but sometimes charming older man was not the person, in public, who would live with her in their own home. Iona had yet to meet the private face of Albert Hammond.

Chapter Seven

The early train from Rotorua was approaching Taumaranui when Caleb began to feel sick. Last night's New Year's Eve party was taking its toll. Must have been the oysters, he thought as he made for the lavatory and vomited – or too much beer. He did his best to wash his face and rinse his mouth while balancing to the rocking train. This box-sized convenience was not the place for a solid six-footer with a dodgy gut. A lifetime of manoeuvring around in small boats served him well, and he was back in his seat by the time they pulled into the station. *I'd better have something to eat. No breakfast this morning – perhaps that's what's upset me.* He was up, riding the bottom step of the carriage as they slowed down, and the first to the station canteen.

"Cup of tea, pie, bread and butter, please." He grinned at the red-faced woman behind the counter and gave her a half-crown.

"Righto, lovey. Coming up."

There was hardly time to pocket his change before she slid his meal across to him and a hungry horde of train passengers crushed their combined weight behind him.

Back in the carriage Caleb finished eating and was sipping his tea and two sugars as the train began to move again. The chap in the window seat came back and squeezed past him with his tea and sandwiches.

"Nothing like a railway cup of tea," he said.

"It'd melt the spoon if you left it in," Caleb answered. He felt much better for the food. They talked for a bit then Caleb settled down to get some sleep. He heard the strike of a match, smelt the first pungent flare.

Iron wheels rattled them over a high bridge. Through half-closed eyelids he saw the deep green bush of the North Island interior, kind on the eyes, flashing past. Then he knew no more until they came into Hamilton.

His stomach felt a bit uncomfortable and he felt sick again. The closer they got to the South Auckland stations, the worse it got. Papakura, Otahuhu – would he make it? He felt like hell.

"You okay?" asked his fellow passenger.

"Not really. I feel as crook as a dog," Caleb grunted and made for the lavatory again.

When he got back to his seat his fellow traveller took one look at him and went to find the guard. With his guts churning Caleb began to sweat. A gripping pain had set in. *What station was that? I think I'm going to pass out,* he thought and was relieved when someone placed a bucket on his lap. He looked up to see a guard inspecting him with world-weary eyes.

"You look very sick, Mr …"

"McKay. Caleb McKay. Yes, I feel terrible actually; bad pain in my stomach and I've vomited a couple of times."

47

"How long have you been like this?"

"Since Taumaranui, I think. Had lunch there and felt better but after a while I began to feel sick again, and it's got worse all the way."

"I'll send for an ambulance as soon as we get into the station." The guard moved off, checking the other passengers as he went.

"I got a blanket for you from the guard's van," his fellow passenger said and spread it over Caleb. "I'll hold the bucket if you like. Just say if you want to use it."

Caleb nodded, thankful not to have to hold the tin bucket. It stank of Jeyes Fluid disinfectant. He spent what seemed like hours feeling ill and trying not to vomit. Then he was so consumed by the pain he simply fought to stay upright. When would this all pass?

"Mr McKay? Mr McKay?"

The guard again. Caleb managed a 'yes?' "Here are the ambulance officers, sir."

He looked beyond the guard, saw two men.

"We have a stretcher here, sir, to get you out to the ambulance, but you're a big man so you'll have to help us as much as possible."

They helped him to stand. It was agony. Even with four men they couldn't get him up and onto the stretcher in such a confined space, so they bundled him along the aisle, down the narrow steps and onto the platform. He had never known such agony. He didn't know how they got him on the stretcher. That was a blank. Once in the ambulance he knew all about it and then ... nothing – until he found himself on a hospital trolley being poked by a doctor.

"Where's the pain exactly, Mr McKay?" a voice asked.

Caleb yelled as a red hot poker was thrust through his left side.

"Thought so," said the doctor. "Get him to theatre as fast as you can. I'll be waiting. Don't waste time and only clean that area. Hurry…!"

He thought he heard a woman's voice. He concentrated, and his eyes opened. "Mother?"

"Hello, Caleb. It's nice to see you awake." He tried to sit up.

Another woman's voice said, "No, Mr McKay," and a strong hand pushed his shoulder to the bed.

"You've been ill, Caleb," his mother's voice wavered. "You've had a very serious operation, and you mustn't move about too much, son."

The voice belonging to the hand said, "You have drainage tubes in your stomach, Mr McKay. You've had your appendix removed."

Caleb turned his head and looked into her eyes. "I'm Nurse Catley," the voice told him.

She was very pretty with blue eyes almost as vivid as, as – no, it wasn't the Creek girl. The nurse smiled and he rested in the glow. He was tempted to try a cheeky comment, but he felt so weak and she sounded so firm he thought better of it.

"There was considerable infection in the operation area so the surgeon had to leave the tubes in to allow the mess to drain away. But you're young and strong, and you'll make a grand recovery if you do exactly what we tell you and don't get clever."

"I'll do that," he managed and drifted away to some place he knew he'd been before, hearing fragmented words – 'needs rest', 'father', 'evening' – fading into the distance.

Three weeks later he was fed up with hospital. He could move around now reasonably well, and they said he was out of danger.

"However," the surgeon told him, "as you know you didn't have a plain appendicitis. You had peritonitis. You've been lucky. Your youth and strength have battled the abdominal inflammation, but I'd rather be sure and keep you here another couple of weeks."

Caleb sighed. "If I have to."

"I'd do as he says if I were you." Lieutenant Archie Meldrew stood at the end of Caleb's bed, black bushy eyebrows bunched above a frown. "This man saved your life, McKay."

"Yes, sir," Caleb answered the naval officer. It seemed he had not much choice in anything these days.

"You know by now the navy won't accept you as fit for war, don't you?"

"I guessed as much. Last time you were here you told me not to get my hopes up."

Silence followed. The older men looked at each other. The surgeon nodded.

"If you are that keen we could find you an office job when you're in better shape."

Caleb looked at him in horror.

"I see. Well, McKay, I'm sorry we missed out on you. If that damned boss of yours in Rotorua hadn't been so clever in holding you over as 'necessary to the war effort', you'd have been overseas long ago."

"I know, sir. I tried to get away but he's a determined old ..."

"Yes, yes. Well, young man, do as they tell you in here, and go and have a good life."

Caleb nodded and watched the naval doctor stride out of the ward, every step sharp, yet soft on the perfectly polished linoleum.

"You're better out of it," the surgeon told him. "You'll be a few more weeks convalescing at home, so chew on that and put on a happy face for that wonderful mother of yours, young man."

"Yes, sir," Caleb answered with a mock salute.

The surgeon laughed. He gave Caleb a light punch on the shoulder and left the ward.

Caleb lay back. He hated the weakness of his body, hated the lack of power over his life. Willing himself to be grateful he got out of bed, pushed his feet into the terrible tartan slippers his father had bought for him and grabbed his dressing gown. In the next ward, in the patients' lounge, Syd, Bill and Roly would be ready for a game of poker. Amputees from the front line they looked like mangled men, and they needed Caleb to arrive in good humour. They were the heroes of the day, poor buggers. What their lives would hold when they left this place was anybody's guess.

Chapter Eight

Monday – washday. By half past six Iona, wrapped in her old winter coat, worked at bucketing the freezing tap water from the tub tap into the copper bowl. When it was two- thirds full she bent to poke more twigs and fine kindling into the firebox. "That should keep you going for a while," she informed the flames and went back to the kitchen to eat her breakfast.

After that she alternated between feeding the fire and hurrying back inside to strip their bed of its sheets and pillowcases and lug them out to the steaming wash house. Next she shaved soap into hot bubbling water. When that dissolved and foamed she shoved the linen under the water with her washing pole, making sure everything was thoroughly soaked.

A month ago Albert had wanted to attach a hose to the tub tap to make the copper easier to fill but she had stopped him.

"It'll get in the way of my handwashing," she'd said. Well, she'd made a big mistake there. Now she'd have to ask him to fix it the way he wanted and put up with his clever remarks.

Sister Grey's warning last Friday had worried her all weekend.

"You watch yourself, girl," the midwife had lectured. "Lifting heavy buckets of water is not normal exercise. You have to use the sense the Lord gave you. Housewifely pride won't do you any good if you damage something inside."

"I'm very strong, sister."

"You listen to me, child. This is not like gallivanting about and climbing trees like you used to be doing. You must take care," and she had pulled down the bottom lids of Iona's eyes to see if she was anaemic and felt the baby's position with tender firmness.

"Make an appointment with Dr Jenkins next week, Mrs Hammond. You want this wee soul, don't you? And so does your man, I'll be bound. Get him to use his muscle on some of the heavier chores."

"Yes, sister," Iona had agreed, letting the rest of the lecture wisp off over her head as she thought how impossible it would be to get Albert to do anything he didn't want to do.

She turned on the brass taps over the tubs and went outside. It was a grey July day, the wind so cold it stung. Leaning against the wash house wall she lifted her tingling face to the sky and closed her eyes. For a few moments there was nothing in her head but peace.

When she went back in, the tubs were ready. Using the pole, she hauled and lifted the scalding sheets up from the copper and into the nearest rinsing tub, and while they soaked she swept the blue bag around the second tub. Smudges of blue powder on sheets would not do at all. Not for Albert. She sang the Ricketts song – 'Out of the blue comes the whitest wash' – and smiled.

The water looked an even, deep blue, the colour of a night sky just before it turned dark.

Albert had paid a woman to keep his house when he lived alone, but now he expected her to provide that service. Not that she minded the work. It gave her something to do, and she could tell by the way he ran out of things to complain about that she did it well. It was just that she would rather have had a job of her own. He had gone as red as a turkey gobbler when she had mentioned the position at the General Store, before she became pregnant.

"What are you talking about? No woman of mine is going out to work. People will think I can't afford to keep you."

No, Albert would not see the last stages of pregnancy as any reason for him to do 'women's work'. Anyway, she was young. She'd be all right. She lifted the sheets into the blue rinse tub, pushed and pulled them about and let it sit. It was time for a cup of tea and something to eat.

Once she sat down in the warm kitchen she felt weary. Perhaps she needed a good walk. It would not be the same as running through the fields. Now she lived on the hill she 'could not go running harum-scarum through the paddocks', apparently. Not that she could run far with this precious load weighing her down. Precious load? She hadn't thought that before. Perhaps Sister Grey was right. Yes, she'd make an appointment with the doctor later on, and she'd ask Albert about the hose for the copper tonight; better to get it over with. But now it was time to get the sheets and pillowcases on the line and make use of the blustery wind.

When Iona came back inside she was frozen. Sitting on the small fireside chair in front of the cooking range she opened the firebox door and held her purple hands out to the flames. 'Don't put your hands that close to the fire – you'll get chilblains.' Her mother's voice rang in her head.

She probably would too, and they'd be itchy and sore and she would regret it. Sore hands could not climb trees! Her thoughts went back to her childhood.

Perhaps she had been more active than girls were meant to be. At the time she had thought her way of life simply natural. Her mother had expected her to be ladylike, and she had tried, off and on, but the mannerisms her mother nagged her to acquire seemed so silly, she had found it better to get away from the house as much as possible. There was peace with the bush and river. Even so, she thought of them now, those schoolgirl friends. For all that they had not been very close, and two of them catty little misses, she had missed them these last few months. Marriage at seventeen had set her apart.

Since she and Albert had returned to Sedgely, flashes of their wedding day kept jumping into her head. Her mother's little workers pressing and primping at her until she looked like a stranger. And that is how she'd got through the ceremony. Yes. Her father's trembling arm led someone else up the aisle of the church. Someone else stood and smiled. And someone else waited while all her mother's cronies and their watch-chained husbands, while Albert's pals and their begowned wives, talked and ate and eyed her up and down as if she were a thing on display for their benefit.

The honeymoon had been like a weird holiday, like being with a grumpy but generous older gentleman who came late to bed every night, intoxicated, to snore soundly in her ear.

But once back at Sedgely, Albert had changed. He was not so drunk at night, and he became the master. Iona's bubble of detachment was blown to smithereens. It began on their first night in his house when he put his hands on her nightdress and yanked it over her head.

"There will be no more nonsense. You are my wife, and you will do what I tell you in my house and in my bed," and he had pushed her back onto the bed and shown her the things that were expected of her and did the things he wished to do.

She had learnt that he was much stronger than her, that he was deaf to 'no' or 'don't' and that her clothing always concealed any bruises that might appear. Her body hurt for a long time until, gradually, she had become more and more docile. She tried hard to pretend it was happening to someone else, but this was not like the wedding day. This was never over.

A pattern developed in her days. While she worked and shopped and cooked, she relived the year before – thinking, questioning. How had it happened? Why had she let it happen? Why hadn't she run away? Auckland wasn't such a bad place. She could have disappeared in a place that size. She could have taken her little birthday savings and found a job down there – or better still, in Rotorua, where nobody knew her and where she could have become someone else.

Disappointment swamped her; anger stalked her, during the days she railed, during the nights she kept quiet, because sometimes Albert went to sleep, and she craved that peace – that release from his physically hurtful attentions and from his anger.

She had to find a way to escape. Maybe she had been too stupid or too young to understand why her mother began having Albert Hammond to their home more and more – but not now. Now she understood, and she would have to escape as soon as possible. So she had made plans. Then she had become pregnant.

By six o'clock she was dressed and ready. Albert had insisted she accompany him to a hotel dinner with business friends. She was used to this. In the first few months of their marriage Albert had constantly displayed her about town, taking her to everything from baby contests to country race days. He had a need to parade her, and his needs must be met.

At these dinners she found his friends frightening. She was almost a generation younger, and she did not understand the looks they gave her or the nudges they gave each other. After a few weeks, however, she remained very still in their presence until they acted as if she were deaf.

While the men manoeuvred and touted over whisky and cigars, crowed about deals and complained about the war, their women conversed expertly about absolutely nothing. When Iona's slim figure disappeared with the pregnancy, the men gave up their snide ogling and touching, their women sat back in relieved revenge, and Iona found respite. She was used to hiding in the grasses of the fields, and now she hid inside the yards of maternity clothing which enveloped her youth and her distending belly. But what about after this baby is born? How many more babies will there be?

The future seemed a nightmare of silent obeisance to Albert. She knew she would be worn away by such a life. She'd seen the faded women dragging six or seven children around and about to give birth to another. How did some women manage to keep their families down to one or two? Surely it wasn't just luck? Maybe she could ask Dr Jenkins. She would make an appointment for next week.

Chapter Nine

As she neared the doctor's rooms Iona became flustered about asking how not to get pregnant again. She tried whispering it. "How do I not get pregnant again, Dr Jenkins?"

No, no, she couldn't say that to a man. She could ask Aunt Maude.

Don't be ridiculous! The woman's never had children. Perhaps mother? For goodness' sake, that would be like putting her head into a lion's mouth. Now she felt as if she were choking.

"Good morning, Iona," said a pleasant male voice. "Oh, good morning," she answered, smiling at the young man while her thoughts cleared enough to recognise a classmate from her schooldays. "Oh! How are you, Paul?"

Good heavens, he'd lost a leg. He stood there with cripple sticks. A picture of the young Paul Sloane leading the field in the boys' race in his last year of school blurred her vision. "Oh, Paul, I'm so sorry."

"Don't worry, Iona. I'm pleased you didn't notice. Here!" he whispered as a tear rolled slowly down her cheek. "Don't be upset, please. Look! Captain Ahab!" he joked, thumping a crutch on the pavement.

"I am sorry though, Paul. I was a bit distracted."

"I think we both were. We nearly collided. That would have made the town sit up," he quipped with such a cheeky light in his eye, Iona laughed. The thought of her bulk and his crutches racketing to the ground while the townspeople watched in horror was hilarious.

They chatted for a few minutes. She would have stayed longer if she'd had time.

"I've got an appointment in five minutes, Paul, so I must go. It's nice to see you."

"Thanks, Iona. It was good to have someone talk to me as if I haven't lost me marbles along with me leg," he smiled.

They parted. Iona hurried along the street. She was beginning to roll like a ship when she walked now, but inelegance didn't worry her – being late for her doctor's visit did. She needed time to organise her thoughts. As she went through the surgery door she realised she felt happy for the first time in months.

On her way home she thought things over. Dr Jenkins had given her a lecture about not overdoing things. Had Sister Grey been talking to him? What an embarrassing thought. And she'd forgotten to ask him about not having any more babies. Maybe next month she would pluck up the courage. These days she found it hard to think straight. Yet it had been easy to chat with Paul. She reflected on their encounter and on the war.

She used to think, when the war first started, that if she were a man she would join the army and be one of those who marched with pride to the other side of the world to fight for king and country. Now she hated the thought of it. The war dominated men's conversations and cast bleak shadows over the faces of the women who waited for newspapers and the wounded lists. Paul's words swirled in her head: 'Bert Swaine and I were both wounded at Gallipoli. He didn't make it. I'm lucky to be alive.'

"And so am I. I have to stop feeling sorry for myself." Yes, she had to get on with her lot. She had to be thankful for a roof over her head and food to eat. And Albert gave her a generous allowance. He liked her to be well dressed. *And he lets me visit Aunt Maude and Grandma Kelly anytime.* Perhaps she wanted too much.

Two nights later the doctor knocked on their door. "I was in the neighbourhood and thought I'd pop in to see how Mrs Hammond is getting along," he told Albert.

Albert led him through to the sitting room.

"Just doing a little check, Mrs Hammond, seeing I was nearby. How are the ankles? Are you making sure to put your feet up once or twice a day?"

"I'm doing my best, doctor. Would you like a cup of tea?"

"No thank you, my dear. In fact, it's eight-thirty already so I don't mind if you take yourself off to bed. You need your early nights, and I'm quite happy to visit with your husband for a few minutes before I get off home. How are you doing, Albert?"

Albert, left to the mercy of Dr Jenkins, felt dazed.

"Seems well, does she? Your wife?" the doctor pressed.

"Oh yes – yes. I think she is – well. Would you like a whisky, Dr Jenkins?"

"Just a tot, thank you, Albert. Can't stay long; busy day tomorrow."

The doctor heard Iona close the bedroom door. He sank into the armchair. His right hand engulfed the whisky tumbler, his left hand dangled over the armrest to graze the floor and his size twelve shoes stretched halfway across the small room. Albert shrank.

"Well, we must be looking after her now that her time is near. Of course, I knew a man of the world like you would be seeing to your woman's welfare. Some men have no idea. Expect their women to work like horses and still be available for their pleasure right up to the last minute. It's no wonder some of my patients don't carry to full term."

Albert was shocked. He had never thought of any danger to the child. "You mean …?"

"We don't want anything to go wrong, do we? The last stage can be tricky, and Mrs Hammond is not a big girl. Some gentlemen do move into the spare room for a couple of months before the child's birth and for the three months after. Makes it easier on a man, eh?"

"Yes, oh yes, of course." Albert's daze thickened with so much pleasantly provided information, and before he knew what was happening, his mouth opened. "As a matter of fact I have a week's business in Auckland starting tomorrow, and I said to Iona yesterday I would be sleeping in the guest room on my return."

Got you! thought the doctor. It didn't matter if his suspicions about Iona's safety were unfounded.

Hammond now knew it could be possible that her doctor had a hunch.

Jenkins stood, finished his drink and edged his way to the door. "Good man. Good man," he murmured. He felt the need of air.

The next morning Albert told Iona he would be away for a week on business and that Sam Newbold would run the store in his absence. The look of delight on her face was terrible.

"When I return, I will sleep in the guest room. It will be better for the child."

She could not hide her happiness. He made for the door before he lost control.

Albert spent his week in the city digesting the doctor's directives, for that was what they were, and he did not want to go down in the doctor's estimation. For the first twenty-four hours the convivial atmosphere of the Central, along with the freedom to use the hotel's well-equipped Private Bar, soothed him.

The rest of the week was difficult. He did not want anything to happen to his son. He wasn't getting any younger, and he wanted several sons to carry on his name. The barman, noticing his discomfort, put him on to a woman at a discreet house nearby, but Albert discovered he no longer had the taste for it and did not return there for the rest of his stay. To keep up appearances he did the rounds of a few hardware premises and put in some small orders. There'd been a run on claw hammers lately, and there was always room for farming implements. After that he gave up. His mind was not on the job. He'd tell Newbold that Auckland stocks were low. The doctor's words kept grinding at him day and night.

Looking back, Albert realised there had been nothing but trouble since the young, untouched Iona had invaded his life. Deep down he'd known she was too young for him, but he wanted her as passionately as he had once wanted a business. In fact it was worse – this need of the girl. The business had never caused him the turmoil she did. He really had believed Iona had feelings for him. That was the mother's doing. It had been her who had got him into this mess.

The barman came his way.

"A bottle of Johnny Walker," Albert snapped.

By the time he got up the stairs and lay on the bed he was shaking. Still he delayed the whisky until, like the break of a branch in a hoarfrost, the truth snapped in his mind. The girl did not love him. That had become more and more obvious.

Albert knew he was not good with women, had never been able to develop a friendship with any of them. He had used a few women on a paying basis, not many, but conversing with women, laughing with them and knowing how to live with them, as the doctor obviously did, was beyond his conception.

"Damn the man," he exploded and knew immediately it was his own fault. He loved her and was haunted by her, and she fought him every inch of the way. Yes, he had subdued her – it was his right to subdue her, wasn't it? But sometimes he was left with the niggling fear that no matter what he forced her to do, he would never own her as he did his business. Something in her eyes now pierced his soul. An icy whisper, a hollow quake that only whisky killed.

The week Albert was away, spring swept early into Sedgely. Magical skies and warm breezes lifted everyone's spirits. Iona's head cleared. She could see the world again. It felt as if she was being revitalised along with all the buds that burst into leaf on the trees. Her cheeks coloured to pink and cream in accord with the blossoms of the season, so that when Albert returned he was amazed at the transformation.

During his self-imposed week in Auckland he had been deliberately trying to shift his focus from Iona to his unborn child. Albert would soon turn thirty-eight, another year nearer the fortieth birthday he had been dreading these last few years. He used to consider a man in his forties to be beginning his decline. Now, however, observing his wife's metamorphosis, he knew that a four and a zero would make no difference to a man's natural inclinations. Still, he tried to be the gentleman that Jenkins thought him to be and concentrated solely on his child's welfare.

But it was not that simple. His carefully constructed peace of mind had been destroyed, and self-control came hard. It took a heavy toll on him that he could not vent his anger. The doctor would be regularly examining Iona's body. Visible marks could be Albert's social downfall. He was terrified. Was that why Jenkins had called that night?

Living a celibate life was hard enough to bear. Living with a woman whose beauty suddenly filled his house, just when he had removed himself from the marriage bed, was like being tortured. 'What did I do wrong?' he asked himself. 'She's my wife, a woman, like all the rest.' But he knew she was not like all the rest. She was an enigma to him, and his life began to creak and crumble. Day after day he watched Iona bloom and could not keep his eyes from drinking her up. Night after night he lay, unsleeping. He was becoming a man scattered within the perimeters of his own mind.

Iona, unaware of the black battle raging inside her husband, could not believe her good fortune. As August floated by she felt she was living a lullaby. Restful sleep for the week he was away had begun to improve her state of mind. Untroubled sleep, now that he had moved into the other room, appeared to be devastatingly good for her skin, her eyes and her hair; and now that Albert again employed a woman to do the heavy chores, her red-rough hands became white and lost their raw cracks. She was unaware of her new beauty. She knew, only, that she began to feel better than she had since she was twelve, when she was free to roam her riverbanks and climb Kotare hills.

She had happiness in her life, never experienced before. She understood it was something to do with the child she carried – but she did not want to think about the child or children. The question she thought she must ask Dr Jenkins remained unasked. The doctor was so kind that at one time she thought she might be a little in love with him. "Goodness, no," she giggled. "He's so enormous and so old, and sometimes he smells, like an old dog." That stopped her. It was an awful thing to say. Yes, I suppose it is, she thought and tried to feel guilty. "But some old dogs are the very nicest of creatures!" She gave up on her own conversation and went for her daily walk as Sister Grey had instructed.

"Rain or shine, girl, a walk will do you and baby good. So mind you get those legs moving no matter what the weather." The midwife was a determined woman, and Iona, for once in her life, was biddable. Now she enjoyed walking almost as much as she had running. She hugged to herself the knowledge that she was once again happy exploring the outdoors.

Things occurred on her walks. The colours in the gardens she passed refreshed her spirit. Neighbours greeted her now, and shyly, she greeted them back. One day the old lady on the corner invited her in for morning tea and fed her on cream sponge. She felt a tingle of kindness – something she had only known when she was with Aunt Maude – and last week their neighbour, Mrs Holly, from across the road, had taken her into their toolshed to show her a new litter of puppies and asked, "Would you like one of them?"

Of course she would have liked one, but she didn't know how Albert would react. He was being very good to her lately – but at times she thought she felt the hunger of his wants below the surface of his words.

"Tell you what," the breeder offered, "you couldn't have one for a while anyway. They're still on their mother's milk, so why don't you pick one out, and I'll hang on to it. If all goes well, you could have a brand new puppy to go with your brand new baby."

A glow of quiet joy made Iona feel something she didn't recognise.

Time floated. Most afternoons she sat in the tattered old armchair that squatted on the back porch. She had come to enjoy the flax that grew in the wet patch of ground beside the open stormwater drain. There, she watched the fantails flit and dart almost quicker than the eye could see, and as long as she stayed quiet they went on with their insect hunting, bouncing from one muscular flax leaf to another in frenetic flights of busyness.

The porch was her favourite place because, being at the back of the house, it looked out over the town of Sedgely and down the winding river.

"Hello, River," she would whisper. "Are you looking after my heart?"

Later, she would remember that spring of 1918 as the heady, quiet time before the storm.

Chapter Ten

Maude Kelly went in to her mother's bedroom on the seventh day of September 1918 with an early morning cup of tea and found that the old lady had died in her sleep.

Maude felt fortunate she could see to all the funeral arrangements without Sybil trying to take charge. Sybil was angry. She had been left her mother's jewellery, but Maude had inherited the house and Amelia's small savings. As the jewellery was insignificant in Sybil's eyes the old lady's attempt to appease her elder daughter might just as well have been abandoned.

Sybil could do nothing about the will.

The solicitor had said, "Your younger sister has spent many years living with and looking after your mother in her infirmity. It would take more than the house and land was worth to try to fight it. Had it been open to contest I would not have allowed Mrs Kelly to make such a will. You must understand this, Mrs Anderson-Keyes: that these were your mother's wishes in repayment for your sister's care, and to provide a home for her."

Sybil had then stalked out of the office as taut as an acrobat's wire about to snap.

Maude endured all the impotent fury her sister spat at her during the next three days and was pleased she had the funeral arrangements to keep her occupied. She was only human, however, and there came an opportunity she could not resist. The afternoon before the service that would lay her mother to rest, Sybil was still haranguing her about the indecency of the bequests. For one split second, as her older sister paused for breath, Maude looked up at her and said, "You will be at the funeral of course, Sybil? People will expect her elder daughter to be there."

Sybil was silent for a few seconds – puzzled. Then an ugly flush flooded her face and throat, and she left without a word.

Maude's little revenge was tinged with regret. It was against her nature to hurt people. The only sense of satisfaction she felt was that perhaps she'd become 'a woman of firm decisions', as Mr Denby kept telling her she must, now that she owned property. She had assisted many families in times of death, and she knew that often the unspeakable was spoken – and what should have been spoken, was not.

Sybil was puzzled again the next day. An extraordinary number attended the funeral. She had been unaware that her mother was so highly esteemed. The priest spoke about a person Sybil did not know.

"We know Amelia Kelly as a woman of wry humour and robust endurance. Everyone here, I am sure, admired her ...", and all Sybil took in was only 'the wry and the robust', both of which offended her fragmented sensibilities.

The man is no gentleman, she fumed silently, talking about Mother in such a coarse manner.

And as the eulogy carried on, leaving no one in doubt as to his late parishioner's qualities and accomplishments, Sybil had to concentrate on the floral arrangements and the sad state of the old church to shut out his disturbing words.

"I should not be here at all," she admonished the arum lilies standing like angel warriors on the side altar. "I am completely devastated by the blow I have received. All last night I had an excruciating pain down one side of my poor head, and I vomited all night. I should not have left my bed today."

Fortunately Edward had come home for the funeral. He had spent the early hours administering cold compresses to her forehead. She did not ask Uriah to assist her, his view being that 'Maude has looked after your mother for almost twenty years, Sybil. She deserves the inheritance'.

The idea was idiotic – typical of Uriah. Her arsenical tablets had not alleviated the pain even after she had doubled the dosage. At eight in the morning she had got Edward to fetch that old fool Jenkins. She knew the doctor would prescribe whatever she requested on the day of her mother's funeral. And so she sat loaded with laudanum – a faint roar in her ears like an ocean wave that got closer and louder the longer the priest talked about her mother.

For the first time in her life, Sybil felt old. For the first time in four days, she realised her mother had died.

For the first time, her eyes drifted to the casket and her mind cleared. It was a beautiful casket. Rimu and kauri shone splendidly together – sawn and cut, shaved and carved, and polished to perfection. Even she, in her state of betrayal, had to acknowledge the craftsmanship and the aura that surrounded it, and she had only just learnt that her husband had built it 'with loving care'. She, the elder daughter, had received that information from the pulpit along with the rest of the common congregation. It was shocking that she had not been made aware of this before the ceremony. Although she vaguely remembered some talk of these matters right at the beginning, but she had been prostrate with the treachery of the will. Now her eyes had trouble avoiding the coffin which held her mother's lifeless remains. She dared not think about it. She had been too delicate to even contemplate viewing a dead body. Not that anyone had assisted her to do so. Everyone seemed too busy making an extraordinary fuss of Maude and Iona – and even Uriah. They had all gone completely mad – the whole lot of them. It was simply a grotesque conspiracy.

She felt suffocated by the perfume of masses of wildflowers strewn at the front of the church. How had they been allowed to do that? It was not decorous. In fact the whole thing was in bad taste, and the requiem mass far too long. Sybil leant wanly on her son's arm and stared at the stained glass window. Between the sword of retribution and the head of the avenging angel she saw the space she had known since childhood – a space of no colour. She kept her eyes on it. She would not look towards Iona on any account. The girl looked positively disgusting and had ignored her mother all morning. Sybil let the drug waves float her into soft insensibility and heard nothing more.

Uriah, sitting beside his wife, felt moved to tears. He had known his mother-in-law since he was a young man and thought fondly of Amelia Kelly. She had tried to help him in the early days. She was a strong woman it did not pay to cross, yet she could be extremely kind at times. The story of her life, so succinctly and simply pieced together by this good man, reminded him of those early times – much of which he would rather forget.

He caught a movement and noticed his daughter, obviously feeling a little uncomfortable, shifting in the seat in front. She would not sit with them, preferring to be in the pew beside Maude.

Uriah had not seen Iona since learning of her pregnancy – the wedding day had been bad enough but the thought of his girl carrying that man's child had nearly tipped him over the edge. Of course Iona had not been pregnant then. That suggestion had been one of Sybil's poisonous darts to put him off the track. He should not think of that time either. Nowadays work had become his only panacea. He laboured long hours, trying to forget the mess he had allowed Iona to be stuck in, until Sybil complained he disturbed her sleep. "What time of night is this to be crawling into the bed disturbing me?" she would grumble. "Good heavens, Uriah, have you no thought for anyone but yourself? It's past one in the morning."

One night she had suggested he might like to take up permanent residence in his shed and had been appalled by his agreement. It had taken her weeks of placatory tactics before he had agreed not to take her up on the offer. However, he had won a victory and had ignored his wife when she stood in frozen martyrdom while he moved his things into Iona's old bedroom. Being in a room of his own, through sleepless night after sleepless night, was the only thing that kept him sane. He knew he had somehow allowed Iona to be used. For the life of him, he couldn't recollect how it had happened.

Now, as he studied his daughter, he felt a small easing in his chest. Being with child had made her even more beautiful. She was not the girl he had seen growing up. This was a stunning young woman. A woman who seemed a little removed from … from the world. "The air of a nun," he mused, and immediately felt the shock of such a ridiculous idea. She seemed well, though, and well cared for, and for that he was grateful.

Whereas Albert, sitting hunched beside her, looked old and slightly scruffy. He sat fidgeting and looking out of place. But then the man looked out of place anywhere in Uriah's opinion, except behind his shop counter. It was strange but of the two of them, Iona looked the stronger. The smell of incense aroused Uriah. It was time for him to take his place as a pallbearer. He stood with the rest of the congregation for the last blessing over Amelia Kelly.

"*In nomine patris et filii et spiritus sancti* …" intoned the priest.

Uriah's mind went completely blank. He didn't know if that was peace or not.

Maude spent two weeks in deep grief. It surprised her. She had thought she was well prepared for her mother's death. Amelia was old and frail and hard of hearing. Several times she had said she was ready to 'move on to the next world, for this one had become a dull affair'. Nevertheless, now that she had died an immense hole had appeared in Maude's life. *Mother has been a part of my life, all my life. I should have known I would be affected*, she thought, *but I must keep busy, as busy as I have been these last years as her health faded.*

And so Maude worked herself hard each day and fell into bed bone-weary each night. Every article of her mother's clothing was laundered and sorted until one day the job was finished.

"Mrs Craig will know where you will be best used," she told her mother's belongings packed in bulging bags and boxes in the front hallway.

Yet she still became upset when they were carted off. In fact she was so choked up she could not thank Mr Craig, and he such a sweet, shy man, he never said a word when alone in the presence of any woman other than his wife. After the clothing exodus, the house suffered so much spring cleaning it groaned.

Maude sat on the piano stool admiring her work. Satisfied, dusty and dirty, she suddenly began to howl, her whole body twisting and shaking as if hit by a storm that left her feeling battered and sore all over. Strangely, she felt much better after that. She slid her aching body into a hot bath and closed her eyes. "The furniture looks so beautiful when it's polished, doesn't it, Mother?" she whispered. "I hope you like it."

Only then did the realisation hit her that it was now her furniture. Everything belonged to her; she, Maude Kelly, spinster of this parish, had become a homeowner – and she now had the right to reposition all that lovely furniture. It was a heady experience.

New things began to colour Maude's days. She had to meet several times with Mr Denby, the lawyer, because she did not fully understand how to conduct her business affairs. The first appointment had been at her house. After that she insisted on walking to his office. It was necessary to show Sedgely she wanted to take control of her life. Maude had known she would inherit the house; she had not known her mother had so many savings. Learning how to manage these investments was not easy. While she knew that on the outside she looked poised and in control, on the inside she felt as if she was living in a tug of war. However, she gradually gained confidence. Good sleep and daily challenges gave her more energy and made her feel younger. The empty space her mother had filled still remained, but she began to accept its presence.

Mr Denby had shocked her by suggesting that sometime in the future she might marry now she was free of her duties to her mother. She was not quite sure whether the widower was making an advance, or whether he had said it in conjunction with a remark about husbands seeing to the financial side of marital affairs. She had tried to hide her reaction. She hoped she had. Marriage had not entered her mind since her late twenties, by which time she had already slotted into the spinster-daughter, maiden-aunt role. His remark made her uneasy; she found she still had some desire for a man's companionship, a male protector and a lover's arms. "No, no!" she muttered and threw herself into the spring gardening season with such exertion she ended up at Dr Jenkins' surgery with a bad bout of what she thought was rheumatics but he told her was a case of muscle strain.

"Don't self-diagnose a digging injury, Miss Kelly," he said. "You'll only find yourself up the wrong garden path," and laughed heartily at his own pun. He prescribed aspirin, embrocation and 'taking things easy'.

Maude went home chastened. The embrocation smelt like horse liniment. Her mother would have said it was 'not at all ladylike'. After a more comfortable night's sleep she saw the wisdom of the doctor's advice. She worked at a slower pace and began making plans for her own future.

In the last week of September, Dr Jenkins summoned Maude to the Hammond house. Iona had laboured through one of the worst births Jenkins and Sister Grey had ever seen. The baby boy was dead, the umbilical cord wrapped tightly around his neck. Albert Hammond had collapsed, and Sybil was hysterical. The doctor would not allow either of them near his patient, so when Maude arrived she saw Uriah standing alone at the side of his daughter's blood-stained bed, pleading.

"Iona, you must fight! Iona, don't give up. Girl! You must try!" On and on he went, only quietening when they promised to 'take her out of this place'.

So it was that while Albert lay stupefied with drink in his own guest room, Uriah carried his dying daughter out of Albert's house. He placed her on the back seat of the doctor's car and held her, while the doctor drove at a snail's pace to the Kelly home.

A week later, Sam Newbold got the constable to break into the Hammond house. Albert had not been seen since the birth of his strangled son, and Sam could not raise a response. They found Albert dead on the bedroom floor, his head face down in a pile of vomit; the room reeked of half-dried bile and stale whisky. The coroner found that Albert Hammond, who would have turned thirty-eight had he lived one more day, had died from misadventure. Three other people knew the truth – the doctor, the constable and Newbold – but they did not burden the townspeople with the information.

Newbold saw to his employer's funeral arrangements. Few people attended. Maude and Uriah were consumed with nursing Iona. They received the news and went on with running their private hospital for one. They could find no trained staff, but the doctor recommended sixteen- year-old Maryanne Stewart, who showed an interest in nursing, to live in and do cleaning and washing.

"That will free you both for the battle. But she must want to fight."

Chapter Eleven

Caleb watched from the back of the crowd as the first of the returning soldiers came down the gangplank of the Niagara. A roar went up. Everyone on the Auckland wharf was waiting for someone they loved, come back from the war. Fighting men fell into their parents' arms and embraced their sweethearts, wives and children. They laughed, cried, kissed and were gathered into the bosoms of their families. It was October 1918 and the war was over.

Caleb still felt out of place when he saw uniformed men. It had taken all these months to get his strength back after the peritonitis. "Oh, dry up, Caleb," he told himself. "If you don't keep an eye out you'll miss Pat."

Patrick Kent Donovan had been called up early. Caleb hadn't seen his friend since the Shelly Beach regatta in 1914. 'That Donovan boy', as the town called him, had been Caleb's best pal since they were six years old. The oldest in a family of eight, Pat had curly hair the colour of mud and eyes 'as blue as Mary's mantle' – as Sister Margaret often said – which always meant a stoush behind the classroom as Pat weighed into anyone stupid enough to repeat Sister's choice of phrase. He'd weighed into Caleb on their first day of school.

"Ger'off me foot, sissy shoes!" Pat had yelled, and when Caleb looked down at the filthy foot covering his black leather lace-up, tiny Pat Donovan had thumped him fair in the stomach.

"Fight, fight!" yelled the kids in line behind them.

Neither of them had won the fight and when both of them got punished for the incident they shook hands like men and stuck up for each other from then on.

"Good to see ya, Cal," boomed the shortest soldier in the army. "Got a smoke?"

"Pat! How'd you sneak up on me, you bastard!"

"Being close to the ground has that effect." Pat laughed but as Caleb went to shake his hand Pat sidestepped and said, "Don't touch me and don't get too near me."

"What the hell?"

"Just start walking and I'll tell you all about the mess that bloody ship's been in!"

They walked at a fair clip past the bottom of Queen Street and headed for Freemans Bay where Caleb had parked his father's car. Neither he nor Pat wanted to get caught up in any crowds. Whether his mate was supposed to be marching, Caleb didn't ask. Pat had got away with many dodges over the years. "I was there," he'd say, innocence beaming from his baby blues. "You probably couldn't see me, I'm so short," and because, in reality, it could have happened, the person being duped would give Pat the benefit of the doubt.

"Now, Donovan, what's all this 'don't touch me' rot?"

"If that ship isn't full of men down with the black plague then I'm a leprechaun," Pat whispered.

Caleb roared with laughter. He looked down at his stocky little friend. "Of course you are. Have you only just found out?"

Pat Donovan stopped. For some seconds he stared at Caleb then shook his head.

"I wish it was as simple as that, Cal." He took a grubby handkerchief out of his trouser pocket and wiped his eyes.

Caleb was shocked. Was Pat in tears? He stood beside his friend and waited.

"Four soldiers died at sea. Others are being taken to hospital right now." He blew his nose. "Some are mates of mine."

"I'm sorry, Pat, but … the plague? What are you talking about, man? If it was the plague they would have kept the ship in the stream!"

"You'd think so, wouldn't you? And I'm selfish enough to be glad they let us dock – but I'm not stupid. I saw some of those men. They were too ill for an ordinary influenza."

"We've had a bit of flu in Auckland this winter. Maybe the soldiers are run down?" Caleb had no idea what else to say. Pat looked terrible.

"Look, don't worry about it, Cal. Perhaps I've got it all wrong – but you should be very careful who you mix with during the next few weeks. They told us to avoid contact with each other on board. As if there was much chance of doing that. Maybe the bigwigs in the cabins above deck could manage it but not us – not the cannon fodder down below."

"I'm sorry, mate. Come on. Let's get you home to your family."

"I'm not going near my family, you dumb ox. Didn't you hear me? I'm probably carrying bugs, and I'll be damned if I'm going to endanger my brothers and sisters," and he strode up and down like a man carrying the world on his shoulders.

Caleb waited until he saw his friend slow down then caught up with him and asked, "What do you want to do then, Pat?"

"I want to go bush."

"Okay, pal. I'll come with you." For a moment he thought Pat was going to punch him. "Look, Pat, we can work things out. In the wop-wops up north we can go anywhere together and not be two yards close at any time. There's nothing but fresh air there. You know that. Can we just get moving?"

So they did. Caleb cranked the car into life. Pat threw his kitbag on the back seat and was sitting up front beside his friend trying not to doze off before he remembered his fear about passing on 'bugs'.

"Too late now, Pat." Caleb grinned.

They talked about their plans for their great 'walkabout' as the Aussies called it. Pat fished a scrap of paper and a pencil stub out of his pocket and made a list of all they would need to tramp the bush and beaches on the edges of the northern river.

They were driving through Henderson when Caleb braked and stopped the car on the side of the road. "Hang on, Pat," he said. "We don't have to tramp up every damn hill and dale. We'll take the *Muritai*. Just think, boat, bunks and shelter in a storm. What d'ya reckon?"

"Can we do that? Will your dad let you off work?" "I've not been working for months, Pat," and Cal told him all about his illness. "I'm little more than a salesman even now. My cousin came in as Dad's apprentice once I went south, and he's damned good. Fully qualified and married with a kid on the way. I don't want to upset their arrangements. I'm still thinking about what I want to do." Their plans took on a different aspect. Living on the launch they could still explore the land surrounding the river's vast waters. Ideas flooded the car.

"We could live off fish and wild turkeys – and pig and puha."

"Yeah, and scallops – or cockle fritters at a pinch!"

They rode in silence for a mile, then Caleb addressed the important issue. "I'll have to tell my folks I'm away for a month or so."

"Yeah. I'll tell my youngest brother. He knows how to keep his mouth shut."

"Will there be trouble from the army? I mean, you're not deserting, are you?"

"Nah! Tod Brown and I had been sleeping near a chap who came down with it two days ago. We went to our lieutenant and asked if we could go straight home before we caught it. I don't know how he did it but he got us an early discharge. Toddy could always talk us out of anything."

"Okay, you slippery sod; haven't changed much, have you."

"Over there, in that disease-ridden mud-hole, if you weren't slippery, you were dead."

Caleb cranked the car up again and got them under way. "After we've squared it all with our folks we'll pack our gear and get out of Helensville. I wouldn't mind a couple of months. How about you?"

"I'd like a year, me boy, but I'll have to find some work at some stage. Let's play it by ear. A couple of months will bring us to Christmas. Might be too long – might not. Let's see what we think by the end of November, eh?"

"Sounds good to me, mate."

"You know, Cal, we'll have to watch it for the next week or so. I could still be coming down with the bot."

"Yeah. Let's get going then and hole up somewhere for a few days. Does it hit hard, this flu?"

"Hard! It can kill you in a few hours or take as much time as it likes. If I do get it, you have to leave me to it. I want your word on that, Cal! I won't go with you if you can't keep this promise – no sense in both of us kicking the bucket. Are you man enough to do it?"

Caleb thought over all the implications of such an agreement. "You have my word, Pat. If you get that ill and you're sure there's no hope, I'll get away. I'll burn the boat if necessary."

"Good man," said Pat. "Right! That's our first plan. I reckon a week will do it. Then, if I'm all hunky-dory, we go. I can bunk down on the boat tonight ... keep my bugs to myself."

"We can work on *Muritai* while we wait. The Kelvin could do with some work. Remember when I bought that motor ...?"

But Pat was snoring. He slept like a baby until Kumeu and woke up starving. They stopped at a fish and chip shop for a meal then talked and laughed all the way back to Helensville.

Caleb was chuffed. He would have a break at the exact time his health needed it, and how fitting it seemed that Pat, who had helped him build the *Muritai*, was the one to be sailing with him on this freedom trip into the winding waters of their boyhood.

Chapter Twelve

Dr Jenkins had not been able to visit Iona since she had started to improve, and it was now the beginning of November. He was run off his feet dealing with the outbreak of influenza that had hit Sedgely. Today he stood swaying with exhaustion on Maude's verandah outside the window of the girl's sickroom.

"Don't come near me. In fact, don't go near anyone if you can help it. She is still weak, and if she catches this illness, all your work will have been in vain," he told the occupants, peering at them from black-rimmed eyes.

Maude was appalled by the change in the man. The doctor sat down heavily on the top step.

"Thank you for all you did for my girl," said Uriah, his voice husky.

"Ah, it's my job, Uriah. It's a tonic to my heart the way you two have nursed Iona. It shows great devotion." He cleared his throat. "You can bring her out here to sit in the sun for a few minutes now. Extend the time gradually. We don't want any setbacks."

"There's a rumour it's the black flu."

"Well … it's very like it."

"Where in hell did it come from?"

"Soldiers coming back from war. The Auckland authorities let them disembark. Stupid decision! It's worse down there."

The doctor headed back to his car. He drove home, his spirit lifted by the thought of those two people. One might say they had willed the girl to live – but then they had been dealing with a body that only needed time and care. Others he now saw daily had no such hope. In spite of all the fumigation stations and medical notices, that Grim Reaper, death, would take his toll.

He parked outside his gate, leant back and closed his eyes. Even in his exhaustion he gave thanks to God, as he always did, for preserving the life of his patient, entrusting the many others to the safe refuge of that Power greater than himself.

Thirty minutes later a horse and rider found him sound asleep, slumped over the wheel of his car, and woke him for yet another call to an influenza victim – the son of Sybil and Uriah Anderson-Keyes.

When Uriah received the message about Edward he knew he had no choice, yet the seriousness of the news would not settle on him, the morning had been so bright with the doctor's verdict over Iona. He moved silently into the sickroom and watched his daughter. She lay in a peaceful sleep. Her first walk to the verandah had tired her beyond belief but at the same time had left a trace of colour on her cheeks.

He was weary from the night watches he had done for Maude. Sybil had been useless. So he and Maude had worked out a system for nursing his girl. During the days Maude had managed Iona, with Maryanne Stewart helping where she could. She showed an astute ability to understand Iona's needs. Remarkable girl, thought Uriah. Worth her weight in gold. Maude had promised Maryanne to help her with her schoolwork and so had Dr Jenkins. At sixteen and living well upcountry on a farm, she had not attained a level of education to get her into either teaching or nursing.

"You need to sit down." Yes, he did. He was so tired he was even talking to himself and sore all over from pushing himself too long and too hard. He moved quietly and sat on the bedside chair. Perhaps a ten-minute doze?

His eyes closed. His mind would not. Behind his lids the weeks replayed. He had gone home and caught a little sleep in the afternoons, returning to see Iona settled in the evenings. Most of those dark hours he spent sunk in this old armchair.

He never slept during those long watches – but sometimes he drifted. If Iona disturbed, he heard her, often before she roused. He held her like a baby while she sipped water or the gruel Maude left ready on the night table. He had helped her on and off the commode and been horrified at her emaciated body. It was easier when she began to sleep through the night without having to relieve herself. He wished he had never felt the protruding bones, the weightlessness of her wasted frame – only a month before she had been radiant in her impending motherhood.

The loss of his first grandchild had meant little to him. The loss of her child had sent her into a coma for a week. A thought struck him: 'She has never spoken about the baby!' Maude had said something about the little boy once, and Iona had not spoken for three days.

The news of her husband's death had, surprisingly, rallied her senses and brought her back to life. 'We nearly lost her!' The words winged through his mind. Yes, that near loss had been the trigger that shocked Uriah out of his taciturn upbringing, had let loose his ability to care and to heal.

They'd shared some gentle words this last week. He couldn't break a lifetime's learning in a few days, and she had almost no energy – a stammered apology, a smile of thanks, a look of love – that was enough. "Almost too much," he mumbled, emotion welling up in him.

"I didn't call," whispered Iona, and Uriah felt guilty for disturbing her rest.

"I was just leaving. I came to see if you were asleep."

"You should have gone earlier, Father. You need your sleep too."

"I know. I know." He cleared his throat, got up from the chair and walked to the window. He had not intended to tell her about her brother, but now he decided she should know. If anything did happen to Edward she would at least be prepared.

"I will not be here now, Iona, in the night times. I have to go home to help your mother. Edward is unwell."

"Is it the bad flu?"

"They fear so."

"Give him my love, Father, please."

"I will." He turned and moved to the side of her bed. She could not see him so well there. He would miss those nights, when the world slept and the hours were soft with woven dreams and the dawn smelt as pure as perfumed dew. Now, with the light behind him, Uriah bent and kissed her forehead. "Always fight, girl. Remember – never give up."

Iona did not speak. Then, as Uriah moved to the doorway, she said, "You saved me, Father ... you and Auntie."

Uriah nodded and left swiftly.

As soon as he stepped through the front door of his own home, Sybil began weeping uncontrollably and accused him of desertion and everything else under the sun, until he was tempted to hit her. Instead he ignored her and made straight for Edward's room.

His son was conscious but he had the bad colour and all the frightening symptoms of influenza. Uriah was struck by the lack of air in the bedroom and by the absence of anything in the form of fluid by the boy's bed. He threw open the windows and strode out into the hall to his wife. He did not look directly at her – that would have tested him too far – and he spoke tersely. "Get water. A large jug – full – and a wide-mouthed glass. Bring it to me in his room, quickly."

Sybil was so taken aback she did as she was told. When she appeared with those things he told her to make up some weak lemon and barley water as well.

"Then bring me a basin of lukewarm water, a washcloth and towels – and clean sheets and pillowcases."

"Don't speak to me like that," Sybil retorted. "I'm most unwell myself."

Uriah still did not look at her but he spoke slowly and distinctly. "Then find someone else to help me nurse your son."

His wife whimpered a little as she explained the impossibility of getting any home help now that people were either sick themselves or petrified of catching the disease from others. "Even the doctor won't call every day," she grizzled.

"Of course he can't be calling all the time, Sybil, he's worn out seeing to everyone in the district!" he snapped – and sighed – as she yelled back, "Well, you should have been here for your son. You've spent enough time all these weeks mollycoddling Iona."

"That's enough! The doctor has only this morning said she could go outside. Maude saw to Iona. You will have to help with your son."

"Oh, no. I'm no good with sick beds. I can't help it." She went off like a banshee, shrieking and crying. "No! I can't bear it!"

"Stop it, Sybil!" he shouted, and when she wouldn't, he grabbed her and shook her. "Stop this nonsense at once."

He pushed her out of the door and holding her firmly by her shoulders walked her down the hallway and into the kitchen. Once there she grabbed him round the waist, burying herself into his chest.

He waited a few moments to get himself under control. Then, in a flat but firm voice, he said, "Leave me alone to nurse your son." He got hold of her arms, wrenched them around to the front of his chest and sat her down on a kitchen chair – shoving it under the table so she could not get away.

She stopped, suddenly, like a tap turned off.

And it was then he thought of a way to make her do what had to be done. It did not seem right. Nor did he like it. But he had no choice. She was right – all home help had dried up. He knew that as well as he knew his own name. She would not have carried on the way she did if there had been any workers about.

And then he thought of the boy and said in a steely voice, "If you don't get off that chair and get on with bringing all the things I asked for, then I'll take you to Jenkins and have him pronounce you insane. I will put you in a madhouse, Sybil. I will!"

She turned slowly – and knew he had changed.

"Get the things I asked for. Just do as I tell you. I will nurse him. Now go. Water, jug, lemon and barley – and then bring all the linen. Go."

Uriah began to shake and staggered down the back hallway seeking air. Outside he sat down on the chopping block. His chest felt so tight he wondered if he might be having a heart attack. He felt dizzy and had difficulty breathing. After a while he managed to stand and walk unsteadily to the back steps. When he put his head back to draw an even deeper breath he saw the first star winking. He sent up a wish – probably a prayer – and went straight back to Edward.

He had been concerned about the effect of Sybil's words on the boy. He was pleased to see that Edward's eyes were no longer twitching and he was resting. There was a jug of water and a glass on the bedside table. He filled the glass and with one arm gathered Edward to him. "Come on, son," he urged. "Sip a little water."

He went to the bathroom to wash and leaned forward on the edge of the basin. He felt an interminable tiredness.

He thought of the difference between Iona's sickroom and Edward's. No loving touches here. He turned the tap on over the bath and shoved his head under. The shock of cold water made his skull ache.

In his bedroom he changed his clothes ready for the night watch and went down to the kitchen to remind Sybil to make weak gruel for the boy. "He needs to get some sustenance. As soon as it's ready, let me know."

His wife, red-eyed and silent, followed him back to the sickroom with a washbowl and cloth.

"The bed linen will need to be changed often, Sybil – and keep as many windows open in the house as possible. The days when they shut sick people up in a fug have gone. He needs fresh air as well as warmth."

He waited a second to see if she had heard. He almost felt sorry for her. "I'll bed-bath him and change his nightshirt."

He washed his son. By the time he managed to get the clean nightshirt covering him, Sybil was back with a fresh sheet. She spread it on the bed while Uriah rolled and lifted the lad – then she left.

Uriah patted a drop of eau de cologne on the back of Edward's neck as he had seen Maude do for Iona and carefully rubbed a little camphor oil on his chest. Then he combed his son's hair. Through it all he talked to Edward as if they were sitting outside in the garden on a lazy afternoon.

Uriah could hear no sounds from the kitchen so he went down and made the lemon and barley water himself. Back by Edward's bedside he managed to get a little into his son. "You can have some tasty gruel soon." The fact there was no answer troubled him not at all. Maude and Maryanne were so natural with Iona that Uriah also felt comfortable talking to an unresponsive patient. He, who had never been able to talk easily with others, had chatted to his daughter sensibly and quietly, and one day she had simply parted her lips – and spoken. And so too would her brother. He had a feeling about it.

As day after painful day slid by, Edward's body performed the usual distressing circus – then turned the corner towards health again. Uriah heard news of Iona's progress from the doctor. He would not be able to go near Maude's house for weeks until he was sure he would carry no germs to the women. Eventually he managed to sleep through the night in his own bed again instead of at all angles on the stuffy armchair. After two good nights' sleep he felt he might be casting off some of his grinding weariness. One day he was able to help his son out onto the sunny porch just as he had helped his daughter take her first walk to the Kelly verandah. It was a turning point for them all.

That night Uriah's throat burned like a fire made in hell, and he dozed fitfully through the dark hours. He knew he had caught the 'black flu'. With Edward so weak and Sybil so unpredictable, he gave himself little chance. By morning, when Sybil gave up calling and came to his room, he was delirious and drenched in his own foul-smelling sweat.

Chapter Thirteen

Iona could not bring herself to go back to Albert's house after she came through the convalescent period. It was not living alone that worried her – it was the sick dreams and the dark memories she knew she would have, should she try to return. Her decision fitted in with everyone else's view, and she enjoyed their support. She was usually so at odds with her family that she was relieved to sink into the arms of their approval, viewing the experience with detached amusement.

Her first outings were appointments with her lawyer, Norman Livingstone. There was a lot to learn. Sam Newbold was teaching her about the shop. At eighteen she had become the sole inheritor of Albert's properties, possessions and monies. So far, no debts had been found, and Iona became determined to learn all she could about the business and the money matters Albert had handled. Livingstone had said there was a bank mortgage over the store but it was taken care of each month by some elaborate method set up between Albert and the bank. All she had to do was sign 'here' and 'there' and not worry. She was angry. She felt she was being treated like a schoolgirl – no, not even like a schoolgirl, like a simpleton.

Christmas 1918 came and went without her Creek family. Uriah was adamant they still didn't know if Sybil might come down with the terrible illness.

"He's worrying unnecessarily, silly man," Aunt Maude told her. "Still, we'll do the best we can without them." And they did – though two people hardly made a family, and sadness settled on the day by late afternoon. They missed the bounce of Maryanne. She had gone north to her family for Christmas leaving Maude and Iona to force their way through tea and go early to bed.

Iona's education as an in-training owner was made easy by Sam Newbold through January and February of 1919. Courteous, with a touch of wry humour, his explanations were clear, open and honest – and his wife Agnes also such a woman. They were not of the business or professional classes of Sedgely society. No. They were real people – what Iona called real people, anyway.

Agnes suggested a break at their small seaside bach – she could see Iona was a quick learner but the effort was keeping the girl as thin as a rake. When Iona said she would like to stay at the coast on her own, Agnes understood immediately, and Sam nodded his pink head, with the thinning auburn curls, sympathetically.

"My family do not like me going off alone," Iona warned them, watching them from under her lashes. "Apart from Aunt Maude. I would be letting it be known I was in the city."

Agnes gave a surprisingly throaty laugh. "Don't you worry, Iona. When you're neither fish nor fowl in the society stakes, and a woman into the bargain, you learn 'toot sweet' how to keep your mouth shut."

There had followed a lively discussion on women's abilities and desires. Iona was intrigued to find Sam joining in. She could see a long and lasting friendship ahead with the older couple.

Sam's words at the end of that conversation bolstered her decision never again to be pushed into being what she was not. "If this war has done nothing else, it has shown this country the true capabilities of our women," he declared.

Not like Iona's lawyer. Yesterday he had told her 'not to worry her pretty little head' about such matters – and patting her shoulder as she left said, "We'll see that you're taken care of, Mrs Hammond."

Sick of dealing with Norman Livingstone, Iona had a talk with Aunt Maude.

"I think if you wish to learn all you can about how to conduct your own affairs, he should help you to do so. Perhaps Mr Livingstone is not used to women clients. Mr Denby is so patient with me. He says I am doing very well. Mind you, your inheritance may be a more complicated matter than mine."

"I know, Auntie, but I believe I could learn. I will not be spoken down to by that man."

"Now don't go getting upset my dear. You don't want to set yourself back."

"Well," she said, "I have been feeling tired this last week, but then it is very hot."

"See! I knew it. You must rest up for a day or two."
"Actually, I would like very much to get away somewhere quiet. Somewhere I could rest, as you say, and get my full strength back. I thought I might slip out to the coast next week and stay at Newbolds' bach. Sam

97

said I would be welcome to use it as none of the family will be there from now until Easter."

"You can't stay out there by yourself, child! That west coast is as wild and deserted as any place on earth."

"I know. That's why I want to go there. I need to be on my own for a while."

"But Iona – by yourself – out there?"

"Don't, Auntie, please. I am not a child any more. And I've seen to myself for years."

At which Maude was miserably silent.

After she had reassured her aunt that her shop manager and his wife would tell no one she was on her own at the bach, Iona got her aunt's agreement in the deception.

"Father, above all, mustn't know. I will be fine, Auntie. I promise."

Iona gave her Aunt Maude a hug and hurried her into preparing the evening meal.

They worked together.

"Have you seen Father and Edward yet, Auntie?"

"No, not yet, but Maryanne talked to Edward from outside the window two days ago on her way back from the farm. She said he looked to be recovering well."

"And Father?"

"She didn't see Uriah. She said Edward was still a bit worried about him. He's up from his sickbed but still very weak."

"I'll call in before I go on holiday. As long as I don't go too near, I should be safe."

Maude glanced at the young woman. Not a word for Sybil, she mused, and no wonder. She brought in the hot food, and they sat down at table.

"Tea's ready. Let's eat, and I will tell you all Maryanne's news over a cup of tea. I am hoping for a good year's study from that girl. We start back with the books halfway through January. We aim to get a jump start on the school year."

While Maude said her regular grace before meals, Iona put her plans to one side. It was safe here. For that she gave thanks.

Before she left for the coast, Iona walked down to Kotare Creek. The morning was warm and she was pleased she had managed the walk without getting too tired. She avoided the house and went straight to her father's shed. He did not hear her arrive so she waited beside the open doors and watched.

He was pottering – that's all you could call it, not working as she used to seeing him work – caulking the old house dinghy, his face as gaunt and grey as the putty he was spreading into cracks and seams. Iona moved quietly away from the door to the outside corner of the shed where he could not see her and composed herself before going back.

"Are you there?" she sang out.

"Iona! How good to see you. Don't come too near."

He made her sit outside in his paint-splattered work chair while he fished out a box to sit on. They talked for a while, happy in their new harmony; but it was like neither the times of her childhood nor the special times of her illness.

"You still don't look well," she said.

"I'm improving slowly, Iona. Don't you worry about me."

"Have you got behind with your orders?"

"Yes, but not too much; everyone got behind during the sickness. It will take a good year for tradesmen like me to recover both in health and business. It is no great problem. Time will see to things."

"Is Edward himself again?"

"Oh, yes. He has shaken it off remarkably well."

"He had a good nurse."

Uriah, always shy of a compliment, avoided looking at her; his blue eyes, no longer bright, lifted above her head and rested on the river at her back.

"Edward did very well. He was only just past the worst of his bout when I went down in a heap. He helped me as much as his poor strength would allow. Mind you we had a great doctor in Jenkins. That was half the battle won. We were very lucky in Sedgely – only two deaths."

He mustered his strength and sat up straighter. "You've missed Edward. He's taking a small tramp up into the bush."

"What about mother?" It was Iona's turn to look away. In the long pause that followed, Iona feared she had been too outspoken for the delicacy of the moment. When she looked back she felt Uriah's eyes fall on her face. She did not know what she read there. It felt as if he wanted to tell her something – something from soul to soul – but she could not read his mind, and while her awareness of him was sharper than it had ever been in her life, she knew he had decided not to say what he wanted to. He brought a fine veil down over his eyes and smiled as if to soften his withdrawal of intimacy.

"Sybil did the best she could, Iona. Things are a little different now. I think you should go up to the house and see her … for at least a few minutes before you leave."

Darn, she thought, *by asking after Mother I've let him know I haven't been there, and he's not going to let me get away without facing her.*

As if he read her thoughts, Uriah said softly, "We can never fully understand another person. It is better not to judge too harshly. Sometimes we make fools of ourselves that way and think we have escaped from our own weakness."

Iona did not know exactly who he was talking about, her or himself. He was shaking a little from the effort of those words, and she felt a trembling in her own chest. Perhaps he suspected the pretending she had meant to do – letting him think she had seen Sybil, because she had planned to leave without doing so once she knew Edward was not about. It must be that. She could not bear it if he was talking about himself.

She got up and began to talk a little too loudly and a little too quickly. "Yes. I was just about to go up. Take care of yourself now."

He moved back towards the door and came slowly to stand above her. He had always been a very tall man, but this flu had left him so thin he looked as if he could not keep his height under control. Gone were his sinewy muscles, his fitness and his strength. She felt a jolt in her heart and had a terrible thought. What if he has given all his strength for the health of his children? She rushed into words again to cover her confusion. "The farmers say it will be a long, fine summer and autumn, according to Sam."

Her father smiled and nodded.

"I have to go to Auckland for a week or two, father … a little business for the store. So I won't see you for a while."

Uriah saw her lie as concern. "I will be fine," he said, using the same words she had used to her aunt. "Go up to the house. Sybil will want you to stay for lunch if you linger too long," he said with a knowing grin.

She waved and choked back tears as she walked across the paddock towards her old home. The visit had been hard, and she had not thought it would be. But he had said something … what was it? Yes, 'time will see to things'. The words gave her a sense of comfort. Perhaps they both needed time to get to know each other in the world outside a sickroom.

When she went into the house she found a change there also. Her mother had become hunched. She was obviously nervous yet did not speak sharply at any time during Iona's visit. She seemed fidgety – unable to keep still for long – and busied herself about the kitchen, touching and pushing at things without any purpose. She spoke of Edward in a distracted manner but enough to reinforce her father's words that he was fully recovered and 'roaming the hills somewhere'.

Then she became intent, in a bird-like way, on making her husband's lunch, hardly noticing Iona's departure until the last minute then hurrying after her and grabbing her against her bosom in an embrace. What's more, she had not criticised Uriah once. Her complaining had been of such things as the poor quality of home help since the war and the inability of the grocer's boy to deliver her orders on time.

As she walked back towards Sedgely, Iona felt relieved and yet at the same time irritated. She was certain her father had been determined she should see the difference in her mother. Perhaps he knew what it was all about; she didn't. It felt as if there was another change to the confusion of her past life. However bad it had been, she had at least known what to expect from her parents. Her consolation was that her mother need not be part of her life now. She hoped with all her heart that her father would get stronger soon. She hoped, too, that for his sake Sybil would be as ineffectual from now on as she had been this morning. Perhaps he would get a little peace.

Just as she was beginning to feel overtired, Dr Jenkins tooted.

"How did you know I needed a lift?" she quizzed him as she got into the big Buick.

"Ha, my girl," he chuckled. "Did you not know I am an angel in disguise?"

A picture of this vast, now balding man dressed as an angel made Iona laugh so hard her tummy felt sore.

"It's so good to see you, doctor," she smiled as she wiped the tears from her eyes.

"And you too, young Iona. Here, have an extra strong peppermint and tell me why you are gadding about out of town."

Which she did, and was a little comforted by his patter of assurances about her father – not that she fully believed him – she had begun to think of doctors and lawyers as 'avoidance men' – a phrase that had come to her during the last few weeks. Then, as she answered his question about her plans with, "I'm away to Auckland for a week or two on business," she thought, *And you're becoming a practised liar, Iona Annabel Anderson-Keyes!*

Oh! she mused, How can I get back to using my own name? Can widows do that? Would everyone be up in arms if I did?

"I'm going to jolly well find out," she decided, "but not before I have my time at the coast. I'm tired of thinking. Soon I'll have sand and waves to walk beside and huge skies to look up to. Soon I'll have some peace."

Chapter Fourteen

From inside the bach Iona watched the wind. It had been born on the morning tide – a light breeze that played with the cabbage trees and ran up and down the stream beside the little house. She welcomed it at first, the movement freeing her in some way from the brooding heat of the first few days at the coast. For most of the morning, sitting at the window mending the skirt she'd torn on yesterday's walk, she had been pleasantly distracted.

Now she felt bored. The holiday bookshelf offered a few well-worn books, mostly of interest to male readers. She chose Kingsley's *Westward Ho!* but found it difficult to concentrate on the story and when Chapter IV was headed 'The Two Ways of being Crost in Love' and started with Lovelace's lines: '*I could not love thee dear so much; Loved I not honour more.*' she gave up and put the book away.

Love, to Iona, seemed to be merely a shadow – always sought, never solid. No! That was wrong because now she saw the love between Sam and Agnes every day. How it worked she wasn't sure. They were happy to be together, a state she had never seen before because her parents surely were not, and as she had no other married relatives to observe, she remained newly aware yet still puzzled.

The Newbolds had brought her out to the bach a week ago after a late evening meal at their home, and they would return in a week to pick her up. She'd watched them go feeling the safety of their friendship catching her like breath in the throat. She had told Agnes she wished she could stay away for two months instead of two weeks, and Agnes had replied, "Well, if you want to become a hermit, now's the time to start, so go ahead. But if you want to play your own tune in this world of ours, I wouldn't buck too hard just yet."

And although they had laughed together like two little girls her friend's words had remained with her.

The older woman was the youngest of a large family. Her mother had died from septicaemia two weeks after bearing Agnes, and her father, 'Pop' Sumich, had been both mother and father to his children. It had been different for Agnes. She and Sam had Harry and Peter, little replicas of Sam. There were no more children.

"I think something went wrong inside me during their birth," she'd told Iona one day in the back of the shop, "but with those two – two's enough." Although she had made a joke of it, Iona could see in her face the ghosts of those unborn children even after seven years.

Her new friends brought their children up in a rough-and-ready fashion with plenty of hugs, laughter and discipline. Iona admired the way the family worked, and after the couple left had been suddenly aware that the older woman was probably the first friend she felt comfortable around. Why was that? Perhaps she took after her father. Although Uriah had earned a certain respect in the district, he was a solitary person, and she took after him in that way. *No, I did make friends sometimes.* There was Mary and Susan, they had started school together. For a minute Iona felt the happiness of that time; but Mary's family were poor, as were Susan's, and somehow her mother killed the chance of any closeness. *No! I must remember.* Ani had continued to visit with her father but refused to come into the house as she had on that first visit, and the friendship became an outdoor playtime. Iona had been very angry. "What about father?" she had shouted. "He has Uncle Toi!"

"Go to bed!" Sybil had said. And after no tea for a couple of nights Iona had not tried again. She had been angry with her father for months over that, because Uncle Toi dropped in to Uriah's shed frequently, and Iona would watch with bad grace as the two men talked and joked. Ani, though, was made of stronger mettle. After acknowledging to Iona that the dislike between Sybil and herself was mutual, she arrived with her father every time he came to see Uriah. Their story of Toi Tira and Uriah Anderson-Keyes, though never acknowledged by Sybil, was well known to Iona and her brother Edward.

Toi Tira had been an apprentice at the same time as Uriah, and the two of them had formed an immediate comradeship from the first day they started in Helensville. They had not quite completed their first year of training when Toi's father died. He went home to his family for the funeral and never came back. His mother needed him to work the farm. This may have ruined Toi's dream but it did not break the tie between the two young men.

Toi was never put off by Sybil's superior attitude, and his friendship with Uriah had been too tight to break. But Toi's wife and most of their children seldom came with him to visit the Anderson-Keyes. Ani Tira, made of sterner stuff, always came. Toi's youngest seemed oblivious to Sybil's bad manners, although after that first day, she never went into the house again choosing to go straight to the work shed and wait until Iona appeared. Uncle Toi's teaching of the Maori language to Ani through greetings and the names of birds enabled a deeper friendship between the girls despite Sybil's nastiness.

Both fathers and daughters knew it was forbidden to speak Maori in the schools and even in the playgrounds. This made many Maori children stop using their language. They became wary of being chastised even outside school grounds. Ani was shy of her father's insistence on teaching the language, but all four knew Uriah's building shed and paddock on his private land by the creek was their piringa, their safe haven.

Instinctively the young Iona never spoke Maori in her mother's house nor did she comment when her father used the odd Maori phrase when speaking with his friend. Ani Tira became Iona's only friend.

The way her mother manipulated people had been a mystery to Uriah's young daughter. Nothing of any relationship content was ever discussed with the children and neither, Iona was later to decide, was it talked over between Sybil and Uriah. Now Iona realised she had never been encouraged to make friends of any girl of

108

whom her mother disapproved. Maryanne Stewart came to mind. Her mother wouldn't approve of her either: 'a farm girl' with 'no social standing' – that would be her mother's judgement. Yet Maryanne had been so kind when Iona was ill, and as she improved they had talked about many things.

Although she's four years younger than me she seems more my age. Maybe it's because she had to be older, living on a farm and having to take her turn at the milking and farm work as well as helping in the house and with younger brothers and sisters.

"So, I'm not good at friendships," Iona decided. Still, today she knew she had a friend in Agnes Newbold, and she knew she sometimes pulled back from the older woman; that fear still tried to stop her getting too close. Now she was her own woman she fought the fear. Those inside quiverings that told her she might lose this delicate new thing were squashed before they did too much damage, and Agnes was patient.

Sam's friendship was different. It was easier. It had begun with the business and remained primarily with it. As to the business – but no, she had promised herself she would not think about the store during these two weeks at the coast.

This was the place she wanted to be.

She wanted to soak up the sea air; wanted to walk on forgiving sands and lie in the edge of the wild Tasman breakers; wanted to be on her own and not have anyone – anyone at all – questioning her, advising her, looking at her, even in concern. She did not want people near her; she wanted to get well and strong and get herself ready to tackle whatever was ahead – like that pompous, young Mr Norman Livingstone. Yes, she needed time, and she needed to do it in her own way.

For the first forty-eight hours she had kept the last few months at bay. After that she found it impossible. Pictures kept popping into her mind. She would remember little incidents or feel suddenly low and lethargic. Then she would feel excited and a little mad. Or she would have an almost uncontrollable urge to clean and scrub and use her body as hard as she could. And she couldn't do that in this little shell of a place. So she had walked and walked and walked.

She saw no one. Except once, when a group of Maori appeared from nowhere and spent the morning digging for toheroa on the low tide. She did not know them, but she felt at ease exchanging a few words. They were from up the coast, they told her, gathering their favourite seafood for their nephew's twenty-first birthday. She was part of their large family for over an hour and went back to her retreat with enough of the shellfish to make fritters for her tea.

Although she had enjoyed being with them, it was a relief to be alone again, even though she now felt like a small child, envious of their family laughter and their family lovingness. Tears fell down her cheeks, but no sound would come from her mouth. She felt frightened of herself.

She decided she would have to go through all that had happened. Ignoring the mixed up messages of her mind was getting her nowhere. She made mental lists; wrote them up in her head; forgot them; and wrote them on her shopping pad –

The pregnancy
My reactions
Albert's reactions
His strange caring of me in the last months
before my premature confinement

and so on. It was perfectly simple.
The list took up half of the small page.

Chapter Fifteen

"Oh my God, the pain!"

She couldn't bear it. It tore her apart and sent her into the dark insides of a huge, seashell, into the peace of that safe 'waiting for death place' – where there was no pain, where there was nothing.

"Iona! Iona!"

Who was that?

"Ahh! No! It's back. No! No! Help me father!"

Then she was awake – shuddering, shaking and gulping in the half-light. Where was she? Where had the shell taken her? What was that whining noise? Ah, yesterday's wind building into a storm.

"I'm at the bach." She looked down.

As always after the no-place nightmare, her hands were clasped tightly together and pressed into her stomach. She unclasped them and rubbed them kindly. Then lifting them up before her eyes, she moved them in a slow finger dance through the air, turning them this way and that and humming an unconscious melody – until her shuddering changed to trembling, and her trembling softened into quivering, and her gulping ceased.

"Thank God."

She got up, wiped away the memory tears of losing the child she had not wanted and got dressed. When she opened the door she found it wasn't all that dark outside. Newbold's old clock said it was half past eight, and it was right. It was the storm darkening the sky that gave the illusion of night.

For breakfast she opened a bottle of preserved peaches, crumbled up some malt biscuits on top and tried not to think about the nightmare, or the birth, or the unbearable pain of being ripped apart. Of course that's what had caused the nightmare. Yesterday she had decided to face up to what had happened. Now all that 'no-place time' had boiled up under the surface.

Well, today was such a dreadful day she would start right now. It was cold. The heavy sky would let no sun through to warm the earth today. She would stay inside and remember.

The air was damp and cold. She pulled on her socks and shrugged into her coat. Taking the top blanket from the bunk, she spread it over her legs.

"That's better, Iona. Now remember." Nothing happened.

It was difficult to remember anything at all of the period immediately after the birth. It was better to persevere though. Here there was no one to come visiting and discover the mess she was in. She shut her eyes and went back to the no-place. Her memories returned in fragments, in the small recollections of sounds and smells. She caught the first time she heard someone talking to her – that little corner of a miracle that was revealed to her as the voice of her father – and she held it as a perfect thing. Her hand flew to her cheek.

113

What was that? Yes, it was the touch of air on her face – and the glimpse of the end of a lace net curtain moving in the breeze from an open bedroom window. Another sound? Was it Albert? Fear fell on her so fast she vibrated like a reed on the bank of the river. Then she knew it was not Albert but her own fear. When the fear went away she felt miserable with guilt.

She was alive – but the baby was dead, and she had not wanted the baby.

She was alive – but Albert, who had wanted the baby, was dead.

She felt the blame, like thick, red blood, flood through her head and blind her to everything; and she saw that her hands, which had come up in front of her like claws, were shaking again, and she clamped them under her armpits for safekeeping. Then she was crying again, and then she wasn't, and then anger crashed in.

Angry! So angry. Things had happened to her that she had hidden in her depths. Things had happened that should not have happened, and she felt betrayed all over again. She felt the attacks, the ravages, the hurt of Albert's hands and Albert's words that trapped her in secrecy and held her in humiliation. She heard her own silent screams and curled herself into an infant ball. Her body hurt with groaning.

"Make it go away! Please make it go away!"

She just wanted a fairy godmother to wave her wand and make the last year and a half disappear ... in a ball of silver smoke ... like in the story books.

"Don't be so stupid!" she whined. She crawled into the bunk and slept.

When she woke it was midday. She made herself eat some cracker biscuits and an apple, and when she stopped chewing she heard the noise.

Yesterday's wind had swollen into today's monster. Gusts wracked the walls. All afternoon she felt like two people. One Iona tried not to remember and wrestled with something trying to take her over – and the other Iona watched the wind. Leaves and little twigs flew about on madly intoxicated journeys. The trees were forced over, more and more, like tortured souls in useless supplication. The noise of the storm ballooned and ballooned and deafened the world while the hurt in her guts grew and grew until she thought she would burst.

She changed into a pair of her brother's trousers she'd packed in the bottom of her bag, and slipped into her sandshoes. Once she'd tied back her long hair – still lank from the effects of her illness even after so long a time – she battled her way down to the first sand dune in front of the bach. She was nearly punched backwards by the wind, but she recovered her balance and forced her legs to adjust as she walked down towards the sea.

"Haaa!" she shouted and felt the wind snatch the sound from her lips. Suddenly she laughed – and she cried out, "Glorious! Glorious! This is glorious!"

She weaved her way towards the north end – not that there was any end to this beach. It was the long coast of the land. It went on forever. But there was a small sand cliff topped with marram and toetoe, about a mile to the north, and she set this as her goal.

The wind raced in from the sea. It forced her trousers flat against her legs and pushed one sleeve up onto her shoulder, billowing the rest of her shirt about her body like a great mad bubble. It plucked out her ribbon so strands of hair flew like streamers. Under her feet seaweed grapes squashed, their flat 'splat' unheard in all the noise. From the throat of the wind came a fury that tormented the waves. It broke them in the middle of their thunder. It bashed them and tore them apart. It sent this part into the air, while another part it flattened back on to the sea. It threw green water and white surf against each other until the screaming and the roaring of the wind joined the screaming and the roaring of the water in an unending, inescapable madness of sound.

Iona found she was laughing and couldn't stop. The 'something' in her all afternoon – that had started in her stomach and grown into her chest – now filled her throat, her head, her ears. It flowed through every hair that whipped around her head and flapped into her eyes. And when the laughing stopped the shouting started. She screamed out to the sea. She screamed at the heavy clouds forming endless, sodden sheets across the sky. She punched at the pockets of wind that puffed and pushed against her and she shouted, "I hate you. I hate you," but had no idea who or what she hated. She thought *I'm going mad. At last it's happening*, then she sang at the top of her lungs. "Going crazy. CRA-AA-ZY!" over and over again like a drunken puppet.

She shook and shook her head – that broken flower – and her tears were the petals falling, but the wind snatched them away up the beach, and the salt spray tears of the sea fell on her face instead, and they, in turn, were snatched and whipped away.

116

Then she heard beside her, and above her, and all around her the sound of an animal wailing and keening. It came into her head and ripped at her throat, her ears, and her chest until it reached her stomach – until she realised it was her, herself, her noises.

All the raw hurting and all the red anger so long held tight and tied up inside her was let loose on the giant wings of the wind and into the womb of the storm.

She leant into those wild wings of wind and rested on them, then turned and let them carry her back. She knew the safety of the sounds of the sea. She knew she was home again – in Iona.

Chapter Sixteen

A few days after she returned to Sedgely she caught the steamer to Dargaville and put her business into the hands of a young lawyer new to that town. She knew by now she was not a woman of such means as she had been led to believe immediately after her illness, but she was confident she would be able to manage her own affairs from now on.

Albert's house would have to be sold to free up the mortgage on the store. Agnes wanted to leave full-time work to be with the Harry and Peter now that her sister had moved away and could no longer babysit. Sam had taken on Paul Sloan two days a week. He had become proficient with his wooden leg, and Iona worked full-time in the shop and did the paperwork for a nominal wage. This way Sam was still free to see to the heavy work he'd always done when Agnes was in the shop. With these changes Iona hoped to be soon saving towards a home of her own.

She was now a paying boarder at Aunt Maude's, as was Maryanne Stewart. The girl's taste of nursing had put her off that career. She had left school now and was a teacher aide at Sedgely Primary School. Next year she planned to go to Auckland to train at the teachers' college. Iona enjoyed the younger girl's company. There was in Maryanne an impishness and jolliness that took Iona out of herself. The little pranks and unaffected laughter that flew about the Kelly house between the three women were good for Iona's soul. And theirs, she realised. It was comforting to know she would have a share in the unfolding of her young friend's youth – a small reparation for the ripping away of her own.

The store and the coming to grips of her true financial position took up most of her time. She would never really know whether Livingstone had a 'sticky finger' in Albert's finances or whether Albert had made mistakes in his business judgements during the last year of his life. As it coincided with their first year of marriage she suspected either situation could be possible. She had her suspicions about Livingstone, but as Sam had said, "You have no proof, Iona, and you'll probably never have the money to pay someone to get it for you. Suspicion is not proof."

The night before Iona's trip north, Sam and Agnes had a long conversation. Agnes had been up in arms about Iona's lawyer and was still angry with Sam. She thought that in his advice to Iona he seemed to be letting the lawyer off the hook.

"She's been robbed, Sam," Agnes huffed when the boys were in bed. "She should take him to court. Oh, come into the kitchen, I've still got the pots to do."

Sam tried to explain the situation as he followed his wife. "My dear, don't you think that if I thought she had a chance I'd advise her to take him for all he's got? It's no good, Agnes, love. I know you think the world of the girl but she'd probably only lose the shop as well. The costs would be enormous. Because that fellow would be able to fight her with the freely given help of his comrades-in-arms, now, wouldn't he? And Iona is just a very young widow who owns a little country store. She may not even own a house of her own after this lot's settled."

Agnes, taking her anger out on the stew pot, was near to rubbing a hole through it. "Sam Newbold, are you telling me that girl's going to end up penniless?"

"Here, let me do that before you do the pot a damage, and listen to me, Agnes, please! Now, you're not ever to tell Iona Hammond any of what I'm going to say. I don't know everything – and I haven't ever heard anything I could swear to in a court of law – so it's no use to the girl in that way."

"Well, couldn't another lawyer …?"

"No! Not in this case, Agnes. Come on, we've finished here."

When they were settled in the sitting room and Sam had eased his slippers off, he carried on. "I don't think anyone could prove any of Albert and Iona's money was misappropriated by Livingstone. As a matter of fact, I have a feeling that even if he has somehow got his hands on some of it, it won't be as much as all that. He's too damned cunning, I reckon. He'd never touch any of the Big Men's money. Money can fight money, you see. But little people don't understand the language of the law.

They only know as much as their lawyer explains to them – and the explanation is only as good as the lawyer.

"I've no doubt Livingstone has got himself perks out of his small clients over the years, mostly from widows. They often don't understand because they've always left that side of things to their menfolk. I am sure he considered Iona easy pickings. She's so young, so unaware of the world. He would have got an awful shock when she fronted up and insisted on reading and understanding all the paperwork.

"I only hope she hasn't already signed a mortgage continuance. That could be a mistake. And she doesn't need it."

"Oh, don't say he's taken her for it all, Sam. It would set her right back."

"No, I don't think so. His records will be clean enough to pass without a court investigation. Bromwell will get to the bottom of it. I've put him well in the picture. Without damning a fellow professional and off the record, he agrees she should get away from Livingstone."

"Bromwell's honest, isn't he?"

"Yes. He's young but he's got a good head on him, and he's got integrity. He's content to wait and let the people accept him in their own time. Not having a wife and family helps – his expenses aren't so high. Joe Houghton's son was at university with him, doing law, and can't speak highly enough of his work. Don't go getting nervous about all lawyers just because of one, my love."

"Well, when you hear about men like Livingstone it makes you wonder, Sam. My dad believed lawyers were so honest and high up in the world. I guess I believed that too, once. It makes my blood boil."

"I'd better not tell you any more then. Can't have you upset before we go to bed …"

Agnes threw a cushion at him and told him to 'cut the cheek'. They laughed together before Sam continued. "There's a reason I wouldn't like to pursue Albert Hammond's past too hard."

"Oh?"

"Yes. Just between you and me, he changed so much. He was a funny beggar at the best of times but he treated me well."

"Everyone treats you well, Sam Newbold. You're such a charmer!"

"Ah, it's nice to know I'm appreciated by such a beautiful woman." He wiggled his ears at her and twirled an imaginary moustache.

Agnes chuckled but wasn't to be put off. "So, about Hammond?"

"Well, when he bought old Jacob out six years ago, the store was not doing well but Hammond was so intense about the business he got the place on its feet and doing a roaring trade for a town this size – and he had other investments, I know. I just don't know what they were."

"Yes, he was a penny-pincher. Remember how he lived at Marie Stone's boarding house for years with the labourers and single men? He only bought the hill house a year before he got married."

There was a short silence.

Agnes whispered, "That was a strange marriage, Sam. She was still a child. Seventeen might be all right for some girls but that girl looked as if she'd been drugged when she walked down the aisle …"

"I know, I know. I can't figure out her parents at all. But wait. I haven't finished yet."

"I understand what you mean, Sam. The girl can't afford to sue Livingstone."

"I'm not talking about Livingstone now. I'm talking about Hammond. Before Iona caught his eye, he wasn't interested in anything in this world except making money. Once he lost his head over her, he changed. He was, well … preoccupied most of the time."

"He was in love, Sam. You told me at the time he was like some callow youth, sick with love."

"And he was. But looking back he got worse. He wasn't as sharp about the books. He … well, he just wasn't as sharp as he used to be, especially about making decisions."

"What are you saying? That he was so lovesick he couldn't run the place properly after he got engaged to Iona?"

"More or less; and that's why we must never tell her. It would only make her feel worse. Anyway, once she was having his child, Albert changed completely. He talked about some deal that would make him and his sons rich and 'people to be counted', and other remarks he'd never have made before. And he had periods of not speaking at all. He'd go very quiet and stare out the office window, and I'd have to speak two or three times to get his attention. He was like a fallen man, a fallen man trying to get up again. Does that make sense?"

"Not really."

"What I'm trying to say is, well … with the state Hammond was in for the last year – especially the last three months before he died – it wouldn't surprise me if he had made some big mistakes in his business dealings. And if that is what happened, Iona Hammond could fight for the truth all the way to Wellington and back and not only be left high and dry but end up looking like a fool. She'd just have another unproven suspicion to live with – the possibility that she was the cause of his poor business decisions."

Iona returned on the steamer that same day. She was impressed with Anthony Bromwell. Before the appointment with her new lawyer she had just about lost her burgeoning confidence. Bromwell had an easy manner but a mind so quick she became confused within the first ten minutes of their discussions.

It was the young lawyer who had been forced to adjust. He did it so well that after an hour she learnt more about her financial circumstances than she had in all the visits she had made to Mr Livingstone.

During the passage back to Sedgely she had time to review their discussions and his advice, and she was satisfied. She fingered the cover of the large book about accounting procedures he had lent her.

"You won't need it long, though, Mrs Hammond. It's my bet you'll be buying yourself something more advanced pretty soon," and he had brushed off her thanks, evenly and honestly.

"My sister lent it to me. She is about to qualify as an accountant herself this year. You'll race through that in no time. I'll get her to recommend what would be best for you after that."

He had not called her, 'dear lady'; he had not patted her hand; and he had not looked at her in any way that could be construed as offensive. He had opened the door for her and smiled at her in a perfectly ordinary, friendly way.

"Make an appointment with me on the very day this chap says he will buy. We'll get that settled, and you can concentrate on the business. Good day, Mrs Hammond."

The steamer was passing Tokatoka Hill, the pub prominent at the foot of the steep incline, a couple of horses tied up outside.

"Not much trade on a weekday," she mused.

Bob Arnold's launch chugged past them going upriver. He was towing a barge laden with sand, his broad, working barrow upside down on top of the mound, his shovel sticking up like a marker beside it. He'd be tied up at the Dargaville wharf before nightfall and probably unload before he went home for tea, working by lantern light into the dark, shovel after shovel, barrow after barrow.

Rivermen worked themselves on a keen edge all their lives. She knew Arnold from her father's dealings with him; she knew most of the men who had anything to do with the river. They knew her too – as the child of Uriah.

He was a nice man, Arnold, hard but happy. He must have been trolling for fish on the way up – kahawai probably, she thought. Birds were wheeling and screeching like pale, miniature witches around the boat. One or two passengers waved to Arnold. He waved back, his head up through the hatch, his shoulders drawn down as he steered. Then he was gone, and they were well on their way.

Iona went to the restaurant and began her tea and scones. One of her ex-neighbours came to sit with her, putting her on edge. She was lucky. It was Mrs Holly, the lady who had taken her to see the puppies last year.

"I'm sorry for your loss, Mrs Hammond," she said, as naturally as could be, so that Iona answered, "Thank you, you're very kind. Please call me Iona," and then they chatted about the puppies. There was still one left.

"Would you be interested? She's an older pup and a happy wee girl. She's well trained. I could have her spayed for you. Our vet is very reasonable."

"You know, I might think about that," Iona replied, amazed at her own words.

"I call her 'Swan' because of her elegant neck," the older woman told her as she got up from the table, "but she'd learn another name easy enough. I must go and sort out my things before we dock at Sedgely. Goodbye, my dear."

Maybe she would have a look at Swan, or maybe not. If she did take her she wouldn't change her name. She got up and went out on deck just as they rumbled past her old home. Her father's work shed had the river doors open but she couldn't see him about. *I hope he's feeling stronger,* she thought, and a childish tremor ran through her body. "Oh, pull yourself together," she mumbled.

Before she left the restaurant she stood watching out the side window. The back of her store and the yard that ended at the riverbank slid past. It might not look the same in a few months. A prospective buyer was coming up from Helensville next week to look at purchasing half the shop and half the backyard. She was more than happy with the price, and Sam reckoned they should get the full amount, or very close to it. If this man liked what he saw, all her immediate money problems would be over. Sam had ideas about how to enlarge the two premises back towards the river if she wanted to in the future.

She came down the gangplank at Sedgely wharf, but instead of going home she turned and walked to the backyard of the store. She made her way down the yard, past a heap of rubbish waiting to be burned, past the empty boxes soon to be broken up or given away, and the old tin shed that served as extra storage. There, at the riverbank, was a stretch of long grass and two ancient cabbage trees struggling to survive. In these last weeks she had often come to this little place by the water. Iona understood why the rivermen loved their work, and she understood why they stayed. She, herself, found some sort of sustenance from being beside the moving waters. It was a releasing place. By this river she found time to catch up on her days and to be the person no one else saw her to be. She got herself back together here; but the rein was tight now and she often felt brittle.

There was also a feeling that something was missing; some pieces that had been there when she was young had been lost. Only in work did she lose that feeling – and it always came back.

Twilight was not far off when she left and walked slowly to her aunt's house, to her one room of privacy. The river sailed on with the thoughts she left behind.

Chapter Seventeen

Iona came down to the store a few minutes before midday. She felt nervous and overdressed.

"You must wear your grey suit, Iona," Agnes had nagged. Sam had agreed with Agnes, and Aunt Maude had agreed with them both. So she wore her grey military with its matching cockade hat and softened it with her powder-blue blouse and the pale blue leather gloves – the only tangible memory of her honeymoon. She would not have gone to so much trouble but she knew they wanted her to look older than her years so she let herself be guided by these people who now filled her life.

When Caleb met Iona for the second time he had no idea she was the child of his Kotare Creek memory. He knew the owner was a woman – and a widow. However, no one had told him that the widow was a young girl. Even her dark costume could not hide her youthfulness – or her looks.

"Good morning, Mr McKay," Iona said, her voice a touch husky, her hand extended towards him, both definite and delicate.

"Ah, good morning Mrs Hammond." Caleb hesitated for a second before taking the small gloved hand. It was a new experience. Most women did not shake hands with men. Certainly most young women did not shake hands with men. He took her hand, tried to shake it gently and felt his face unexpectedly flush. He executed a sort of half-bow towards her and turned towards the side wall of the store, asking another question of Sam Newbold to hide his nervousness.

This left Iona slightly behind the men. She followed them, not knowing what else to do. She knew Sam would have given McKay all the information he would need before she arrived. By now he would know the exact measurements of the building and the area of the land out the back. He would have been given the average weekly and annual takings and a rundown on some aspects of goodwill.

While the men talked, Iona had the advantage. She was able to study the back of Caleb McKay.

His neck, above the stiff, white collar, seemed vulnerable–which was a silly thought for her to be having in the middle of a business deal.

Iona had gone through so much learning during the last months and dealt with so many older business men, she had expected Caleb McKay would also be an older man. He was not. He was average height. His hair was brown, with lights of red shining through in the sunbeam from the window where he stood with Sam. There was something about him, even seeing him from the back, that threw off an air of command, of energy – an aura of control. Iona made herself look away.

Sam and Agnes had arranged that she would be brought into the scene a few minutes before it was time to have lunch at the hotel. She knew what they were doing. She was not happy about it. She was not a confident conniver – but she let herself be led this time. She moved quietly behind the weathered shop counter, put away a box of staples Sam must have had out and made herself stroll back to the shop doorway. She felt the two men turn from the other side of the store and walk towards the door. When they were nearly upon her she turned and smiled as naturally as she could. They could not say she let the side down.

"I hope you have liked all that Sam has shown you, Mr McKay. Would you have a hot lunch at the Orion with us? Mr Becombe does a wonderful midday meal, and you must be hungry after travelling."

Caleb had no option. Not that he wanted to decline the invitation. He had settled himself down after his first surprise at Mrs Hammond's age and had himself well in hand for the rest of the business. He was impressed with the premises and the size and layout of the land behind. But he wouldn't let these two know that. A reasonable purchase figure had to be arrived at. He would not go too high even though he wanted to buy into this town. His father's money as well as his own would be in this venture, and he needed to show his father he could deal sharply, right from the start. Besides, now that things were progressing he was only too happy to sit at the same table as the attractive Mrs Hammond. The last couple of years had changed his opinions on many things but not about which type of looks he preferred in a woman.

At lunch, he was seated opposite Iona. While they waited for the food to be served they talked of the state of the country after the war, the hoped for resurgence in business, and politics. He was surprised. This young woman was well informed in business matters and the current economy of the country. Most of the women he had known didn't bother to inform themselves of these topics. Not that she took a great part in the conversation, but when she did she obviously knew what she was talking about. And her eyes! God! They were beautiful. With that blouse they were storm blue. Or were they? It was hard to tell. She was facing the window, and the sunlight, muted by the rich crimson drapes of the hotel's dining room, played with her face like an embrace.

Then their meal arrived, and they ate with little conversation.

After they had finished, they discussed the asking price for half the premises of Hammond's Hardware. It was such an easy transaction Caleb wasn't sure it was all over until Mrs Hammond left them. He shook hands with Sam Newbold at the wharf. "She's very young – Mrs Hammond," he said.

"Yes," Newbold answered.

Inwardly, Sam smiled. He liked the young man well enough. He'd make a good businessman – but he knew he and Agnes had staged the business deal well. Not that they thought it wouldn't go through, but having Iona arrive at the right moment in the proceedings had kept the ball firmly in their court. He had thought McKay might have turned the screws a little tighter over the asking price, and he smiled at how subtly Iona had encouraged his concentration to wander. Yes, she was a beauty, and bright, but it was her ability to be still at the right moment that captivated a man. Of course, she was a habitual bird-watcher – you had to be still for that occupation, for sure.

"See you in a month, then," said Caleb as he climbed down into his father's launch.

"Yes, in a month. Pleasure to meet you, Mr McKay."

"Call me Cal, please."

"Sure," Sam agreed.

He waited to hear the motor cough into action, waved as Caleb moved out from the wharf into the stream and watched the *Tara* glide away in front of its ribbed and shining wake.

As the noise of the engine faded Sam stood with the smell of diesel still sharp about him and was content. He felt secure in Iona's future now and in his own job. He himself would never have the money to own a store; he would always be a wage man. That was a fact of life. And he was so used to his own lot he doubted he would be able to manage any change.

Sharing his knowledge and experience to assist the advance of a young woman such as Iona Hammond gave a little more meaning to the value of that experience. She was a good owner to work beside, and she would improve, he had no doubt, until she got caught up by some chap and married again. That would test her. A family would be inevitable – and children made a great difference to how much a woman could manage well.

"Never mind, Sam," he said to himself as he walked back to the store. "Sufficient unto the day – and this day has been good."

Iona was waiting in the office when Sam, trying to hide the grin on his round face, strolled in. Agnes had arrived. She stood arms crossed, sparking with impatience. "Well?"

"Well what?" Sam tossed back.

"Oh, for goodness sake, you know what I mean. How did it go?"

"Didn't Iona tell you?"

The two women looked at each other but before Agnes could erupt Iona spoke like the child from the creek.

"Is it really true? Has he really bought it?"

"Yes, my dear. He has really bought it. You can order your new stock now."

"I – I didn't ... I didn't quite understand ..."

She rushed out the back. Throwing her hat and gloves onto a crate by the back door she ran halfway down the yard then stopped and turned. Like a small girl remembering her manners she waved at the couple watching her from the doorway then spontaneously clapped her hands together and hugged them to her chest.

"She's in tears," said Agnes out of the corner of her mouth, then lifting her voice called, "I'll make a cup of tea, Iona. Join us when you're ready, eh?"

The girl nodded, and then turning away, walked towards her scraggy old cabbage tree. She watched the *Tara* become smaller and smaller as it travelled downriver towards the Kaipara Heads. Panic set in. *Stop it!* she commanded and reached her arms to the sky. What was the matter with her now? She didn't know. Probably relief about selling half the business, she supposed. "Yes, but ... I don't know ..." The words were hardly out of her mouth when she did know. "Yes I do. It's the reeds and the mud and the river air. I can smell again. I think I've been holding my breath all day."

Well, that was all over now and she could think again. She hugged the scabby cabbage tree trunk. She giggled. She stood up straight, shouted across the river that was settling back to calm after the wake of the *Tara*'s take-off, and with her hands on her hips she told the waters, "I shall go and see Mrs Holly this afternoon."

She flew back to the shop, grabbed her hat, grinned at the Newbolds and, as she skipped out of the shop, said, "I'm going to buy a dog. Her name's Swan."

That night Iona found companionship. She'd stayed an hour making friends with the two-year-old Irish setter that no one had wanted. 'The runt', Mrs Holly told her, and proceeded to give Iona her first lessons in being a dog owner. As she packed up Swan's plate, some cooked bones, her sleeping blanket and her chain, she smiled and said, "Lesson 1 – familiar things."

Both owner and dog were a bit nervous by the time they arrived at Maude's. Turning a corner of the shed into Swan's sleeping quarters took so long, Iona was worn out. By the time she got through Lesson 2 – 'give the dog a small meal tonight' – Iona was exhausted. Even though the food was supposed to help settle Swan, the night was hard. The big pup was lonely; missing her mother and the scents of her old home, she cried off and on for hours. And Iona cried in sympathy. However, with Lesson 3 – 'be firm' – ringing in her ears, she stayed in her own bed and let Swan go through her own grieving. Eventually they both slept.

Next morning when she went out to let Swan off her chain, the dog was as pleased as punch. She jumped up and down, barking with love and wriggling for joy. When Iona hugged and patted her she ran everywhere, sniffing the grounds, dancing about, her long, russet coat gleaming in the morning sun.

"Yes, I shall brush you until your coat shines like the sun, Swan," laughed Iona. "You're my beautiful, beautiful Swan."

The young dog pranced around her as if she understood the words her mistress spoke and barked out of sheer happiness. Then Iona remembered Mrs Holly's advice. 'You need to watch your own feelings. Dogs pick up on how you feel and can easily get overexcited or miserable, according to your moods.' Trying to make her voice calm, kind and authoritative, Iona called, "Come, Swan, breakfast time."

She fed the dog and then rushed through her own breakfast. When they left she had a kit packed with an old mat for Swan to lie on at the back of the shop, an old brush to groom her coat and a meaty bone that Aunt Maude, already enamoured of the dog, provided from the safe.

"Walk!" Iona ordered at regular intervals on their way to the shop.

Mrs Holly had been very serious about training a dog to walk at your left heel. In between orders Iona made a mental list of things to buy. Water dish, food dish, old toys from the second-hand shop, and she'd ask Sam if he would make a shelter at the back door.

"Come, Swan," she said crisply. "We have to be at work by half past eight."

Chapter Eighteen

On his trip back to Helensville Caleb's brain was working overtime. Now that he would have a place of business his life took on a whole new meaning. He was determined to make a go of this venture. Sure, times weren't so good at the moment. The war had just about bled the country dry. Some were crying recession. He didn't think so. There were farmers up here hard hit – but for him the time should be right to buy into commercial property. "Probably should have tried to push the price down a bit more," he muttered.

Still, it was within his means, and Coates would see them right. Homegrown was Gordon Coates. A force, that one, a strong man to have representing the north in parliament. Caleb reckoned business would soon be onward and upward, and he wanted to do well for himself. He was not a young lad now, wanting to prove himself to all and sundry. The war and his illness had put a stop to that–but he did want to show his father, who had backed him with half the asking price, that his faith was well founded.

Caleb's brow ridged slightly as he thought of his dad. Henry McKay was in his fifties now. He didn't look that old. He looked tired though. Well, his father could retire tomorrow if he wanted to. He and cousin John had got that place running so sweet that this year his dad had managed to help with backing Caleb and keep his own investments intact as well.

On second thoughts, it would probably keep the old man active to help John. A man could only catch so many fish and grow so many cabbages. *At least he's accepted the fact that I'll not work in Helensville.*

"What the heck!" Caleb shouted, doing a little left-right twist of the *Tara*'s wheel in celebration. "I'm a businessman and a landowner. Thanks, Dad!"

Time had worked miracles between father and son although Caleb never knew if it was his absence down the island that had made his father respect him or whether his own views had changed. *Could be you that's changed, Cal McKay. After all, you got to work under a different boss and to come close to death with peritonitis.* Then there was the real version of the war he'd heard from Pat Donovan on their trip up north. Not that Pat moaned about his experiences. He just told it like it was, and Caleb saw, now and then, the effects on his mate's mind and body.

"All that blood," he'd wept. "All that rotten waste of so many young lives."

It was like listening to an ongoing lament as only the Irish could tell it. Pat never spoke of those years again.

"That's enough, Cal," he'd said one day. "No more. It's gone – over and done with."

And when they'd eventually got back to Helensville his best mate had headed off down Nelson way – said he felt like being 'a grower of things worthwhile'.

138

Caleb chocked the wheel and ran to the cabin to get a bottle of beer from under his bunk. He took a pee over the side, opened the bottle with the rusty opener, hurried back to check the course and lifted the beer to the wide Kaipara skies. "Here's to us, Pat. See ya in 1930, like we promised on the *Muritai*!"

And they would, somehow. He pulled a face at the warm beer, shook his head and swamped some more down. "Not half bad, Pat. How's yours?" Then he laughed and laughed until all the tension and excitement left him.

His mind turned to the *Tara*, such a smooth-running ship. Built by a local man, she was a trifle too fine for a workhorse so Henry McKay had bought her at a very reasonable price. Her work for the business side of their firm was light, and his dad had said he wanted Caleb to have it for Sedgely. If he'd had his own way he'd have driven his dad's Tin Lizzie up to Sedgely. His father didn't use it much. The roads north were still not wonderful, though. That's what put him off. All the same, cars would be the transport of the future. As sure as he stood at the wheel of the old *Tara* this day, Caleb McKay knew that, and he had his eye on a Ford himself, now that his father had saved him money by giving him the *Tara*.

"And you're a grand boat. Look at you – safe as houses and steady as a rock."

He threw his head back and drew in a deep breath. The immensity of the skies over these waters made him feel like a speck under heaven. "God, the ships these waters have seen," he said in awe. "Sail and steam, ships of glory and ships lying wrecked under the water."

Now engines drove the water white with their churning props then tarnished it with their oil trails. Men loved their ships, pampered their yachts and now polished their motorboats. With the war no longer eating up money, the railway and the automobile would soon push further and further north, changing everything. Once money-power realised there'd be no need to wait on wind, weather and tide it would be a different world.

It was a shame in some ways. River life had something you never found elsewhere. Living with the elements gave an extra quality to people. It stamped them with a natural strength – with an unassuming self-reliance. The Northern Wairoa had serviced them so well for so long, their whole way of life was intertwined with it. This long river had carried generations on its saffron back, while the huge Kaipara Harbour sent them out to sea and brought them back for more. Water, boats and people had joined together from the beginning. Maori, the tangata whenua, the people of the land, had paddled in canoes. Pioneers rowed, sailed and steamed it. Now came the kerosene and diesel engine boats.

Everything from firewood to Aunt Fanny's furniture and whole buildings for removal chugged up and down this giant waterway. Kauri, gum and flax had been scrounged out of the belly of the north and been sacrificed to the coffers of the bankers of Auckland. This river was something you were born to – or born upon. The old ones said it never left your soul. Muddy, rotten water sometimes, blessed beauty another, it was always there beside you, constant to its own majestic moods. "You're a great old river, aren't you, eh?" Caleb whispered.

These days, though, the mills were getting fewer, shipbuilders less plentiful and so many butchered boys buried in foreign soil were no longer here to settle and work the land.

"Oh, God. Leave it alone man," Caleb told himself. "Don't go there. They're Shorty's nightmares."

Caleb had thought about starting up an engineering yard beside old Anderson-Keyes at Kotare Creek. But then he thought better of it. It was a sidetrack area. Better to be in Sedgely on the main road north, and although he was marine trained he'd taken to the auto engine as fast as anyone in the field. His future lay with the roads. He could service both marine and auto engines from the corner site that backed onto the water at Sedgely. The land was high enough to beat a river flood. That was his dream – land right in the middle of a town – far better for him than the block out at the creek.

The creek! By God, yes! That was where he'd seen her before. She was the girl in the field that day. No, she would only be about twenty now. Yes, she could be nineteen, and yes, he remembered hearing something about the storekeeper, Hammond, marrying a girl just out of school. He vaguely remembered Hammond. He must have been nearly twenty years older than her. Why hadn't he realised before? Those eyes of hers – of course – they were the same colour as the child's – purple-blue – and she still seemed slightly removed from the world. Even though she'd become a beautiful, confident young woman. Caleb shook his head. She was still a mystery.

Chapter Nineteen

Crack! ... went the starter's pistol; engines choked and screamed, revved and roared, and three boats, judged to the moment, crossed the start line. The race for working launches was under way.

"Arnold's made a good start," Anthony Bromwell smiled, blocking out the sun as he handed Iona a tiny glass of sherry. "Yes, but the *Kuaka* and the *Anstead Bee* are keeping up with him," she replied.

"Do you think he'll win?"

"Well he should, according to my father. But he's just as likely to stop halfway and give all his passengers a swim, knowing Bob Arnold."

Iona looked up at the dark shape of her new solicitor, skipper of the *Celeste*, now anchored with the other spectator boats on the edge of the course.

She thought; *he's just a black shadow. I can't see anything at all. I could be looking at a hole in the sun,* and laughed.

"I've never seen you laugh before," said Bromwell, so quietly against the engine noises Iona hardly heard him.

She lifted an eyebrow then clutched her drink as the wake from the racing launches reached them and the

Celeste danced, pulling on the anchor rope, her girth groaning in protest. As they settled down, Anthony's elongated black arm reached out and patted her lightly on the shoulder, then he moved off to attend to other guests.

The sun fell on her again, raw, hot. She drew her hat brim forward, feeling the tenderness of the satiny French straw, watching the sherry sparkle. She took a tiny sip. Sweetly tart, it tickled in her throat; it drew her mouth and made her eyes moist. She was not used to drink. She was not used to this sort of company either. When Anthony had invited her to join his boat party for the Pahi Regatta she had agonised over her decision – making excuses such as unknown business dates – keeping him at bay until she found the courage to accept.

The *Celeste* was a new boat – a pleasure craft – Anthony's latest big acquisition. She hadn't had much to do with pleasure boats. Edward had a small sail boat. Father had built it years ago, and they had enjoyed skiffing around the river – two children gauche and grubby. This launch had everything – and everything seemed to be either upholstered, varnished or made of brass. Anthony had already raced her to a credible third earlier in the day, giving an exciting ride to his guests.

Iona glanced around at the others. They were chattering and laughing and getting on so well. She supposed that when she chatted and laughed she looked just like them. She liked Anthony Bromwell. But the Anthony of the office chambers was so different from the Anthony of today. His friends were obviously from his university years – or from the wealthier farming families. She had met his parents and his sister on their own boat and had taken a liking to his sister, the accountancy student, immediately – but she could not hang on to his sister's hand all day.

"They've turned!" shouted one of the men, and at once the crowd on the wharf picked it up, yelling and shouting and ha-hooing.

"The *Bee*'s in the lead!" a gentleman with leather binoculars and white suede shoes informed them.

Five years ago I would never have been asked into this company, thought Iona and smiled at the young woman opposite who was slightly tipsy from too many sherries on too hot a day, and who smiled back with a fallen face. Earlier in the day she had been sharp – entertaining them with her witty stories of a girl's life in the mostly male lectures at university. Iona had laughed along with everyone else, not understanding always what she was laughing at. The girl pushed herself out of her deck chair and wobbled over to Iona.

"Having a good time, are we?"

"Yes, thank you, Marion."

"You live around here, don't you?"

"Well, I live upriver a good way, but I do live in this part of the country. Where are you from?"

"Oh, I'm from Remuera, Auckland. You know 'the land of the bright little girls and the bloody boring boys', and I've got a bloody beautiful headache from all this crass Kaipara sun."

Iona looked at the blotched skin and the lip rouge caking at the sides of Marion's mouth. For some reason she felt sorry for her. Grandma Kelly had often said,

'The only thing worse than a drunken man is a drunken woman.'

Iona thought it wasn't worse. Sadder? Yes, sadder. This girl looked as if she might burst into tears any minute.

"Would you like to sit down?"

"Well …"

Just then everyone started yelling. The boats were coming down towards them on the last lap of the race.

"It's Arnold, Iona!" Anthony sang out, standing on tiptoe to call to her over the heads of the other men in the stern.

Arnold's *Wairua* was forward of the *Anstead Bee*, and Iona forgot all about Marion. She shouted at the *Wairua* and danced up and down. One minute one boat forged ahead. Another minute the other took the lead. The wharf crowd started to call for The *Bee*, and the spectators on the flagship responded by calling for the *Wairua*.

"Come on, *Wairua*!"

"Come on, *Bee*!"

"Come on, *Wairua*!"

"Come on, *Bee*!"

The shore crowd now yelled with the wharf contingent, and the small boats joined in with the flagship, which went well over on stream side as everyone rushed to see the finish. As the two boats converged, bow to bow on the finishing line, it was …

"*Wairua*!"

"*Bee*!"

"*Wairua! Wairua*!" "*Bee! Bee! Bee*!"

No one knew which boat had won.

Comments and opinions now flew about the head of the crowd like feathers in a turkey fight. A ship's hooter stunned everyone to silence, and a race steward roared through a loud hailer that the *Wairua* had taken the honours by a hair. That sent the crowd off again. The whole scene made Iona chuckle. They all look like large children on a school picnic, she thought.

Then a loud and terrible wailing came from Arnold's boat, and everything went quiet. From the *Wairua*'s cabin staggered a man playing the bagpipes. Behind him came Arnold in long striped togs, wearing an oversized false moustache and an enormous cardboard crown. As the spectators began to catch on, Arnold's passengers hoisted their captain on top of the *Wairua*'s cabin and began to bow and scrape in homage as the piper played '*Hail the Conquering Hero*'.

Not to be outdone the *Anstead Bee* produced a board and made their captain walk the plank. This he did with much pantomime at the man who was walking behind him pretending to jab him with a boat hook. Sticking out his chest he then made a magnificent run, dived and surfaced toothless. "Ya silly buggers, I've lost me teeth down there!" he yelled and dived again while two of his mates jumped over to try and find their captain's false teeth.

Tears streamed from Iona's eyes. She could not remember laughing so much in her life. Somehow, in all the uproar, Anthony had moved to her side, and she threw her arms around him without thinking, then quickly drew back. *He must think me a child.*

"'Scuse me, I'm sure," mumbled Marion, squashed beside them and the cabin door. She stumbled down the steps and disappeared into the gloom.

Anthony whispered in Iona's ear, "I hope she finds the bucket!" and they both started to laugh again – as did everyone else watching Bob Arnold's antics as he prodded his subjects until they too fell overboard. And Anthony Bromwell, as he laughed along with all the rest, realised he had fallen in love with Iona Hammond.

Later, Anthony guided her up the wharf steps, wanting to take her around the regatta grounds. The crowd was thinning on the wharf. Two lads fell off the greasy boom as they passed.

Parents called from the beach to their children swimming under the wharf. "Watch that current, Jane!" – and – "Jimmy, you little tyke, stay by the poles!"

They caught the end of the wood-chopping competition and stood under the big fig tree talking to the other passers-by. A man began to play '*Roll out the Barrel*' on his mouth organ, and men, women and children sang along. When he switched to '*Danny Boy*', Solly Burton sang it solo. He had them all watery-eyed by the time he'd finished.

Iona and Anthony moved on, taking everything in. There were sideshows, stalls, plenty to see. This was a special day for the north.

Iona had come down on Bromwell's launch but she was sleeping the two nights with the Newbolds in their family tent and going home on her father's boat, hoping to keep everyone happy. She did not remember enjoying a regatta as much as this one. Perhaps she was seeing things in a different light after being so sick.

Anthony was trying to guide her towards the refreshment tent, but they had to stop and watch the antics of the young boys, from opposing towns, straining their guts out–copying the young men, determined to win their own tug of war and ending up in a heap on top of each other, grass-stained britches, feet and arms entangled – one of the tiniest in tears. Anthony moved her on, circling the crowd, and headed for the afternoon tea tent.

Iona found her parents and Aunt Maude in the tent, sitting with friends, giving her no choice but to introduce Anthony to the whole table. She cringed at the calculated appraisal her mother gave him and moved away, although Anthony hadn't seemed to notice. He was more interested in jamming something under one of the legs of their lopsided table. The grass floor was usually a paddock.

"Country etiquette requires much invention," he smiled up at her.

At this moment Caleb McKay came into the tent and saw Bromwell kneeling and gazing intimately at Iona. He could not see Iona's face. Bromwell's was enough. Caleb was surprised at his own reactions. Rage boiled up in the pit of his stomach. He turned and left, passing but not seeing the toffee-apple children, ignoring the shouts of his mates on their way to the Pahi pub. The day was sour enough, he told himself, without a belly full of booze as well. He got in his new speedboat and howled off over to Whakapirau. His father and his friends were there, and he told himself that was where he wanted to be anyway.

It was a shame that halfway over the motor ran out of petrol and he had to be towed to shore by a course steward.

"What ya doin' over here then, young Cal?" drawled Billy, the railway guard-cum-regatta steward. "These new fandangle motorboats ain't a patch on the mulleties."

"Right, Billy," muttered Caleb, paying the price for being rescued. He prepared for the inevitable ear bashing, and as Billy settled into his stride Caleb was probably the only person at the regatta who was thinking 'I'll be glad when this day is over'.

Chapter Twenty

Iona took a few days off in Auckland to look for some new working clothes. The outfits she had were starting to look shabby already.

She booked in at the same boarding house she'd stayed at with her father when she turned fifteen but she asked for a room with a road view.

Looking out at the road and busy cars was at least interesting at times. Pedestrians were more wary now that motorcar traffic had increased. Noise and exhaust fumes seemed to dominate the roads – Cal was ever enthusiastic about engines. She went to the window and looked out on the black asphalt. She missed Swan, who was nearly full-grown now. "Ah," she sighed, "I'm ready to go home. But am I ready for Caleb?"

Cal – with his brown, penetrating eyes and his lopsided grin that she longed to see and did her best to ignore. "He can't surely be interested in me. Not that way," she whispered to the faded roses on the wallpaper, where, close to the left side of the mantelshelf above the coal scuttle someone had smeared something that now looked like a face with an open mouth, talking.

"You look like my mother," she told it. 'Sit up, Iona', 'Don't clump, Iona', 'You really are so-o stupid,

Iona'. And the latest 'You have surely not refused Anthony Bromwell – you are such an idiot, Iona!'.

She didn't care. It had been difficult but necessary to show Anthony she did not want him too close – and like a gentleman he had taken the hint. She had found it an impossible chore trying to fit in with his family and friends. "They're all such clever people. They talk about art and music as naturally as they talk about cows and rugby," she told her wallpaper mother. "And I was fond of him. At least he listened to me as if I had a mind as well as a face."

Nice Anthony Bromwell. She sometimes still missed their little friendship that had begun to grow into something more. Had it been love? No! Iona thought she knew a little about love now. There were different sorts of love, that's all. "Oh, stop it," she told herself.

Getting up, she emptied some coal onto the small fire. Dinner would be served soon. One thing she couldn't fault was the food. They had a great cook here. That's probably why father liked it, she thought. That and its proximity to Queen Street and the waterfront. Tomorrow she would have to tramp Auckland's main street looking for a serviceable costume. Yes, and a new frock for Maryanne's wedding.

That had been a shock.

Barely three weeks ago Maryanne had arrived at Aunt Maude's front door looking sick and miserable and babbling like a bewildered child.

"Mum said I can't have a white wedding. She says a white bride is a virgin bride and that I'm not, now. So would you let us have our little ceremony in your garden, Miss Kelly? Mum's sewing me a dress I can use after for good occasions – but the last of your pink and white roses would make me so happy, especially the climbers. I love your climbers. They never stop reaching for the sky."

"You'd be most welcome, Maryanne," Aunt Maude had said, putting her arms around the girl and guiding her to sit on the verandah seat.

"There'll only be my family and Seth's brother," Maryanne gabbled on. "His folks said they can't afford to travel up at such short notice. And oh! I'd like you to be my bridesmaid, Iona. Would you? Please, be my witness? Seth's brother is his."

When Iona said she'd love to, Maryanne had gulped and continued, "And Seth would really like Caleb and the Newbolds to come. He thinks the world of them even though he's only met them once or twice. Would you ask them for us? Yes? Oh, thank you, Iona! It's got to be a little wedding, you see, with no advertising. That way Mum will tell them up the line that we've been married for ages, and when I go back home from training college no one will be any the wiser. It'll stop the tongues wagging, Mum says."

"When's baby due, Maryanne?" asked Maude. "September, I think …" The girl stopped, looked down at her dirty old farm boots and whispered, "Dr Jenkins is going to see the training college principal and ask if I could do my final term by correspondence. I'll stay in Auckland with Mum's cousin until the baby's born. Seth will get down when he can …" and in a ragged sigh, whispered, "We've made such a mess of things."

"No! No you haven't, Maryanne, not at all. Don't you ever think like that. This child just decided it wanted to be here and to belong to you and Seth. See? It loves you already."

Iona, watching Maryanne's tears disappear, had felt very proud of her aunt.

A week later Iona was back in Sedgely in Maude's kitchen washing the family crystal ready for Maryanne's wedding. The end of March day was warm, and through the window she could see everyone decorating the back garden for the ceremony. The glasses sparkled from the sudsy water, and when she'd dried them she carried them into the dining room and arranged them on the sideboard. Back in the kitchen she took off her apron and hung it on the back of the door then stood watching the Stewart children finish twisting their crêpe paper streamers.

All the guests were busy. Sam and Caleb were fixing tiny silver bells around the edge of a small canvas canopy, and Ollie Wallace was carrying out the side table to set it in front of the makeshift bridal shade. Her aunt stepped forward, flung her Irish crocheted cloth up and out and guided it down to settle like a spider's web over the polished table.

And just as Agnes Newbold finished arranging the climbing roses in front of the table, eleven-year-old Rory Stewart came rushing up to the women yelling, "The minister's here! The minister's here!"

Swan began capering around everyone's ankles, and Iona thought *that dog is too excited. She'll knock something over any minute...* when Sam Newbold shouted, "Be quiet! Everyone take their places, now! Sit!" and Swan sat straight down on Sam's black polished shoes, making everyone laugh.

Iona left them to it and walked down the passage to the main bedroom. When she knocked and opened the door the most beautiful bride she had ever seen stood there. Her friend wore a silver dress with a sweetheart neckline picked out in cream pearls, and when she took a step towards Iona her bouquet of pale pink and white roses quivered.

"Oh, Maryanne, you look so ... so beautiful."

"Thank you," smiled Maryanne.

Mrs Stewart fixed a circlet of identical roses on her daughter's shiny curls, kissed her and gave last-minute instructions to her husband. "Wait for Caleb to start the record and remember to walk slowly." Then she was gone.

Iona took her place behind Maryanne and they waited – and waited.

All of a sudden Caleb appeared at the door asking if they were ready.

"Yes. All present and correct and awaiting orders," joked Mr Stewart.

"Well, it's time to start, right? Now wait for the music – and ah, Mr Stewart? Mrs Stewart says to remind you not to gallop," and he took off leaving them on their own.

"Your mother has spoken, Maryanne," grinned Mr Stewart.

They heard the gramophone begin '*Here Comes the Bride*' and three right feet stepped out as one, Mr

Stewart giving a salute with his left hand sending Maryanne into giggles.

"Stop it, Dad!" spluttered the bride. "We're not marching off to war."

"How do you know, girlie?" said her father, and the bridal party broke into gales of laughter.

Caleb appeared once again, took in the situation and said, "It's nice to see you all so happy but Seth and your guests are waiting out there. I'll go and restart the record, shall I?"

"I think we've just been reprimanded," snorted Mr Stewart, and while Maryanne doubled up and Iona stuffed her hand in her mouth they heard the wedding march blare into life again.

"Right! It is now time to stop laughing, girls," Mr Stewart said firmly, and somehow they did.

In a magic moment in Maude Kelly's rose garden at ten past four that afternoon Maryanne Stewart became Mrs Seth Wallace. She was a radiant bride. The groom looked handsome in his uncle's suit, the only one he could borrow that fitted his six-foot-five frame – and no one noticed the patch in the coat elbow Granny Stewart had woven with fine needle and thread the night before.

Maude Kelly, Mrs Stewart and Agnes Newbold put on a wonderful evening meal; Sam Newbold made a speech to the bride and groom; Ollie Wallace stumbled through a few words; Mr Stewart spoke kindly about his daughter and welcomed Seth into their family. And Seth took everyone by surprise by speaking as if he had been doing it all his life.

"Maryanne and I thank you all. You've given us a really grand day to remember forever." He cleared his throat. "My brother Ollie has never had a piano lesson in his life but he can play anything. Just ask him. He'll play it. If he doesn't know it you just start singing and then he'll play it."

"*Old MacDonald Had a Farm*," yelled Rory Stewart.

"But, little brother-in-law," continued Seth, "the first song is for my lovely wife. Mrs Wallace?" and holding his hands out to Maryanne he took her towards the house where they could hear Ollie playing and Sam's tenor voice singing '… *If you were the only girl in the world and I were the only boy. Nothing else would matter in the world today. We would go on loving in the same old way. A garden of Eden just made for two …*'

"Hold it!" ordered Caleb, and he took a photo of them with his box camera.

It was so lovely Iona took off to the bathroom to mop her eyes, and by the time she made the sitting room the kids were bellowing out '*Old MacDonald had a farm, Ee i ee i oh!*' Then the adults went off into '*the bells are ringing for me and my girl*', and all the young Stewarts were up dancing. And did they dance! When Seth coaxed Maryanne and Iona into doing the Chicken Walk and the Shimmy, even the old Kelly house was fair shaking.

Maryanne and Seth and Iona and Caleb were the last still dancing when the old hallway clock struck eleven. Sweat-soaked, exhausted and gloriously happy, at Sam's bidding they joined hands and sang '*Auld Lang Syne*' and wished the newlyweds good luck.

Iona then edged Maryanne and Seth aside and gave them an envelope. "Open it together, right now!" she ordered them.

Inside were bookings for the two of them for a cabin on the passenger steamer leaving on the tide at midnight and for a room at Helensville Hotel the following night.

"Oh, Iona!" whispered Maryanne. "I've never been in a cabin or a hotel before."

"Well, you're going to now, and you'd better hurry up. Your cases are in our car."

Caleb and Iona watched the steamer move off down the river. It was a mystical sight. The lights from the boat turned it into a fairy ship. Rippled reflections skipped over the water while the full, white moon and the stars looked as if you could reach up and pick them out of the sky.

"What a night to start a life together," Caleb murmured.

Iona, frightened of what might be on his mind, made for the car.

"Come on, Cal, we have to get back and help tidy up," she told him in her best businesswoman's voice.

Chapter Twenty-one

When Caleb asked Iona to go with him to Whangarei for the day he did so out of desperation. He did not think for a moment she would agree, so he was lost for words when she accepted the invitation. He had requested she help him buy curtaining for the small house he'd had built. It was the last day of April, a little showery, but pleasant.

"I've looked all through Creighton's Drapery here," he said, "but I can't find anything I like. I'm not too marvellous at that sort of thing."

Playing the helpless male had worked. He had refrained from telling her his mother would have been happy to select and sew without him having to lift a finger. Caleb found it difficult not to 'wear his heart on his sleeve'. Not that it mattered much by now. Every man and his dog, it seemed, knew he was interested in Iona – at least that's how Sam put it to him the week before, after the Wallace wedding. Sam Newbold had assumed the role of protector where the young Mrs Hammond was concerned.

"You know what small-town talk is like, Cal. You need to watch yourself."

"I'd not do anything to compromise her, Sam."

"I know that, Cal. It's … well, it's not just 'doing'. It's looking and it's proximity."

"She's not interested in me. It sticks out a mile."

"She's walked away from Bromwell, hasn't she?

Caleb felt embarrassed but he respected Sam for speaking up. He thought the pressure might have come from Iona's father, but Sam denied that.

"Uriah doesn't hear much talk out at the creek. His wife may have. I doubt it though. You would have heard from her if she'd been told anything. On second thoughts, maybe not! Word is she's pretty much becoming a recluse. It's me and Agnes who are concerned. We live in town and the whispers are starting, Cal."

"Right! I appreciate what you've said. I'll speak to her soon. It's gone on too long. It's … well … it's going to be awkward if she slaps me down – the premises being so close."

"Faint heart never won fair lady, lad. You'll survive."

They set out, Caleb leaving the shop in the hands of his apprentice, with some trepidation, while Iona, secure in Paul Sloane's capabilities and Sam's expertise, had no worries at all about her business.

The conversation was stilted at first.

"Have you travelled much by car, Iona?" Cal asked.

"No," she said. "We've always been a boating family. I have been in a service car though." She stopped, just on the point of also mentioning her trip with Anthony in his new Buick last summer.

"I like a Ford myself. They're reliable …" volunteered Cal and carried on talking about his favourite subject. Iona didn't know what vanadium steel was, and she got lost in his explanations of side valves and pistons; however, she found she appreciated his knowledge of the background of the four-cylinder engine and could see why the Model T was so popular, with its higher ground clearance and ignition allowing it to cope with getting through wet roads and even streams.

They made good time to Maungataroto and topped the Brynderwyns with only one stop on the way up to let the radiator cool. Caleb backed them off the road and parked by a farm gate. The view from the summit was spectacular. He experienced a tender pleasure in Iona's appreciation of the panorama. She brought out the thermos flask and a small cane hamper filled with fresh scones wrapped in one of her auntie's starched table serviettes. He set the folding canvas stool securely on a patch of grass and perched himself on a spare nail box. Morning tea slipped in time.

There was a little stab of excitement whenever they looked at each other – a hint of magic in their isolation. A virgin sun fired the auburn strands in Iona's hair. A fantail danced in the bracken. 'Fantail is piwakawaka,' Iona's child-voice sang in her head; somewhere from the valley below a dog's muffled bark lifted.

"Iona …?"

"Nice cuppa, then?" boomed a man's voice from the gate behind them. Caleb looked up into the eyes of a grinning farmer about to open the gate and let a straggly band of cows through.

"Sorry to bother you, but I've got to get this lot down to my other spread."

Damn, thought Cal as they packed up quickly and got under way again. *If I'd only spoken sooner.*

The downhill run into Waipu jolted them about a bit. Some of the stones looked like boulders and a long, lying puddle made the Model T skittish. They laughed a lot, the two of them a little reckless with tension, before settling down to the long drive over the flats.

They were hit by the level of energy in Whangarei. It took some time deciding on which material Iona liked best, and when they came out the pale sun had disappeared leaving an icy sting in the air. They found a fish and chip grill and ordered the fresh east coast snapper. Rain started as they entered the shop and rapidly became a downpour. Conversation ceased as sheets of water fell like shale on the tin roof. When their meal arrived they signalled each other to eat. The shop soon became full of people in various states of dampness taking refuge from the deluge – eating while the world outside overflowed.

They finished their meal and Iona shouted, "Shall we go?"

"We'd better wait until it eases off a bit."

She nodded. They went to the window and watched the rain. Passers-by sheltered under the shop's bulging awning. The street was invisible. Rain crashed down and water splashed up making a liquid curtain between one side of the road and the other. Soon the drains couldn't cope with the runoff, and small, angry rivers spilt themselves across the footpath. Then as suddenly as it had begun, the rain ceased. The silence caught everyone by surprise. People still shouting at each other, stopped, smiled at their own folly and self-consciously slipped into whispers.

"I think we'd better make our way back, Iona. The roads will still be bad after this downpour, but we can't afford to wait about. The trip home will take much longer."

"Of course."

"It's a flood out there, sir," offered the young girl behind the counter. "I'd wait a bit if I were you."

"We really must go," said Caleb, paying the bill. He went over to help Iona with her coat and they left.

But when they got outside they took one look at each other, and Caleb led her by the elbow back into the grill.

"Thought you might be back," said the girl. "My dad says we'll need a rowboat to get down that street if it rains any more. Why not have another pot of tea on the house? Everyone else is."

One or two showers passed over while they waited. They talked with other customers about the rain. One man was jubilant. Said his wife wouldn't expect him home in that lot so he'd take the afternoon in the billiard saloon.

"I'll tell on ya, Bert Reilly," quipped the waitress.

"Don't be such a spoilsport, Nellie. What a wife don't see she don't get mad over."

They were surrounded by people and Caleb lost another opportunity.

After an hour the shop started to empty. Cal went out to check once or twice. The third time he decided they should be able to walk rather than wade to the car. A stopover at a restroom was the only other delay. It was getting on towards late afternoon before they left Whangarei, and Caleb's courage, like the rain that had once been a torrent, had disappeared.

Iona could hardly believe they were travelling over the same roads. Any metal still on the surface was useless, and the bulging ditches threatened to flood. Still, the road between Whangarei and Waipu remained passable, if slow.

At Waipu a constable stepped on to the road and waved them down. "Going over the hill, are you?"

"Yes, constable. Is it out?"

"No, not yet. Any more rain and it will be. If you have to go over I'd get straight on. Take it easy though … she's greasy on the bends, and there could be a slip or two on the other side any time. We may have to close it before dark if she sogs up any more."

"Thanks for the warning. I'll watch out," said Caleb.

They went on and soon began to climb. Iona knew what Caleb was thinking as she sat beside him. It would have been safer to stay over at Whangarei, or even Waipu. If she'd been a mate of his they would not be attempting this journey. Etiquette demanded he bring her home to her family that night. They would be late arriving – much later than they had intended – much later than they had told her aunt. They would struggle through this journey because her honour demanded it. Even as a widow her honour demanded it – and should her honour be blemished she would get most of the blame. Cal would gain respect by getting her through this and home. She would simply feel guilty because she was a woman.

"Sorry," said Caleb as yet another patch of mud sent the car slithering, whipping his passenger about.

"It's all right. Don't worry, Cal."

"We're nearly at the top."

"Yes, you're doing very well. It's a different road to the one we came over this morning."

"Isn't it? It's more than time they did something about it. Southern main roads are not left in this condition."

"No. So I've heard."

Iona said nothing after that for a long time. She did not want to be a hindrance to his driving. She tried to rest back in the seat as much as she could, which was difficult. She was used to sitting in a tossing boat when men had to handle dangerous seas, and she thought she would prefer a boat in a storm to this sort of jolting about. Perhaps she was being perverse. She probably just knew more about boats.

She knew more about Caleb McKay now also, and she knew she liked being with him. He was very dependable and not a man to rant and rave. He seemed too even-tempered to ever roar and yell, to ever do what Albert had done. He was comfortable to be with.

Some men were so nervous of women you couldn't say you needed go to the lavatory when you were out with them. She'd heard of girls who came home in agony, holding on so long, not wanting to ask to relieve themselves – or asking and then feeling embarrassed because the boy was embarrassed. Caleb was a nice person. She had no fear of him even when he made her feel a strange sort of excitement.

They crested the top of the hill. This time there'd be no stopping and no view. Cloud and drizzle blanketed out farmlands, houses, animals and the expanse of sea in the distance. They were crawling and sliding downwards and Caleb, worried about the radiator, which had been overtaxed on the way up, warned, "We're in a mess if she blows."

"Do you want to stop?"

"I think if we stop she'll sink down and we'll not get her out."

"Oh. Oh-hh!"

There was a short bang and a grinding, and they did not move.

"I think we've stopped."

"Yes," said Iona and they looked at each other and both began to laugh.

"It's all ridiculous really," she said.

"It's more than that," laughed Caleb, "it's damned crazy."

They settled down, the tension broken.

Half an hour later they got under way again, covered in mud, and wet, but more than pleased with themselves. The car had gone into a deep rut, made deeper by the rain and camouflaged by a top layer of watery clay. The sacks Caleb always carried had not been enough to drive the car out on, and he had cut brush from the down side of the road. The drop was nearly sheer and not easy to work, so Iona had insisted he tie the tow rope around his waist and fasten it to a tree as an anchor. The rope proved an added weight but at least it left both his hands free to cut. He slithered up and down while she carried the dripping bundles of brush and bracken and pushed them under the wheel above the sacks. He got plenty to avoid climbing all over that slippery slope more than necessary. The surplus brush they pushed under one back wheel to give the car a good first chance of coming out. Then Caleb gave her 'all she'd got', and Iona, standing ahead on the road, had shouted in victory.

Now they were rattling along over the plains nearing Sedgely. The mud on her clothes made her feel heavy and cold as it dried on her skin and on her stockings and shoes. Iona began to feel drowsy even though the car jittered. She felt happy, though. Yes, very happy. She did so like being with Cal, hadn't known anything like it before. He was both safe and exciting – which was something she didn't understand.

The car made its own mad rhythm, and the night began to pull down all around them. A soft rain set in making a quiet lulling sound on the roof. Perhaps the night would go on forever and she would never have to worry or strive again – just be comfy and warm.

"I'm stopping here, Iona. We need to clean up a bit."

She sat up straight. "Oh, yes. Yes, clean up."

Cal pulled them in just before a bridge where a creek had grown large with rainwater. He got out and went to the toolbox at the back. Then he disappeared down by the side of the bridge. He came up carrying a full tin of water.

Iona got out and stood beside him, thankful the rain had stopped. "What shall we wash with, Cal?"

"I don't know. I used the rags I had to clean up back on the hill."

"I know! We've got the table napkin from our morning tea. It's in the hamper."

They found a tea towel as well at the bottom of the basket. They stood in the car lights and, dipping the cloths into the water, they began to dab away at themselves and each other trying to make their appearance presentable before arriving at Auntie Maude's. In the end, with faces and hands reasonably clean and some of the muck scraped off their clothing, they called a halt to the futile exercise.

Back in the car Iona shivered. The night had thickened; the dampness was through to every part of her.

"You're cold. I shouldn't have stopped."

"It's all right. I'll warm up soon."

He took off his coat and draped it around her shoulders. "No," she said, "you'll only get cold yourself."

"I don't feel the cold much," he mumbled.

Then he put his arms around her and held her so close she could smell his warmth, and her shaking began to subside.

It was very quiet in the car, except for the sound of their breathing.

It's drizzling. Drizzle has no sound. It floats down like shiny bits of cobweb. It's soft and silent while our breathing sings like a rhythm of the night of cobweb rain. It is so quiet it hurts – it's too strong – I'll cry if it hurts much more.

She felt the pressure of his arms and did not resist. When Caleb lifted her chin and kissed her closed eyes and then her mouth, Iona was aware of nothing but the need to draw closer – and the relief of hearing Cal break the soft, unbearable pain of silence.

"I love you, Iona Annabel Anderson-Keyes."

Chapter Twenty-two

"What a warm day for May, Iona!"

"Yes. It surely is Agnes."

Agnes walked on in the opposite direction. That was a help. Iona kept on going. Time was precious when you had someone looking after your children. Nina Stewart, Maryanne's youngest sister, turned twelve two months ago; did very well, looking after the children, but Miriam, at seven, could kick up bobsy-die when she had a mind to it. *Mustn't worry, Nina is old for her years. She's extremely capable.*

"Off for a stroll, love?" Caleb called.

Everyone seemed to be standing outside their shops this Saturday morning, even her husband.

"Yes, Cal. Nina's with the children so I mustn't dawdle."

"Ward's resigned his position from parliament. Just heard from Stephens at the Post and Telegraph," he called out.

"Has he?" she shouted, then "Come on, Swan!" to show she had to get on with walking the dog. Although Cal was right – Swan strolled now that she had grown old. She'd be twelve in August, quite an age for a dog, and Iona worried about the pain of her arthritis. As far as

Caleb's news went, she was not at all interested in politics this morning, even though the country seemed to be going backward economically again. No. She had other things on her mind.

Agnes was right. It was a warm day, and it was hard to believe they were nearly halfway through 1930 as well. The new winter sky glinted so brightly it hurt her eyes. Everything glistened: the few dry leaves left on the ancient maples down Underwood Street, the faded surface of a suspended high-tide river, the rusty iron roof of the wharf shed. Everything that could, flirted with the fickle young sun. Iona ambled across the road at the end of Underwood Street and on, past the wharf. If you went through the back of Syd Martin's timber yard and down the bank, the makings of a stream ran inland from the wharf.

Solly Burton's uncle had lived round the corner in an old shack down there for many years. He was dead now, Solly's uncle, and the shack was falling to pieces. She and Teddy and Solly had thought 'Tiny' Matich a wonderful old man. She didn't know to this day whether he was a widower or had never married. He had simply 'been there', living alone in his falling down shack, sometimes filling the three of them with camp bread and dripping, or with stories from his days on the gum fields, whenever they went to see him. None of them realised just how much time they'd spent with 'Tiny' until he'd gone. He always said he'd die with his boots on, and he did – dropped dead digging his garden, the shrivelled old spuds with their hanging-out eyes still waiting to be planted on the ground beside his stiffened body. That was before their wedding.

They were married in January 1922. New Zealand had slid into a slump the year before, and now, nine years later, they were into a depression again by the looks of it. Things were getting so bad in the country these days, it made 1921 look like a party. People were doing their best but they felt helpless and angry. Who could blame them? The government expected too much of hungry people.

She walked on around the bend, stood looking at the ruins of Tiny's iron castle then wandered back to where she would not be seen. In this little dip she could catch a glimpse of the river sailing past the wharf. She sat on an old log. Swan came to lie at her feet and began to doze off. Iona drooped with tiredness herself. Two school-age children and a toddler were hard going at times, and sometimes she had to get away for a while. Nina would manage till lunchtime and be pleased to have a shilling for her work. Her parents were in a mess. Losing the farm would be the end of Mr Stewart. Maryanne and Seth Wallace were down to their last farthing as well. God knows what they would do with that brood of kids – nearly enough to make a football team. Well, seven-a-side anyway.

This wasn't much of a stream when you came to look at it. It was a bit of a joke – a trickle that didn't even warrant a name. She gave a chuckle for the three kids who had thought it such a wonderful place. She felt better. The sun was shining; its warmth lifting her out of greyness, lifting her head higher, lifting her eyes to the sky. She sniffed the paddock grasses.

Along the other side of the ditch on a farm paddock ran a line of old men tea tree. Dusky green against a fawn hillside, they were a scrap of leftover autumn. On her side of the ditch grew a wilderness of rambling inkweed, bracken and dried needle stems. Even splotches of new grass poked up here and there, living dangerously in the middle of the bully-boy bushes. On a faraway slope black-and-white cows munched their way from patch to patch.

This creek – always alone – made its own music beside the open river. Perhaps one day they might have enough money put aside to buy a house by the river – her river which didn't need to look after her heart any more. Caleb and the children held her heart now. It was not the time to think about her 'no-mother'. She'd had her father's love. That was enough.

She watched a gentle cloud form and reform into willy-nilly shapes and whispered to it – addressing God – as if his shape, all-powerful and ever-changing, might be somewhere contained in the fluffy whiteness rolling along above the earth.

"Why does everything have to change? Why, when things are going along reasonably smoothly and a person is reasonably happy, can't you let things be?" And into the hollow of the creek's sound she let her own images float – the closeness that was her and Cal, their children, blood of their blood, flowing so richly through their living: Miriam, Danny and Jimmy. The colours of her family eddied around her until they settled into a peaceful throb and were replaced by the solidness of the shop.

It had to go, of course, her hardware. She had known for the last year it would have to go. Business had plummeted then levelled off into the dust of beggary. And it wasn't as if she didn't have enough to do, with the children and a home to run. It was just that the shop had been there since before she married Caleb – since Albert had died.

Sometimes she wondered why she had taken to Hammond's Hardware so well. It had been so strongly Albert's. Everything else connected with him she had sold, burnt or buried, but the store had wrapped itself around her and become hers. *My shop*, she thought. That was the crunch of the whole matter. From her businesswoman's point of view she didn't begrudge the selling of the hardware. It was her silly pride – needing to know she contributed financially to the family.

"We have to survive!" She had spoken out loud and it was true. To survive in this present dearth of trade they needed to sell Hammond's Hardware while they could.

"You will still have a trading corner to call your own." And that was true too. Caleb and Sam were building an attractive area for her right inside the doors of McKay's Garage. It would not be so much to manage, and it would provide household tools in the small town. People would not have to travel to bigger centres for everyday implements. *A new start would be refreshing, wouldn't it? It's only your silly pride hurting*. Iona smiled, remembering Sister Grey, all those years ago: 'Housewifely pride will get you nowhere, my girl.' And neither would business pride.

"Well, I'm losing my feeling of independence," she said to the God of the clouds, "which is silly. Cal will always do the best he can for us. So why am I so grizzly? Why do I feel pulled and pushed? I'm like a child. I just don't want to lose anything. Look at all the people who have lost their farms and their homes. You should be ashamed of yourself, Iona McKay."

And she was. She felt warm tears creep down her face and knew they would wash away her confusion and indecision of the last few days. The needful place that had been filled by Hammond's Hardware was now filled by husband and children.

"But I will keep a part for myself!" she growled up to the heavens and then laughed self-consciously. For by now she could hear herself talking into the ear of a being she could not see, a being that might not even be there for all she knew, but a being who gave her strength she didn't know she had and peace she found nowhere else. Sometimes she doubted – but all His little miracles compelled her to believe. She only had to walk this natural earth, away from man-made places, to know there must be a Creator. Lucky Caleb – he had always believed.

"Thank you," she whispered to beyond the cloud as she wiped her face and began to erase the evidence of disappointment. Relaxed now, revived and in control of her thinking, she also thanked this place for welcoming her in her need.

Then a gift happened. A family of goats arrived, big goats and little goats, old, middle-aged and young goats, all white – all sparkling in the sun – all quick, sure-footed and so crazy they made her smile. They jumped and flashed, twisted and turned and danced, leaping and bucking and kicking their joy like a jubilant dance of prayer under the heavens.

"You are all mad," she shouted, "and I love you for it."

They shouted back, grinning teeth twinkling, goat voices baaing at Swan's barking.

She waited until they moved off to graze around the small hill, then she too moved, walking a little lighter past 'Tiny's' memorial ruins, back up to the road.

She walked, quickly now, past the wharf and along Underwood Street, back to the shop to tell Caleb she was pregnant again.

Iona walked into the shop planning how she could get Caleb out the back. He needed privacy for this news.

"Hello, Iona," Sam greeted. "You'll never guess who's out the back with Cal!"

"Oh?" she stopped, stunned. What was this? What was he talking about?

Out the back Caleb's face was filled with enough excitement for ten little boys.

"Pat! Pat!" he yelled. "Come on, you two. Come and meet Iona." In an instant he had her in his arms. "I told you he'd turn up in 1930. I just didn't know when. And I didn't know he'd have a wife! Don't react. Just smile. You'll love them by lunchtime," he whispered in her ear, "Here you are, dear. Please meet my best friend, Shorty Donavan, and his gorgeous wife Jonquil."

Iona's mouth fell open and turned into a smile – while her brain spun.

There, walking up from the riverbank, were two of the shortest, roundest, ruddiest people she had ever seen. So, this was Pat. Cal had often told her everyone called him Shorty, but he'd never mentioned Pat had a wife, nor that she was even shorter than Shorty.

Suddenly Caleb squeezed her so hard she shrieked and then shut up as he hissed, "Say something good. Now!"

"Ye-ess! It is so good to meet you both. How lovely. How long do you have in Sedgely? Would you like to come home and have lunch? Do you …?" Another sharp squeeze stopped her twittering, but then Swan galloped down and leapt up all over the pair.

"Get down, Swan!" shouted Cal.

"Come! Sit!" yelled Iona. Then "Oofff!" as a pair of small, hard muscular arms grabbed her waist and Jonquil's head squashed itself firmly between Iona's tender breasts. *Goodness, she's strong. And she's not that much taller than Miriam.*

Iona's mothering instinct took over and she patted Jonquil's broad shoulders and made what she hoped were welcoming sounds.

Then Pat moved in. "It's so bloody grand to meet ya, love!" he boomed. "Here, Jonkie, move over and let the woman breathe."

And he immediately enveloped Iona himself, shouting into her shoulder, "Bloomin' heck, we'd be pleased ta have a bite o' lunch with ya."

"Pat and Jonquil have their truck arriving at three this afternoon, dear," roared Cal, forgetting to whisper and nearly deafening Iona's other ear, he was so caught up in the Donovan moment.

Iona disentangled herself from the trio, who somehow reminded her of the happy goat family she had just left, and ushered them all into the shop where Sam, having shamelessly listened to everything from the back door, asked in his squeaky 'I'm not laughing' voice, "Will I make a cup of tea for Pat and Jonquil, Iona?"

"No, no, Sam. They are lunching at home with us." She turned to her husband with a grim smile. "You will be with us, of course, Caleb? I'm sure Sam would shut the shop for you," and she swept out of the door, burying her own laughter, with an exit even her mother would be hard-pressed to emulate.

"Jonquil," she said, as she slowed down to allow Pat's wife to catch up. "What a lovely name!"

"Yes," boomed Pat, trailing behind with a bemused Caleb. "When she was born her mother said she was the prettiest little flower she had ever seen and named her Jonquil straight off! Didn't she, Jonkie."

"Too right!" huffed Jonquil.

Iona slowed down a little more and took Jonquil's hand in hers. Caleb's words sang in her ear: 'You'll love them by lunchtime.' And she would. They were so refreshing.

By three o'clock, when the mechanic arrived with their truck, Pat and Jonquil had won a place in Iona's heart forever. Apparently they had met in Nelson hop-picking, got married then moved back up north where they bought a Returned Serviceman's farm in the hills.

"We've just sold the farm – so that was all a waste of money. Too hilly, too rocky and too greedy a mortgage," Pat had spat, thumping his fist on Iona's well-scrubbed kauri table in frustration.

However, when Cal had asked what he was going to do for work, the stocky little man turned into the most confident businessman Iona had ever met.

"We're going to buy into the second-hand trade, aren't we, Jonquil?"

He succinctly outlined their whole plan of action down to the last pound and their ten-year plan of purchasing their chain of shops by 1940.

Just before they climbed into the truck, their one remaining possession, Pat said to them both, "Never put down a second-hand man. Even the rich buy from the experts. The army taught me that."

Jonquil gave Iona a tender hug, saying, "Thanks, Iona McKay. I damn well knew I'd like ya ta bits if I ever got to meet ya. But I think that bubby you're carrying has other fish to fry. You'd better get inside and into bed. You've got a hard night ahead, darling."

"How did you know?"

"She's fey, Iona. For real."

"And, Iona girl, I ain't been the best little cow midwife in the north for nothin'. See ya in 1940!" she yelled from the cab, and they were gone.

Iona lost the baby in the early hours of the morning.

Chapter Twenty-three

"I think you should tell Iona."

"I don't agree."

"I think she needs to know."

"Why should she? It's not Iona at all, is it? It's you. It's you, Maude, who wants her to know."

"No, Sybil, it's not that. That miscarriage last year has left her most unwell. I think it reminds her of when she lost Hammond's child and then her dog dying in the winter. She was very fond of Swan. It's as if she's lost her way, and I think if she knew, she might understand herself better. She's a woman now, a mother. I really do think ..."

"I think. I think. It was a dog for goodness' sake! What twaddle! You really must consider me a numbskull."

In the long pause that followed Maude reached for the teapot. Sybil was an expert at silent intimidation. As the younger sister, Maude had learnt to wait her out, and today she didn't want to send her sister into a coughing fit. Even though Sybil had not caught the bad flu like Edward and Uriah, she had become nervous and weak and prone to bronchitis. *Should I be pushing this?* Maude wondered. She poured the tea, black, just as

Sybil liked it and squeezed in a few drops of lemon juice. As she passed it she said, "Iona hasn't been well enough to come down ..."

"I know. I know that. I know what it's like to be anaemic, remember? I've had a miscarriage too, you know. For goodness' sakes, I'm not stupid, Maude."

And Maude remembered. Sybil had miscarried – twice; once before Iona and once after Edward. The memory of the second loss now clear in Maude's mind brought pictures of their mother waiting on Sybil hand and foot for weeks. Then suddenly, with mother exhausted and she herself worn out, Sybil had recovered. Then again Sybil probably didn't remember that part of it. Her sister's memory stretched only to the things she wished to retain.

As the silence continued, Maude thought the wordless gaps in their conversations were like a dance. Sybil's thoughts careered above her head, darting and diving and waiting to fling themselves at any moment, while Maude's thoughts bowed this way and that and waited to counteract the surety of Sybil's attack.

"I don't know why you keep pestering me about her, Maude. The girl has everything. A good husband, though not the husband that young solicitor would have made. However, Caleb McKay does seem to do reasonably well by her – he has given her a good home and healthy children. He even put up with her playing around in that wretched hardware store. She's quite all right. She needs to take a pull at herself, that's all. She's better treated than better people."

It was Maude's turn to invoke silence now. Maude forced herself to think slowly – her feelings were rising in defence of Iona. She did not want to let Sybil know that Iona still took off from time to time around the countryside. It had ever been Iona's way to sort herself out. But lately she had taken to going off for walks out of the blue, much like she used to run off into the bush and down the riverside track as a child. Not that Caleb seemed to mind – used to it probably – but a woman, in Maude's mind, could not get away with what a child could.

"She's never quite sure of herself, Sybil, never quite happy. I think she would be far more at ease if she knew."

Sybil drained her teacup, set it down with trembling hands on the starched cloth and looked up. Probing eyes, wobbling head and all Sybil's mind still worked overtime. All this nonsense. She rejected everything Maude had said. Maude had always been a ditherer, always let her feelings lead her by the nose. Besides, she did not want Maude's words around her – jumping at her, not leaving her alone. She toyed with the silver and bone handle of the tray, fingers quivering, flipping against the edge of the cloth.

"I am not well, Maude, and I will not hear another word. You are deliberately trying to upset me."

"I am not, Sybil!"

Sybil tried not to smile. It was most rewarding getting a rise out of Maude – one of the few delights she had left, now that her body and half her mind seemed to have played a dirty trick on her. Uriah, that cold fish, never sparked back now. But Maude, there she went, red face, blazing eyes, so …

"Leave things alone, Maude. Iona has a very good life. It seems to me all you want to do is cause mischief."

"Sybil! You know me better than that!"

"No, I don't, Maude. I don't. Look at you, all done up like a sore toe. You've changed since you married old Denby – and not for the better."

"He wasn't that old, Sybil. You say the most hurtful things."

"Maude, he was over fifty years old."

"So! So? I was over forty."

Maude stopped. *For goodness sake get yourself under control, woman,* she thought. *She's doing this on purpose. She always does this. She gets you worked up about some other topic altogether, and then you sound like a hysterical idiot. Calm yourself, Maude. Get back to the subject.*

"Look, never mind about that. It's Iona …"

"Leave things alone! I made a promise all those years ago, and I intend to keep it."

"But sometimes things change. People change."

"And sometimes I think you have never grown up. You keep out. Do you hear me? Keep out!" and Sybil began to cough, clutching her chest, gasping for breath.

Maude found Sybil's cough tincture and gave it to her. She packed the cups and saucers on the tray, went out into the kitchen, closed the door and cried like a suffocating cat. The dishes were washed with her tears as they dripped into the suds, tears for the years filled with the frustrations of being Sybil's younger sister, and tears for Iona. She covered her muffled mourning by bashing the soap container against sink and tap and water, so that she didn't hear Uriah come in the back door.

"Maude?"

"Oh! Uriah!"

"What … ?"

"I'm sorry, Uriah, I upset her, but she's all right now. She's in the sitting room. I … Oh Uriah … I just wanted her to tell Iona …"

Uriah Anderson-Keyes closed his eyes and stood swaying slightly – but he did not walk out, as he would have done over the tears of Sybil. Sybil's tears tore and cut like the claws of a vicious beast in control of its power. Maude's were simply the tears of hurting over someone else.

"She will never tell Iona, Maude. You know that. Your mother knew that. It's no use my dear – and sometimes I think she might even be right – but whatever you or I or the Pope himself thinks, she will never change her mind. Just give it up, my dear. You'll only get upset." He patted her shoulder awkwardly and passed her his own clean handkerchief.

Maude mopped her face and straightened herself up, pocketing the handkerchief to launder at home. She turned on the cold tap, soaked the huckaback hand towel she had bawled all over and wringing it out pressed the cold cloth to each of her eyes and against her hot forehead.

"Yes," she whispered. "You're right." She gave him a weak grin. Her hat and coat were hanging on the back of the kitchen door. She walked over, patting her faded curls into place, without much success, and reached for her things. Uriah was drying the last of the dishes.

Maude turned. She had forgotten he was there. She watched him as she wrestled into her coat. *He is very bent over now*, she thought. She placed her hat on the back of her head and her fingers, from long practice, pushed the hatpin in through the thick felt – along the top of her scalp – and out through the felt again.

Uriah turned. They stood, reading in each other's eyes the weariness of past knowledge. This was a family monster that had been around so long it did not need words.

"Goodbye, Uriah."

"Goodbye, Maude. Give my regards to Tom."

"I will."

"Could you give Iona some beans for me? I've left them in a paper bag at the gate."

"Of course."

The air now seemed cool. The beans made the afternoon sane. The hot and sticky red breaths of a sisters' argument had disappeared into a moment already called the past.

"I must go. Call me if you need …"

"Of course. But she seems to be recovering quite well from this last bout. Yes, quite well."

Maude sang out, "Goodbye, Sybil."

Tom wouldn't be along to pick her up for another ten minutes so she took her time, ambling out to the end of the limestone drive.

There by the big gates, on the smooth old macrocarpa stump, were two brown paper bags filled with fresh beans. They lay neatly together in the middle of the stump, where Uriah knew she would sit and wait. One or two beans protruded, and tight little brown ears stuck out on each side of the bags, formed by the size of his thumbs when he had twirled the full bags round and round to keep them closed. On the outside he had written 'Iona' – and 'Maude', obviously before he had put the beans in, because the writing was large and the letters perfectly cursive, quite beautiful in fact, as was all Uriah's handiwork.

"Beans!" she muttered. "It's not beans she needs."

Sitting there holding the bags made her feel hot and sticky. She dabbed at her throat with her sodden handkerchief, trying to wipe away the red mottles she knew would be there, and looked up at the sky. It was a cool blue. An early summer sun had kept the day clear despite her tumultuous afternoon. *He is a clever gardener to have these ready so soon. I wonder how he does it.* She pulled one of the beans out of the bag, snapped it in two and began to eat. It tasted sweet and tender.

"It's not fair!" she exploded, nearly choking herself on the juice, and swallowed the half-chewed bean as the last of her tears ran down her face, onto her hands and the cuffs of her too-hot winter coat, the coat that covered her cuddliness.

'Cuddly' was what Tom called her now she'd lost the streamlined figure of her forties. She accepted her age – most of the time. What else could a body do? Look at her hands! They did not look like her hands at all. They were no longer the smooth hands of the young woman who had been Maude, during all the years of caring for mother. Now they were growing those brown patches people called kidney spots, whatever that meant, and when she held her hands up the knuckles frowned back at her like eight tiny old faces.

She put her hands away. She was glad now that she and Tom were leaving Sedgely – and everyone in it. She'd certainly had more than enough of Sybil. Maude felt a twinge of guilt. Sybil had been very ill with prolonged bronchitis this winter – but Sybil had been ill so many times, mostly in her own head, Maude suspected. Sometimes over the years, Maude had wondered whether Sybil was quite right in the head. She was an extremely determined woman, and her fury did have a mad edge to it. As the younger sister, the one generally on the receiving end of Sybil's tantrums, Maude had even thought there was something evil in her attacks. When Sybil made her mind up, the world could explode around her, and she would still sit there, glaring or smiling her cruel, sinister smile – and she got a look in her eye that fairly made you shiver. Yes, Sybil could make your life a misery.

Yet she wasn't happy being like that. Why wasn't she happy? If she was so right – so very right – about her decisions that everyone else had to fit in with her way ... like about Iona, for example.

"Me-oww!"

Uriah's latest in a long line of cats squashed itself under the gate, and with its eyes fixed on Maude, leapt onto the stump then shoved itself onto her lap haughtily.

"I've never heard her laugh," Maude whispered, as she held the cat's paws to prevent its sharp claws from gouging her thigh. She stroked its soft fur, trying to calm herself down before Tom arrived, and she did feel a little quieter, lulled by its mystic and monotonous purr.

"You're such a comfy cat, you dear thing. Don't let her hurt you, will you?"

Tom arrived and they drove towards town without mentioning Sybil, because behind the smile she had ready for him, Tom Denby could see the traces of her recent tears. He reached for her hand for a minute as they approached Sedgely. Maude simply sighed.

At home that evening, sitting amongst the packing cases, sorting piles of linen, wrapping things ready for removal to Dargaville the next week, Maude told Tom about the afternoon.

"It's a difficult situation, Maude."

"I know that."

"Have you ever considered that Sybil might be right in this business?"

"Yes – and no. I don't think she's right. I think she's taken it all out on Iona, and on Uriah … Uriah, 'the disappointment of her life'. You know they've slept in separate bedrooms for years now?"

"No. No, I didn't know that," he mumbled.

Maude knew he was embarrassed but she was determined to talk about her sister before she exploded. "Yes. Edward let it slip one day when he came to visit. Some remark about being grateful for the long truce since his dad had moved into the other bedroom … before that bad flu years ago."

"Hmmm. Do you want to take this vase, dear?"

"Yes, it was mother's favourite – that box – behind the door."

They wrapped in unison, selecting pieces of china and ornaments. Some went into chests marked

'Dargaville'; some were put aside for family to choose from at the weekend.

Semi-retirement upriver would give Maude a new life, and Tom had a good agreement with young Bromwell. Part-time work in Anthony's burgeoning firm, to be reviewed on either side in two years. It should be a pleasant life, and maybe not seeing Sybil so much would be better all round. She watched Tom, carefully packing, so patient.

"I'm sorry, Tom. I'm ruining your evening."

"Not at all, my dear. I just hate to see you upset."

"She is just so selfish, it makes me mad."

"Yes. But then Sybil may feel very bound by that promise."

"Bound by … Oh, Tom, you still don't know our Sybil, do you? She may or may not have made such a gilt-edged promise to Father – but I didn't. I didn't make any promise at all. I suppose I was so young no one bothered. I suppose they thought I'd just fit in with them all – as was expected of the younger and not so clever daughter. But whatever …"

"Maude, darling – don't." Tom moved to hold her firmly, hoping to halt her distress.

"No, Tom. I mean it. One day, if I think it is the right thing to do. If I think it is necessary. I will tell Iona myself, and Sybil can go hang!"

"Yes, dearest, but not now. Not just now. Let it be. It may take care of itself. Some problems do, you know."

Maude drew back, trembling.

"All right. But I mean it, Tom. One day …"

"Yes, one day we might have to make such a decision."

Maude felt soothed by his words. What a nice man she had married, so late in life.

Chapter Twenty-four

It started on the wharf, the regular gathering place for this early morning group of townsfolk to share the newspaper, and it finished with frontline, word-of-mouth news about one of their own people.

The relief worker strikes and riots in Auckland and Wellington were still the top stories that May day in 1932. Now some ratbag journalist had been bad-mouthing Coates – their Gordon Coates – and they didn't believe it. Still, Coates had promised the delegates in Wellington he would make an announcement on 8th May. He'd been their hope. And now there were rumours flying about everywhere; but the north demanded loyalty to its man.

"You know about a week and a half ago the police lay about with clubs at those relief workers in Wellington, even though some of the wives and children were with them," said Willie Floyd, heating up the moment for all he was worth. "And what's the truth, I ask you?" He threw his paper on the ground. "Ya can't trust journalists."

Floyd always blamed the journalists. He'd had an aversion to newspapermen ever since a visiting reporter had whisked his best girl away from under his nose –

and then let her down without ceremony a year later. It didn't help that Willie had got himself married in a huff in the meantime.

"Yeah. You can't trust townies. They'd say anything," agreed Izzy Wood, throwing his paper away as well. And Izzy knew because he'd done a stint in Wellington on the boats. "Worse than sheep they are, those city slickers," he'd told them this morning at the Road Service Office when the papers came in. "Believe anything they would."

Sam Newbold pulled his bike over to the back of the group in time to hear Mavis Smith say her brother had rung from Taranaki to see if it was all true.

Then Angus Casey joined in. "More likely those Reds stirring up trouble," he muttered, and this time they took notice of him. He was just getting into his stride, working himself and the breakfast bunch up into a decent lather, when someone strolled up and whispered in someone else's ear and the next thing it was all – 'No!', 'You're joking!', 'Who told you?' and 'When – when did he go?'

Angus, his Celtic blood still on the boil, did his best to keep their attention, but his own curiosity was so aroused that, "Who's gone where?" slipped out before he knew it.

"It's Livingstone. He's done a bunk."

"When?"

"Last night!"

"What … ?"

"Lost the lot – hasn't he!"

"But …"

"Ya silly beggar. He's been found out in a fiddle. He's got out of town in the dark before we lynched 'im."

"My God," whispered Bandy. "I told ya years ago to give that smarmy sod a wide berth."

"Yeah, I know, Bandy. Hell, I'd better go and see if the old girl's heard anything. See you lot later," he muttered as he took off, doing Underwood at over the thirty and swearing to himself all the way, the thought of losing his mum's little nest egg worrying him more than a traffic fine.

Sam Newbold had heard enough. He spun his bike full circle and rode back to Cal's garage. Cal made a few phone calls to check the news was genuine and let Sam go to tell Iona.

"Go on. You and Agnes saw her through that time. That was well before I came onto the scene. It'll do her good."

Iona was in the middle of scrubbing the kitchen floor when Sam arrived. All she could say for some time was, "We were right. We were right."

Sam had already phoned Agnes, who walked into Iona's kitchen and made a pot of tea, still puffing and panting from her fast walk over. They sat around Grandma Kelly's table talking for a good two hours. It enlivened Iona to the point where she couldn't remain still. Her anger at the man who had so nearly used his position to lighten her bank balance in 1919 welled. Then she thought of his present-day clients and got worried for them and angry all over again.

Around eleven, Caleb rang.

"They've got him, Iona love."

"Livingstone?"

"Yes. Herbie called in. The Auckland police picked the dirty scoundrel up at the wharves early this morning. His wife potted him. Apparently he'd even had a go at her inheritance."

Agnes and Sam left not long after that. They could see Iona looking better than she had for weeks. Iona stood gazing at nothing when the phone rang again.

"Could I speak with Iona McKay, please?"

It sounded like Anthony! Tom Denby sometimes gave her news of him, but she had not heard from him for years.

"Speaking," she said.

"Iona? It's Anthony Bromwell. How are you? Are you well?"

"Yes, Anthony – I'm fine."

"I wanted to reach you, Iona. I know you will have heard about Livingstone, and I felt it might upset you. He will stand trial! I don't think he has a chance of getting off."

"I see."

"You're upset."

"A little. He was very good at making me feel brainless."

"You were never that, my dear."

There was a pause.

"Thank you, Anthony. It's good of you to think of me."

"Well, you weren't the only one he tried it on – but I am certain we saved everything of yours. I won't discuss it any further now on a party line. Perhaps next time you're up this way you might call in and we'll chat about it – just to tidy it up."

"Yes. I'll ... I'll try and do that."

"Goodbye then."

Iona put the phone down. She felt she was in such a kaleidoscope of memories she gasped. They had jostled and changed and slipped about all morning.

"Jimmy!" she called.

He came up from the backyard and got into his pushchair happily enough, shoving a dirty thumb in his mouth. She automatically called for Swan before remembering the dog had died last year at thirteen, old and worn out. How she missed her companion of the years. How upset the children had been. She would never have another dog. They were too hard to lose. Fighting back tears she could not shed in front of Jimmy, she set off down the back road singing his favourite lullaby ...

"River river raupo rye-ee
I see the sun
I see the sky
I see the tui bird flying by
River river rau-aupo rye-ee."

... before he dozed off.

Iona kept walking at a slow pace so he wouldn't wake, while her thoughts raced. *Yes I did know he wasn't honest but it seems so far back now. And yes, I haven't thought of Livingstone for many years.* She'd thought of Grandma Kelly though, often. They lived in Grandma Kelly's house now, had done since Miriam was an infant and Aunt Maude and Uncle Tom were married. They had been so happy in Cal's little cottage with its sunshine curtains that she'd sewn after … after Cal had kissed her that rainy night … and in a voice so broken she'd thought he was crying, told her, 'I love you Iona Annabel Anderson-Keyes.'

It had been hard to shift from their first little home. Still, Grandma's house had made a fine family home with its big kitchen and sitting room, wide halls and four bedrooms – well, three really, but they'd glassed in the sun verandah to make a fourth. Four years they'd been there now. Miriam would be ten in November – so, yes, about four years. She'd be thirty-two herself this year.

The roads were uneven this far out of town. It slowed her up having to ease the pushchair over ruts. Lowry's farm wasn't too far off. They knew her there. They never minded her using their track down to the river. By some miracle Jimmy stayed asleep even over the grass track. She left him under a pine and moved away a distance.

"Fancy being thirty-two in December," she whispered to the running water. "It's nearly fifteen years since Albert died – poor Albert; poor Mum and Dad too, now, neither of them strong." Sudden, hot anger rushed through her head. "I hated Mum once," she acknowledged.

"Hate's not worth it
Don't throw stones
You're for me and he's for seas.
Dead in a thrice
Brought back to life …"

The old skipping rhyme they'd sung at school. What on earth did that mean anyhow?

"Thank you for friends like Sam and Agnes and Maryanne. I do see love in your people sometimes now, don't I?" her voice low, addressing the space above the water – the space of breath and newness.

She checked Jimmy then moved a little further away, again making sure she could see if he moved or woke, then sat on her jacket and made herself stop – but the mind does not stop as readily as the body, and the heart doesn't let go as quickly as the 'self' wishes.

What was getting at her then? It wasn't that she had any silly thoughts about Anthony. There would always be a certain fondness for Anthony, but she loved Caleb – and always would. It was just that she had been so fragile these last two years after the miscarriage. Yes, the miscarriage had left her weakened, but Anthony's call had brought back the past. He came from a time before Cal – a time when life was freer, opening up for her, vibrating with new, unfettered things.

The bulrushes were magnificent this year. Their proud, brown heads stood warrior-like, guarding either the line of the land or the line of the water, whichever way you saw it …

> *"River river raupo rye*
> *I see the sun*
> *I see the sky*
> *I see the kuaka flying …"*

… too many years, too many people.

Two little people … "My little people."

Two of them – now – never breathed the river air. She remembered her first son. People never mentioned him – neither did she … talk about him. She had talked to the river though. She had talked to God – that first time she had gone to the coast and rode it all out with that mad storm – and even now she could feel those screams in her throat. The second time she'd gone to the church to talk to Him – and found Father O'Rourke. He had listened. He was very kind, very patient. She didn't really know how he could understand, never having borne a child – but he had helped, in his way, and he was right about it being easier with time; though it never went away.

"After that I talked to you, as well, didn't I?" She addressed God. "Like I did at Tiny's hut. It still feels strange, that day – the light afternoon with Pat and Jonquil – the heavy night. And the poor little thing – nothing but blood and guts when you look at what came out of me – but I know it was a person."

The raupo moved a smidgeon, daintily, and the rising tide sang 'wishes, wishes, wish-sh-sh' through the strong, thick stems of the bulrush brigade.

"I wish it would be here in my arms."

And once again tears poured from her body, as the blood had poured that not-to-be-lived-life from her body, and her tear water met with the river water at the feet of the raupo warriors.

Chapter Twenty-five

"Can we help them at all, Cal?"

"Well, I've spoken to Joe Lowry. He's got an old cabin on the back of his farm. He'll stand for Seth and the boys staying there for a few weeks with this good weather. No rent. He's not keen on the womenfolk being there though. It's pretty rough and ready."

"Oh, they'll stay with us, won't they? Mr and Mrs Stewart are already living with one of Maryanne's brothers. He can't take this lot in as well."

"I told Lowry the women would be here."

Iona looked at him a long time.

"What's the matter?"

"Nothing's the matter. I'm just thinking what a good man you are, Caleb McKay."

"You don't always think that, my fine Iona." He was flushed with pleasure all the same and teased. "You don't like it when I go against your royal wishes."

She smiled up at him. It was true. She did like her own way. Sometimes they seemed to argue for no good reason – until the reason came clear. "But today is special. Today I think you're good, and we're so lucky to still have money coming in."

Their arms reached for each other, and they stayed close for some time.

"It won't be easy if it goes on too long, my girl."

"I know."

Surely it wouldn't be too long. Seth and Maryanne would find something ... given time. Seth was so down. He took it as such a personal failure to have lost the farm. He couldn't seem to rise above the sheer size of the tragedy even though the same thing was happening to farmers all over the country. Depression, they called it, and depression was what everyone had sunk into to some degree or other. Hearing bad news day after day for four years and having even the bare necessities of life torn from them into the bargain took the light out of living altogether.

The Wallaces arrived two days later in time for morning tea. The strain showed on every face, even the littlest, telling its story better than words. Fifteen-year-old Nina Stewart, carried the baby. Maryanne would not leave her husband's side. Seth looked older than his years, pale and tense. Iona took nine-month-old Lucy Wallace from Nina's brave young arms and forced out the most cheerful words she could muster.

"Come on in. There's hot scones and apple jelly waiting in the kitchen. Don't let them go cold," and it worked so well that two hours later, full of scones, hot tea and cocoa and empty of talk that had been stuck in their craws for weeks, every Wallace face looked pink and alive.

Caleb made a special trip home for lunch to be with Seth. The two women watched their husbands walking around the back garden. Cal had become a pipe smoker now. Seth was trying to give up his cigarettes, but Cal had slipped him a packet of Park Drive and some papers, knowing how hard it could be to give up smoking at a terrible time like this. They puffed and talked, and stood silently together, Cal feeling the pain of the man beside him.

"He looks better already," said Maryanne.

"Yes."

"I can't thank you enough, Iona."

"You'd do the same for us."

"Yes, I guess we would."

"Take the little ones out the front in the fresh air, will you, Nina?" Iona asked, giving the girl a look that said, 'Your sister's about to break.'

Nina and Maggie, with Miriam chattering like a magpie, guided the Wallace girls out to the backyard. Iona found it amazing how young her Miriam seemed in comparison to Maggie Wallace. There was a year and a half between those two, and both were the eldest in their families. But then Miriam had never had Maggie Wallace's responsibilities on her shoulders. No. Miriam had a privileged childhood, and Iona wondered if it was good for their daughter. The old adage, 'Time will tell', stopped her thinking about it. *Now is not the time.*

She called to Nina, "Take our lot with you too, love?"

"I will, Aunt Iona."

The glance she gave her sister told Iona the girl knew exactly how things were and how relieved she felt to be leaving the women's company. Nina saw her nephews standing around Seth and Caleb looking fidgety and awkward, trying to be little men.

"George!" she shouted, back in command mode. "Come and give us a hand!"

Oh, Nina, thought Iona, *you should be off with girls your own age, dreaming of dances and pretty dresses and princes on white horses, without a care in the world.*

Today was the girl's last day with the Wallaces. She had been living with Maryanne and Seth for a year, helping her big sister with the children; but tonight she would go back to her parents, to an all adult household. It had to be. This house was already bulging at the seams – enough to burst, thought Iona as she watched the young ones wander off past the rose gardens and down towards the back paddock.

The big kitchen became still as the men strolled off to keep an eye on the kids. Maryanne started slicing cheese to go on the children's sandwiches while Iona cut into the huge fruit cake she'd made yesterday, 'ready for the invasion' as Cal put it, trying to make the old joke work.

"She's been wonderful, Nina has. Maggie too, and the boys," sighed Maryanne.

"They're lovely children, Maryanne."

"I know and they should still be children."

Iona had no words to say. *Stay quiet*, she said to herself.

"It's not fair, it's not …"

Now Iona moved. She grabbed Maryanne and let the slices of cheese fall to the floor. She held her friend while the soft, plump, beautiful body heaved and jerked and choked and splashed tears over both of them. Maryanne was clutching her so tight Iona thought she might get a couple of broken ribs out of it. The woman felt like a frenzied anchor in a crazy current, feeling everything ripped and torn away from familiar sands. Her friend was a strong woman. But too much is too much, even for the strong, thought Iona.

"Thanks, Iona."

"That's okay, love."

"I bet I look a mess."

Iona nodded. "A beautiful mess – but definitely a mess."

They smiled. Like rainbows after rain, Iona thought.

"I'd better go and clean myself up in the bathroom."

"Take your time. The men are still talking."

Alone, Iona leant over her dear, scrubbed bench and held onto the taps as hard as she could. Gradually the stone in her throat went away. She straightened, forced her face back into place and reached for the tonic on the windowsill. It tasted like cow dung and rusty nails but she had to keep pushing it down. She had been battling anaemia since the miscarriage and was surely nearly on top of it. Turning on the tap she bent and drank from her cupped hands. She splashed some of the cold water over her face as she finished and mopped herself up with her apron.

The children – I'll get them in. They can help. If they put jumpers on they can have a picnic lunch under the old oak. They'll love that.

As it happened the Wallaces were only with them for a month. Seth went off to a relief camp determined to help his family somehow, ready to use a shovel and pick, anywhere, to do anything. Mr Lowry, the cabin lender, came up trumps. He had put off his hired milker a few months before, unable to afford full-time wages. He now became so impressed with the Stewart boys, he offered Maryanne and Maggie and the baby the single milker's quarters on the end of the house, and the boys the cabin, rent-free if the family helped with the milking and general chores. For Lowry, a widower with no children, the years were rolling on. Cal reckoned Maryanne and the boys probably made the place feel like a home. He winked at Maryanne adding, "And I bet someone's wonderful cooking doesn't hurt either!"

Maryanne asked if Iona would consider having Nina come and stay with them at Sedgely. "I think she's missing the young company. Mum and Dad are getting on now, and my brother is a real sober-sides. It's … well, it's a bit boring for Nina."

"Oh, Maryanne, what a good idea. We were thinking of having a girl in to live. Cal says we could afford five shillings a week and bed and board. Would that be all right, do you think?"

"All right! Iona, that girl will love you forever. She's never had a penny all the time she's been helping me. I'm so relieved. It's a bit of a squash on the farm, and I didn't want to push Mr Lowry too far but I have been worried about Nina."

They were good weeks for Iona, the next ten or eleven. Nina was a chirpy girl, happy to be helping with the three little McKays and, Iona suspected, happy to be in a secure place. At first she acted like a miniature woman. It took a month or two of licking her wounds and the news that Seth had complied with the bank eviction from the farm before Nina forgot to be old and became her peppy self again.

Caleb made sure his garden supplied the Wallace table until Maryanne told him they were doing well off the Lowry garden and had started their own patch too. Edward incorporated them in his fish round; Edward had several hard-hit families to whom he gave fish. He and a mate netted regularly for their own tables, being family men themselves now. Agnes Newbold had been down to Auckland recently seeing to their older son. Harry boarded with Agnes's brother so he could do his last two years at a secondary school that specialised in technical courses. Boarding school fees were out of the question for the Newbolds' purse.

Agnes told Iona that some of the city families were having a shocking time. "Some of those kids look as if they're starving." The sight of a queue of sad-looking souls at a soup kitchen had turned her heart over. Agnes reckoned Harry was not too badly off with her brother and his wife, and neither was Sedgely, compared to Auckland. "At least we've got plenty of good soil to grow vegies, and we can swap rabbits for fresh fish from our neighbour."

Once, when Seth got back up for a weekend, Iona had the Wallaces over for a Sunday roast. Seth was home for two days and over the worst of it all now. Mixing in with the other men at the camp had made him realise his smallness in the world of grinding poverty. Conditions were harsh for the men, and there was no chance of having their wives and children with them. Seth had everyone and his dog looking out for work. He 'had his dander up now', he told them, his toothy grin firmly back on his face.

Chapter Twenty-six

In the August of 1933 Caleb took Iona and their three children down to visit his mother and father at Helensville – they were in their sixties now. Mr McKay had sold his business just before the depression and half of their hard earned money had dwindled. At least Henry had managed to get the rest out as fast as he could. They lived frugally. Caleb wanted to check they were being sensible and not going without necessities.

"I know my father. Probably eating weevil porridge and not lighting the fire."

Sure enough, when they'd finished tea they all had to sit in the kitchen around the range while they talked.

"Not using the sitting room fire then, Dad?" asked Caleb with a side wink to Iona.

"No use wasting kindling and the good embers," declared the proud Henry McKay – and glared at Cal when he joined in his "Waste not want not!"

When they went to bed that night Cal whispered to Iona that he was right.

"What do you mean?"

"I watched him set his porridge in the kitchen before we came to bed. Weevils!"

"Oooo, Cal. I'm not having any porridge then. And neither are the kids!"

"Good protein, my girl, good protein," he grinned evilly at her while he tickled her – until she laughed too loud.

"Stop it, Cal!"

"It's okay. They won't hear a thing."

"Are they all right?" Iona asked later.

"I think so. I'll try and check things out a bit more tomorrow. Independent old devil!"

"Like father like son, Caleb McKay, and did you really see weevils? Truth now!"

"Well, no – but it wouldn't surprise me."

Iona spent the next day with her mother-in-law while Cal and his father visited old business friends. She liked Ada McKay. Old-fashioned and a little regal; she spoke precisely and liked everything done as it had always been done. Although she suffered from her legs terribly now, she never talked about it – never grumbled. Sometimes she spoke with asperity if she thought you were talking nonsense at her, but not often, and she had the gentlest smile Iona had ever seen, a smile that gave the lie to the weathered toughness within. The youngest daughter of a landed father, she had been privately educated and was musically talented. She came from a generation when women were generally dominated and expected to entertain. Although she skirted around opposing the two men in her life, you knew where you stood with Mrs Henry McKay. She was a fragrant lady in Iona's book. Today she gloried in being Granny McKay to Caleb's children, and they gloried in her love.

The next day the children wanted only Grandma 'Kay' so Iona and Caleb had a day to themselves. They decided to take the waters at Parakai. Old Josh, Henry's fine-lined roan, trotted them down past the dairy factory. The McKay gig gleamed and sparkled from all Henry's spit and polish and looked fit for a queen. Cal could never understand why his father had not taken to the automobile. Once he'd retired his father had sold the Tin Lizzie, bought Old Josh from a farming friend, and the gig, which had been wasting away in the shed. He had cleaned it and painted it and brought it back to life. Engineer or not, Henry loved his gig.

"A horse is half the price of an automobile, as well as being a friend and a supplier of fresh manure for the garden. What more can a man ask for?" he quipped when pushed.

"Is he right?" Iona asked Cal as Old Josh trotted them down the road.

"To a point - a horse might indeed be a lovable old friend but it could never be as efficient as an engine. Animals tire, get sick and die."

"Efficiency isn't everything," Iona pronounced. She loved Josh and the gig.

The hot mineral waters warmed and soothed and sent them into a dreamlike state as they soaked. Among the other bathers they chatted with was a couple up from Riverhead who were helping their crippled son exercise in the restorative waters. Watching the effort the little fellow had to make made Iona grateful that their surviving children were fit and healthy. Maybe Dr Jenkins was right when he told her that a miscarriage could be nature's way of removing an imperfect baby.

Then why do some get born imperfect and all? She wondered as she saw the pool masseur working on the boy's deformed legs.

"Poor little wretch," Caleb mumbled at Iona. "Yes."

"This is too hot for me. I'm going in the cooler one. Coming?"

"No. I think I'll stay here a bit longer."

Iona's body dissolved with the water, and her mind wandered.

Some people drank the water from these springs – said it helped their rheumatics. Uriah did when he came down. Although her father was eight years younger than Mr McKay, he looked just as old. He'd had trouble with his chest since the flu and been down with pneumonia several times these last few years. Iona didn't think having to work and look after her mother helped matters. Her mother had been sick in the autumn, really sick. Aunt Maude had helped Uriah nurse Sybil this time and Edward and Jane looked in when they could.

Teddy had built a small home on the block across the road from the family home at Kotare Creek and bought the adjacent block. The way he'd worked clearing all that land was a credit to him, and they survived quite well. Jane was a city girl with a country girl's heart, endowed with a high-cheeked beauty that would never fade. Iona smiled. Her rough-looking, land-working brother adored his wife and readily showed it. Lately Edward and his neighbour had begun fishing commercially as a sideline as well as cropping extensively. The son had inherited their father's flair for growing superb vegetables.

"Growing vegetables is an art, Sis," he maintained. "I find it a chancy business producing enough chou moellier and ensilage for the herd – and even hay's a bit of a gamble weather-wise – but a well-grown pumpkin or a perfect cauliflower does something for the soul and the belly."

Edward had grown into a lovely man. His rose gardens were a feature in the district. He would have bought the block next to their parents as well by now if the economic times hadn't turned so bad.

Edward and Jane would have their third child by Christmas. Jane said she didn't want any more after that, and no one blamed her. The poor woman had morning sickness for the first five months of her pregnancies. Then she blew up to an immense size and produced nine- and ten-pound babies. She looked like a skeleton when she came through labour, and she was so exhausted she couldn't see to the baby once it was born. Her mother came to stay for three months or more after the births. Edward didn't want to take the chance again either.

"I love the children, Iona, I do. But I'm terrified every time that my lovely Jane might die. We should have been more careful over this one."

Edward worried as well about Uriah and their mother. "She doesn't look at all well," he'd said, and when she'd made some a flippant remark about their mother's ill health, Edward had jumped down her throat. There had been no time to check Sybil out before they'd come away.

She's always ill, Iona thought. *She's never able to do anything for my children – or Teddy's. I wish she could have been more like Jane's mother. Well, she wasn't, and she never would be. Aunt Maude said Sybil was a replica of their father – only in a dress.* "I'd better go down next week and see for myself, I suppose," Iona told herself.

If their afternoon was a delight, their evening was not. Old Henry had lit the fire in the sitting room in honour of their visit and their last night in Helensville. They played five hundred and were having a bedtime cup of tea. Everything appeared fine. Caleb had warned Iona that his father could blow up on occasions but she didn't really believe him. He never had when she visited.

It all started when the conversation turned to the news about the coalition. Later, she realised she had seen Cal's warning stare but didn't heed it.

"Never vote for any fly-by-nights," Henry announced, looking at her over the top of his glasses like a teacher at a backward child.

"I wouldn't call them fly-by-nights," Iona said.

"You women don't understand politics at all, do you now?"

"I think I have a good grasp of the political situation," Iona replied with a sting in her voice. She should have been aware by the way Ada McKay got up and started clearing the supper things that it was time to shut up and play dumb.

"In fact I think some women understand the political situation better than some men who just vote for the same old party because that's what they've always done."

"What a lot of poppycock, girl!" Henry looked as if he was about to burst a blood vessel. She'd set him off on a tirade. He ranted and raved and thumped the arm of his chair and gave her a long, loud rundown on the history of government in New Zealand. He had 'no time for this coalition party'. He was not a 'Coates man' – and he had 'known him since he was a boy'.

"Rapscallion. Just a rapscallion, that one!"

"Well, he's not a boy now, Mr McKay, and I think he does a fine job. He might do better if his own party would let him."

"Women! I tell you girl, the worst day this country ever saw was the day those stupid blighters up there gave women the vote. It's ruined the nation."

Iona was so astounded she sat with her mouth open – stunned.

Caleb came to the rescue. "Dear creatures, though, aren't they Dad? No more politics tonight, eh? This wonderful wife of mine is very tired. We'd better be off to bed. Got a train to catch tomorrow," and he had her out of the chair by the elbow while she was taking breath to go another round. "Never, never bring up the subject of politics when my father is around, Iona," he whispered between clenched teeth as he steered her past his parent's bedroom, where Ada could be heard getting ready for bed.

"I … I didn't know he …"

"Why do you think I never discuss politics in the home?"

"Yes, but he's never …"

"Well, now he has and now you know."

Iona pulled her elbow out of Caleb's grasp. "What right has he got to talk to me like that? Did you hear what he said? I'm going back in there and tell ..."

"You'll do no such thing, Iona McKay."

"Whose side are you on, Caleb? You heard how he spoke to me. You heard what he said about women."

By this time they were in the bedroom. Caleb managed to get hold of Iona's elbow again and shut the door with his other hand.

"Let go of me!"

"I will if you promise to listen to me for a minute before you go down and cause a worse scene in my parents' house."

"I did not cause any scene in your parents' house."

Caleb opened his mouth – then closed it. He looked at her and hugged her to him. "No, you didn't, and I don't blame you for being angry, but you will cause another scene if you push it any further."

"I've never seen him like that before."

"No. And I'm sorry, love."

"It's not you should be apologising, Cal. It's your father. He's a rude, self-opinionated old man. No wonder you grew up unable to discuss politics."

"I am not unable to discuss politics, Iona; I merely will not discuss it in our home."

"Well, that's an inability too."

"Maybe it is. At least I don't shove my opinions onto you now, do I?"

"No."

Iona considered this. He was right. He gave her complete freedom in her views but he never discussed them. He would never behave like his father, and his

213

father's views were sending them into an argument of their own. She made herself cool down. They had been so intense in their whispered exchange, neither of them realised Caleb still held her elbow.

"You're hurting me, Cal," she said softly.

"I'm sorry, love. I'm so sorry."

Iona sat on the bed with a heavy bounce that could have been heard all over the house. Involuntarily, they both 'shushed' each other and Iona began to giggle. "It's a wonder we didn't wake the kids."

"It's a wonder you didn't get the bit about 'brainless women having to be told who to vote for'."

"I never thought he was one of those. No wonder you wanted to leave home. He's out of the ark and growing barnacles, Cal."

They collapsed back on the bed trying to laugh without making a sound. Eventually they stopped, their stomachs sore, their jaws aching.

In bed, snuggled up, safe in their love, Iona asked, "How does your mother stand for it?"

"She nods her head when he tells her who to vote for."

"She does?" She thought a moment. "Do you think …?"

"I don't know, my love. Can you imagine living with my father in that angry state? But it's her choice behind the screen, and I do not talk politics in the home. Okay?"

"Okay, Cal. 'Night love."

"Goodnight, dear."

Poor Cal, thought Iona. *I knew his mother was reserved. Now I know why. He and his mother must have been on the other end of Henry McKay's angry outbursts many times and kept their family secret. An only child has no one to talk to – at least I had Edward, even though we hardly ever talked about Mother and Father. I shouldn't have pushed at the old man. It's not my home.*

Drifting off to sleep she tried to be sorry, but couldn't. "I love you even more, Cal, for knowing," she whispered, cuddling into the warmth of his back as he slept solid and steady within her arms. Agnes Newbold would say, 'You don't know what's inside till you lift the lid, kid.' Iona went into sleep smiling.

Chapter Twenty-seven

A few days later Iona and Caleb went down to Auckland alone. The children had ensconced themselves in the senior McKays' home, and Iona was grateful. A beetle-browed Henry had everyone tiptoeing around the kitchen during breakfast the morning after his heated words to Iona, then, as he realised the episode was not going to be mentioned, he thawed out, and by the time he and Josh took them down to catch the train, he appeared the same, ordinary man he usually presented to the world. Four-year-old Jimmy came with them for the ride. He had his grandfather in the palm of his hand and was showing incipient signs of becoming a real charmer. Miriam and Ben, intent with Ada – writing and drawing their own storybook about 'Jumping Josh the Kaipara Hoss' – said goodbye with a preoccupied air.

Caleb and Iona went straight through to Auckland central from Helensville. Caleb had an appointment with the owner of a firm he'd been dealing with for years. He wasn't happy with their service during the last few months.

They were still a little early so they sat on a sturdy old wharf seat, their bags clutched between their legs, and watched the activity on the Auckland waterfront.

"Seems funny without the kids," Caleb said.

"Yes. They'll be all right with your dad, won't they?"

"They will, Iona. They have each other. They are not alone like you and I were as children."

There was an overseas passenger ship in. Disembarking passengers looked purposeful, adventures of the day spurring them on.

"I sailed on a ship that size once; did some business for Dad in Australia. I was too young really but he insisted. It certainly added to my experience."

"Did you enjoy the trip?"

"Not much. It was too jolly big to feel you were even on the ocean and nothing to see but water. No, I'm a small boat, river man, me."

Seagulls were screaming and squabbling on the oily asphalt surface of the wharf. On a bench further along two drunks dozed in the watery sun, their booze in lemonade bottles, the corks wrapped with dirty bits of newspaper to make them stay in place. *The magic and the mess of a city waterfront*, thought Iona. *Just like life – intertwined.*

"I need to go now," Cal murmured as he pecked her on the cheek. "See you for lunch at one o'clock, love." He picked up their two bags. "I'll leave them with Jacko in the office. He won't mind holding them for us."

"Won't they be too upset – when you tell them you're not doing business with them any more – to put up with our luggage?"

"Jacko stashes them under his lunch table. His boss will never know. Bye."

He made off in one direction while Iona walked up Hobson Street to the Farmers. Her shape had changed after Jimmy, and she needed a couple of new dresses, cheap as possible. She sewed for the children because she had to - not for herself.

They met for lunch on the top floor, both disappointed. Iona had only been able to make the money stretch to one frock, while Caleb had heard such a horrendous story of the firm in trouble since the Wall Street Crash he'd left his business with them for the time being.

"I didn't have the heart to take it from them."

Iona looked out over the roof to the dark green September harbour. "How are we doing, Cal? Can we afford to be so kind?"

Caleb had his head in the menu.

"Cal?"

He put the menu down. "If we're very, very careful we should make it through."

"Should I have bought this dress?"

"Of course, love. You needed it."

"What about your garage?"

He flicked his eyes at her, played with the salt and pepper, undid his serviette. "It was just a dream, Iona."

"It would have come true if this depression hadn't hit us."

"Maybe."

"I'm so angry sometimes ... and so sorry."

He looked at her, his eyes moist. She rested her hand on his for the softest second. Caleb could hardly believe, sometimes, what her skin transferred to his insides. His guts came alive in the closeness of this special woman. He cleared his throat. "I'm luckier than a lot of people. I've got you."

Iona smiled, frowned, chewed her lip. Cal watched the emotions wash over her face.

"Yes, well – but I wanted you to have your garage and workshop."

"You haven't got your hardware shop."

"No."

"So, if you can manage, so will I."

"I'm grateful we haven't lost anything else, Cal."

"So am I. We've still got our home. I still earn money, and the kids will still eat. The garage dream can wait."

"Yes, and I have a new dress for the party. Two and six off the bargain rack."

"Oh God, Iona, what the hell does it look like?"

Iona couldn't help laughing. His face was a treat.

"Terrible," she spluttered. "I'll tart it up with Grandma Kelly's glass beads. They're just the right bluey-green. Don't worry, I'll look stupendous."

"You always do, my love."

Indigo eyes rested on his face. Brown eyes held her being. They were one.

It turned into a mixed few days. They were standing in for Henry and Ada, who were now stubborn about keeping close to the comforts of their own home, and had delegated the younger couple to attend a twenty-first birthday party in Point Chevalier. As well as the celebrating son the couple had five daughters, all older than Caleb. They were jolly women, who teased Caleb all through supper by telling Iona stories of how they had spoilt her husband when he was a boy.

"They did not, Iona. They fussed and bossed me worse than my mother."

It was easy to enjoy the uncomplicated fun of this family and their friends. Hard times were forgotten in the celebrations of 'their Walter's reaching the age of manhood'. Walter did seek Caleb's advice, though, asking about the availability of work in the northern west coast region.

Caleb had not much encouragement until the young man shyly offered, "I'm trained in orchard horticulture. Might there be anything in that line, sir?"

Caleb looked at Iona, and together they said, "We'll tell Edward about you!"

Walter's face shone with hope.

"No promises," added Caleb, "but Iona's brother is certainly worth an ask. Give me your particulars and your address, and we'll see what we can do."

That night and the next they stayed with Agnes Newbold's brother on the edge of Grey Lynn. Their hosts were so warm and welcoming Iona left Auckland feeling she had been treated like royalty.

A week later on a fine September night, they chugged upriver towards Sedgely wharf, Jimmy dozing on Iona's lap, Miriam and Ben leaning, half asleep, each side of her and Caleb, with his head up through the hatch, steering carefully with his night-eyes. Children aboard always made him extra careful. A bite in the air warned of a change in weather. Their clear sky holidays were over. The woman and her children were all covered with a dark grey blanket, sharing each other's warmth.

Iona's eyes were on the stars. Her head, holding no everyday thought at all, full to the brim of river and giant sky. Her soul drank the depth of darkness. Her eyes sipped the dusty stream of stars called the Milky Way. *In this pure place the stars dazzle and throb, yes,*

> *There's the Pot – and the Southern Cross.*
> *Its tail flows down into navy blue.*
> *I see Venus – I see you.*
> *I see my lover in the morning dew.*

The *Tara* made a perfect sweep and nestled against the wharf pile like a cygnet finding its mother's side. Iona would never forget that night arrival at Sedgely.

Edward was waiting on the wharf to tell her their father, Uriah Anderson–Keyes, was dead.

Chapter Twenty-eight

"He wanted to be buried by his boatshed."

"I know."

"She can't refuse him that, can she?"

"I'm not sure, Sis."

'Sis'. He hardly ever called her that now. The familiarity of their young years warmed her soul, drew her back to those fragile moments in the distant past before she grew into a woman and the entire world changed forever. Uriah had occasionally called her 'girl'. The memories, sweet with sadness, clung in whispers around her, tugging and distracting. She pulled herself back into the day, into thinking of hymns, hearses and how to bear the losing.

"We're going down tonight. I'll speak with her."

"No, Iona. Leave it to me. Please. You know how bolshie she gets when she knows you're after something."

"She'll be more than bolshie when I get through with her, Teddy. She's no right to prevent Dad's wish to lie there. No right at all."

Edward put his arm around his sister's shoulder. He smelt of grass, sweat and fresh air – unlike Uriah who smelt of wood, oils, paint and putty. Her little brother had grown almost as tall as his father by the time he turned eighteen but heavier in the upper body. His face, which as a child had been a smaller version of Sybil's, had altered completely into a squareness of its own. It suited him well, and his outlook on life had changed after the influenza epidemic of his youth.

Edward and Iona had talked about that year the three of them had been so ill; talked about the emergence of that part of their father neither child had encountered before; talked about their mother's collapse. To his children Uriah had appeared to shrivel in size yet grow in mental stature during his long convalescence. But they had never quite seen the intimacy he had shown while nursing them – and after a while they did not expect it.

It dawned on Edward some months after his own illness that his stentorian mother had declined into a vacillating and vacuous woman, and that gradually he had ceased to be her puppet. There was a consequence, however, to this family shift. That he had disappointed his mother, by turning to the land, had been made clear to him frequently over the following years. Sybil had wanted a lawyer or a doctor for a son, not a common farmer. Edward was relegated to second place, behind his father, in her increasingly quarrelsome queue of life's disappointments. She did, however, take a liking to Edward's wife Jane. Lovely Jane, who came from solid parents, had an easy outlook on life but never let anyone push her into an argument.

This liking of her daughter-in-law had created a small ray of brightness in Kotare Creek. It had lightened, somewhat, the sullen atmosphere that emanated from the only woman who lived in the big house.

Nevertheless, there were times when the turbulent emotions of Edward's early years pinned him into the middle of that metaphorical 'tow rope', that emotional tendon that quivered at him and dripped guilt when there was another bout of pain-pulling between his parents. He wanted his sister to know this was not one of those times.

"Edward! Are you listening?" Iona snapped. "Tom says it'll carry legally if she doesn't kick up a fuss. Dad was well thought of here …"

"I'll get around her, Iona. No matter what it takes, I'll get her to agree."

"Promise me, Teddy."

"I promise, Sis. Just button-up on this one, will you?"

"I don't like subterfuge. You know that."

"Come on, Sis. It's either subterfuge or the local cemetery for Dad. Give me a chance with her."

Iona looked up into his broad, strained face, into his night-pool eyes, dirty with lack of sleep, and knew he would do his best. "All right, Teddy."

He gave her a squeeze.

"But they need to know by tomorrow. They can't be digging the grave ten minutes before the service."

"Don't worry. I'm going to see her now. Jane's already there softening her up."

"Perhaps I won't go down tonight," she mumbled, slumping against his solidness. He felt like the only member left of her first family who meant anything more to her than what good manners and duty demanded.

"Might pay to keep away. Did you go to see him again?" Edward's voice vibrated over her head.

"No."

"He looks not too badly now, you know …"

"So I've heard."

"I better get back and sort things. You okay, Sis?"

She nodded. He went off, loping down to their gate like a rangy animal too big for town spaces. She felt grateful to him.

She knew they were all concerned about her – and she did know Uriah would look 'not too badly' with old Warren Jacob's further ministrations. They could not understand that her need had been to see him immediately, three nights ago, when she'd got off the launch. In the end Caleb had taken the children home, and she had waited and won.

Jacobs, the town's undertaker, had not been happy about it though … "Your father drowned, Mrs McKay. I would not recommend you see him until I can prepare him for you. Perhaps tomorrow?"

She had insisted. He'd given in but made her wait until he had fixed him up a little. She had insisted because she knew if she didn't see him she would not sleep at all that night. It was as simple as that.

Looking back, she supposed she'd been in shock. Torn out of the wonder of the night into the news of her father's drowning she could not have moved herself out of the funeral parlour anyway, even if she'd tried. Yes, she supposed it was shock that made her sit there in Jacob's tiny waiting room, but suddenly he was there, tut-tutting, saying he'd done the best he could and, "Will you come through, Mrs McKay?"

And yes, he looked bad. It was a cold river to die in, the Northern Wairoa, in early spring. She could see that on his face. His poor face – set in the same stillness she had seen on dead birds she sometimes used to find on Kotare Creek ground, where she had wandered as a lonely child. Her father's thin, old body looked decrepit. Yet not as bad as some animal carcases the river sent ashore from time to time. Of course, her father had died on the edge of the water – not in it. Nothing had attacked his body. And that was just what it was – a body.

It was not Uriah. It was not her father. She could see that. This was the outside walls – his frame. Like a cicada's shell; like the bark of a fallen tree. She had not even looked at him when she said aloud, "Well, you're not there, are you?"

Caleb came into the room and saw her gazing out the small, high window behind her father's body, as if she was yearning to go out into the velvet night.

"Iona?"

"Oh! Caleb!"

"I'm sorry I've been so long. I had to wait until they were all asleep and they were upset. And then Maryanne took a bit longer to get there than she'd said."

They stood close, holding each other up. "Don't worry, darling," Iona whispered.

"I am worried. You've come back to this awful news."

Iona took his hand and stepped aside for him to see her father's body. He was very quiet.

"They haven't fixed him up very well, have they?"

"No. I didn't give them enough time. Jacob's done the best he could, Cal. Don't blame the old man. They'll have to do his mouth better before Mother comes in, though."

"You told me Sybil never views a body."

"I forgot. How silly of me. Well, at least he's free of her now."

Shocked, Caleb looked down at her, but she was oblivious of her words.

"Come home, Iona. You need some rest."

"In a minute."

"There's nothing you can do here, love."

"No, there isn't really, is there?"

She turned. "This isn't him, Cal. Is it? He's not here."

"No, love."

"He wouldn't want to be in this poky little room anyway," she snapped; and left …

Iona had woken at five o'clock the next morning so alert she thought, for those first few seconds, she must not have slept at all. Everyone else was still asleep so she crept down to the kitchen in her dressing gown, got a glass of milk and some biscuits and sorted the facts she had been given the night before.

Two ten-year-old boys from the farm above had got off with their family dinghy without permission, 'to catch a load of mullet like Dad'. The boat was much too big for their scrawny arms to control but they persisted in their adventure. They got the net down but once it was wet it was too heavy for them. The late afternoon breeze grew into a wind. They were blown out into the main river, oars tangled in the dragging net. They capsized. Iona could imagine them frightened, screaming for help, those little boys …

Two wood pigeons flew out of the puriri tree, heavy on the morning, their strong wings 'froom, froom', beating the air. Yesterday's waves swept one boy away. Uriah saw them. He was walking home across the swampy river paddock from Edward's farm. Had he been in his shed he would have used his own boat, would have been there in a trice, without effort.

The first boy he rescued – weeping, shuddering, blue with cold – said of his friend, "He was so cold he couldn't hang on to the boat any longer. He let go and tried to swim but the water took him away."

In her mind she saw her father tearing the boots from his feet, pushing his way through the water – a frail body, a frantic mind – determined to save the second child. Iona grabbed her mouth, shook off her slippers and ran down the back behind the tool shed where no one would hear the sounds of her pain.

The phone rang all morning. Between that and the children, Iona was never still. Agnes arrived with fresh cooked food, and Maryanne returned from seeing to her own tribe. When the parents of the boy who had survived arrived with eggs and baking Iona felt every muscle in her body tense. She and Maryanne and Agnes hugged the still trembling pair, fed them, soothed them and listened. It was pitiful – their whispered gratitude, their gnawing guilt over her father's death.

Word came through to the McKay house that the body of the drowned boy had been found miles down the river. The whole town went into shock. Death was part of their everyday lives, even children's deaths – but the loss of an old man while saving one child dropped like a heavy weight on all their shoulders.

Three days later Uriah was farewelled in the same church where Iona had said goodbye to her grandmother. They could have done with three churches. It poured with rain several times. The extra crowds stood under umbrellas, still and silent, some able to look through open windows, others unable to hear or see anything. Although she was with everyone else, Iona had little recollection afterwards of any part of it – except the lowering of her father's body into the fresh dug soil of the home paddock and the words of Toi Tira, Uriah's Maori friend from their youth.

"He wairua hauta a ia." Words which sank into her soul even before Toi repeated them in English. "He was a brave spirit."

Yes! He was a brave spirit. But will he lie, forever sightless, in sight of his small measure of river? *No! Surely his spirit is flying as we stand bound to this ground.*

Chapter Twenty-nine

Sybil made it to the church service but not the burial. Iona had to admit her mother looked unwell. Her eyes were sick, and she had lost more weight. Perhaps Edward was right about her health.

Iona, feeling twinges of guilt, made a visit two days after the funeral. Aunt Maude and Tom were staying with Sybil for at least another week. Both of them looked the worse for wear.

"She's not going to rest until we get all Uriah's things out of the house," Aunt Maude whispered as she moved down the hall with a bundle of Uriah's clothes.

"Where are you going to take them?"

"For now we're storing them in his shed. He was a tidy man, but you can't get a lifetime of machinery and bits and pieces out of a place in a few minutes."

"When did this come on?"

"Last night," said Tom, backing into the kitchen to let them through. "She came up for breath after tea – and announced her orders."

Iona smiled. They looked so funny, the two of them, moving in unison in and out of the doorway like two crabs in a backwards-forwards dance.

Tom caught her amusement and gave her one of his rare grins as he said to his wife, "Can you get that kitbag we saw in the back of the wardrobe? Some of his gear will pack down quite well in that."

"I'll come and help as soon as I've been in to see her."

"Good luck," whispered Maude.

In the original bridal bedroom Sybil lay fully dressed; her lower body covered with the lavender satin eiderdown which made her look sallow. Iona went over and gave her a kiss on the cheek.

"You're looking well, Iona."

Iona had not slept properly since her father died. She knew she looked terrible, but she smiled and said, "I'm fine, Mother, and you?"

"I'm not at all well. Maude and Tom told me to take a rest this afternoon. They seem to be busy."

"Yes. They're seeing to ..."

The next thing Sybil threw herself into Iona's arms, pouring out her distress to a daughter who had never in her life seen her mother cry in such a fashion – snivel, yes – weep, sort of, once or twice, but never howl as she was now and all of it peppered with breathless, choking words that had been buried through the public days of the news and the funeral.

"He's gone, Iona. I've lost him. What was he doing going out in that river at his age. He should never have done that, leaving me all by myself. He's gone." And raising her watery face she wailed, "What am I going to do?"

Luckily Maude had been hovering, suspicious of what her sister might do when she had Iona alone. She swept into the room and brushed the scene out the window before Sybil realised what had happened.

"Ah yes, now, a little bit tearful, are we? Well, that's only to be expected. Iona, can you give Tom a hand with those books your mother wants taken away? And do you know, Sybil, I caught a glimpse of Jane and the baby coming down the road. We must tidy you up for your visitors now, mustn't we?"

Iona watched in amazement. She'd never seen Aunt Maude show such adroitness in a Sybil situation before. She found she had been holding her breath and went down the hall concentrating on steadying her breathing and bumped into Tom again.

"I'd better put the kettle on. Auntie said Jane's on her way down."

"Jane?"

"Isn't she coming down the road with the baby?"

"I don't know. I haven't seen her."

They looked at each other and laughed. "Let's put the kettle on anyway, eh?"

"You and Dargaville seem to be agreeing with Aunt Maude, Uncle Tom."

"We do our best, Iona. We do our best."

The afternoon proved good for the three of them. Iona, let off lightly by their presence, felt the cramps leave her stomach. However, the respite was short-lived. Maude and Tom thought the same way as Edward – that Sybil was looking most unwell. They decided to get Dr Jenkins down before Maude went back home.

"He's cut back on his hours now that his new partner has settled in," Iona told them. "Do you think he'll come this far out?"

"Yes, I asked him at the funeral. He said to let him know as soon as we are ready. I thought I'd phone him in the morning. Sybil doesn't get up until late so she won't hear me."

"She'll like Jenkins visiting, Auntie. She'll think she's really sick."

"I think she is really sick, Iona. I'm sorry. I know she's always kicked up bobsie-die but this time I think she's very ill."

"With what?"

"I can't say, dear. That's why I want a word with the doctor."

Maude's suspicions were confirmed. Tom went back to Dargaville five days later leaving Maude to stay on yet another week. The townsfolk imagined she remained to support her elder sister a little longer after the death of her husband. In reality, she stayed to help the younger people adjust to the fact that in the doctor's opinion it would only be a matter of months before they lost their mother as well. Sybil did not yet know and, in conjunction with Dr Jenkins, the family decided this was not the time to lay such bare facts before a newly widowed woman.

"She'll never cope. Not straight after Uriah's death. I'll watch her without her realising. I've already told her I've a patient just past here I visit once a week. She'll accept my popping in for a wee while yet," Jenkins told them.

"Is she in pain?" asked Iona.

"No-o, she's more than likely suffering a little discomfort most days. The cancer, as far as I can tell, has developed steadily over the last months and is quiet at the moment."

"You said there's nothing you can do?" Edward began.

"No. No lad. It's way beyond stopping."

"She's been saying she wasn't well. I should have …"

"Let's talk straight here, Edward?" and the doctor, who had known the family most of their lives, proceeded to do just that. "Your ma has always been a great one for being unwell. We won't go into that any further. But living as a semi-invalid and dosing herself up on her own remedies has not helped. It's just the way things are. Don't, for pity's sake, go feeling guilty for something you could never have prevented in a million years. See it for what it is. It's bad news, especially at this time. But we must get on with it. We must do what we can to help your mother through what time she has left – and know we did the best we could."

Iona would never be able to look back on the following three months with any sustained clarity. There had been no time to grieve for their father. They set up their turns of visiting their mother; her wishes to have all Uriah's things removed giving them good cover for their frequent calls. So that when Dr Jenkins finally told Sybil the truth about her illness, the family were at least, in a practical sense, well into a sickbed routine.

Surprisingly, Sybil made a reasonable patient. Surrounded by one or other of her family at all times, she floated towards death, the centre of attention. She saw to her own affairs, arranged the making of her own shroud and refused to be buried next to Uriah 'in the back garden' as she put it. She instructed Edward to find a 'nice plot' by the side gardens of the cemetery, near her father's grave. It took Edward a week of going up and down drawing little plans of the plots and their surroundings before his mother was satisfied.

She even treated Iona reasonably. It helped that Iona put herself out to be agreeable to Sybil – the only thing outside her own home on which she could concentrate – being nice to mother. Being nice to mother even invaded her dreams.

The family, the town, the world went on around her while she walked on a parallel path. It felt as if she lived in two compartments: the family at Sedgely and Sybil at Kotare Creek. Now and then something from one compartment crossed over into the other, leaving her holding her breath again until she worked out where she was and what she was supposed to be doing. At the Creek she would stop in the middle of making up her mother's bed with clean linen and be stuck in the fear that she hadn't made the children's lunches. Several times she set off for the Creek only to find herself standing outside 'Newbold's Emporium' – that Aladdin's cave managed by Sam but set up by Shorty and Jonquil Donovan was a wonder world of everything the partners could buy in the second-hand and bankrupt business stock trade. The town loved it, and Iona escaped there as often as possible.

In the middle of October of 1933, Sybil left her home for the last time to be nursed in the small hospital in Sedgely. Now Agnes, Maryanne and Ani supported Iona by cooking, cleaning and minding the children. Iona's neighbours sent in supplies and often took in the children, while Caleb felt as if he was living in everyone's shadow. He said as much to Father O'Rourke.

"I feel as if she doesn't want me near her," Caleb muttered to the priest one day in the garage. "I don't know where my wife has gone or what I'm supposed to do."

"Wait! Just wait, man! It's a difficult path, the road to spiritual amendment."

Caleb, sure there was no spirit left in his woman, hoped – and hoped it was not evil to hope – that his mother-in-law would hurry up and die.

When she did, on 1st November, her death hardly made a ruffle on the sea of Sedgely's populace. All her arrangements went so smoothly it was over before Caleb realised Iona could now come back to him, and for a whole week she seemed to be doing just that.

So that when he walked into the house on a backlash wintry night, seven days after his mother-in-law's funeral, ready to be greeted by the woman he knew was returning, to find her sitting at the kitchen table staring at nothing, he was stunned.

"Where are the children?"

"Hmm? Oh, the children. They're outside getting in the firewood."

"What's wrong now, Iona?" His voice tired, his mind blank, he threw the local rag on the table and sat down.

"Oh," she said, her faraway eyes gradually wandering back to him. "Oh," she said again. "It's Sybil."

"Sybil? What are you talking about?"

236

"Edward was here this afternoon in a terrible state. She's left everything to him and Jane – the house, side block, money, everything. Poor old Teddy, he didn't know anything about it. None of us did. Ha …"

"Everything?"

"Yes, Cal, everything. Isn't it hilarious? I never thought about it … never entered my head," and she began to laugh in short, sharp shards. "It's so funny. She made a new will a week after Jenkins told her she had cancer; the sly old witch. She's showed me, hasn't she? What a sneak! Oh! And what a laugh!" Iona stopped for a moment, panting for breath.

Caleb opened his mouth but no words came. He wrapped his arms around his woman and held her secure but the words still fell between them like a sword.

"And you know something, Cal! We were all so flat out looking after her we never even thought about her silly old will! Apparently she saw Dad's will after his funeral and read that everything was to be split down the middle when she died. She rang the new lawyer who took over from Livingstone and got him down the day we cleaned up Dad's shed. Remember? Lily Grantham came to sit with her so we could work all day. Oh dear, it's so funny. Lily would have known about it," and she went into such a spate of mad laughter Caleb thought she would never stop.

"Don't, darling. Hush, hush now, she's not worth it. Iona …?"

But Iona had gone somewhere else.

Chapter Thirty

Iona began stacking the second lot of dirty dishes on the bench and groaned. Baking! She'd been at it most of the day. Cleaning up afterwards made her so tired these days. Now she had dirty cake tins and bowls as well as the lunch dishes to wash. She ran the hot water, hurried through the living room to the back verandah and called for Miriam, then raced back to the kitchen to turn the water off. The sink was full of hot, soapy water when Miriam came through the kitchen door. Brown, curly hair, freed from its school pigtails, winged her face like a wild bracken bush. She watched her mother turn off the taps, and her face flared red in anticipation.

"Aw, Mum. I helped with the breakfast lot."

She looked so comical Iona wiped her hands on her smeared apron and hugged the girl. "Don't worry, poor little Cinderella. I'm not asking you to do any more dishes."

"Thanks, Mum," Miriam beamed. Head thrown back, throat muscles taut, she tried to pull away but Iona held her a little longer, the sweet scent of her child filling Iona with pleasure and pain.

She'll be twelve in November.

"Get Benjamin and Jimmy. We'll fix fairy sandwiches for your afternoon tea, shall we? You can take them to your hut. You can only have the bits, mind."

Miriam shot off down to the empty section that backed on to theirs, yelling like a lout out on the spree. "Danny, Jim-mee! Come home! Mum SAYS!"

Then they were all around her, helping with the treat one minute, getting in her way the next.

"Can we have an afghan as well, Mum? Can we?" wheedled Jimmy.

"No. You've already had one. But if you get a teaspoon each you can finish up what's left in the icing bowl."

"Oooo, yea!"

"Thanks, Mum."

"They're going too fast, Mummy. There's none for me." Eventually they took off down the side of the house with their treasures, not running, but wanting to – scurrying, as they concentrated on not dropping anything. There would be no treats tomorrow. Things were tough with the business. And they knew it. Though they were luckier than most. And they knew that too.

Iona watched them go, thinking how little it took to make children happy – a few teaspoon swipes from a bowl followed by guava jelly sandwiches with multi-coloured hundreds and thousands; a feast of iced, broken, patty cakes and a bottle of homemade ginger beer. She went back to the bench to get the washing up out of the way before she made a cuppa. The suds had shrunk so she took the soap shaker – a tin with a wire handle and holes pierced in the bottom – off the tap again, reached into the cupboard underneath, cut another chunk off the Sunlight Soap and shook the water up a storm again. The water began to disappear. "Botheration! Where's the rag gone?"

Some minutes later, with a new piece of rag wrapped firmly around the plug, she started washing the dishes again. "Look at the time! This is so silly – using bits of rag for months on end. My husband's an engineer, for goodness' sake! And you're talking to yourself again. You'll have to stop it, Iona." *I will. It worries Caleb when I talk to myself.*

She stopped and eased her aching back against her hot dishwashing hands that left imprints on her dress. The spring sun shone gently through the window panes, through the steam rising from the sink, and made tiny rainbow colours in the bubbles, little jewels on froth. Precious sight! She played with the bubbles as if she were a child, eyes glazed, body falling forward. She knew she would fall asleep if she could only lie down. "Finish the dishes – braise the sausages – cup of tea – then you can sit down."

The sausages seared and simmering on the stove, she was about to put the kettle on when she caught a movement outside. She wiped the patch of steam off the window and saw Aunt Maude and Tom coming down the path.

"Hello, the house! Anybody in?" shouted Tom.

"Come on in," Iona called, drying her hands on a towel as she turned the sausages off then went over to the kitchen door to embrace her aunt.

"Tom's dropping me off for an hour or two while he calls on an old friend who's up from Auckland for a few days. Is that all right with you?"

So Maude was worried about her too.

"Of course it is. It's lovely to see you, Auntie. I'll put the kettle on. Have you time for a cuppa, Uncle Tom?"

"No, I'll get going. Bye."

The two women sat at the kitchen table and drank hot tea with and a slice of warm currant cake while they talked, catching up on the news and observing one another.

Maude has not weathered Sybil's death well, thought Iona.

The girl is overtired. She needs a break, thought Maude. "Where are the children?"

"They're down the back, building a grass castle and eating the leftovers from my baking. I'll call them up if you like."

"Don't worry, dear. There's plenty of time."

They talked about how pleased everyone was with the headstone on Uriah's grave. Iona caught Maude up on the children's progress at school and exchanged news about Tom and Caleb. Maude talked about their trip up to Paihia. Tom, standing in for Anthony, who was away in England, had taken Maude with him on a northern business trip for two nights. They'd had a look at the Waitangi Reserve.

"It's very suitable land Lord and Lady Bledisloe have given the Maori people."

And Iona remembered Toi telling her about the Waitangi Reserve at Sybil's funeral. Most news had slipped by her since her parents' deaths but today she even remembered what he'd said. 'So many tribes, eh Iona? So many tribes all together. Must be good for us Maori, eh Iona?'

And she had smiled and nodded and remembered thinking, Toi Tira, you're talking to me like you used to talk to Uriah. You're the same age as my father, aren't you? Yet he's dead, and you look like an excited boy.

"Iona? Did you hear me?"

"I'm sorry, Auntie. What were you saying?"

"I said I still can't believe Sybil ... changing that will!"

"Oh, that! Don't worry about it."

"But I do, Iona. There was no need ... I've spoken to Edward. He says you don't want anything from the house."

"I don't need anything."

"But surely ... isn't there anything you like in the house at all?"

"Well, no, not really. My tastes were so different from hers. I'm not being horrible or anything."

"I wouldn't blame you if you were. I wondered, though... Edward – well, perhaps he'd feel better if you had something from the place."

"Oh, I see. Oh, heavens to Betsy, I hadn't thought. Edward. Look, I'll go down and pick something out this week. That might help, do you think?"

"Yes dear, I think it might help him a little – just choose a token – so he knows there's no ill feeling."

"Is that what he thinks?"

"Oh, I don't know."

"I would never feel like that about Teddy. Surely he knows that? I just can't be bothered thinking about her any longer."

Iona leant back, her arms dangling down each side of the high back chair, her eyes closed when she said, "It's not the house, or things, you know. It's not worth so much, Creek land, but it will enlarge Edward's holding, and that's good. Cal and I have the workshop and our home. It's ..."

And here, if her eyes had been open, she would probably not have gone on.

Maude was looking at Iona, tired, beautiful Iona, who had once had so much fight in her that everyone would get out of her way when her boil was up – and Maude was in agony.

"... it is just that I never knew why she didn't like me," Iona sighed. "Once, when I was very small, I would have done anything, anything at all, if she would only like me. And once, when I was about Miriam's age, I believed that one day she would tell me she really ... did ... love me. Now I know finally, and forever, that my mother ..."

"She was not your mother."

For a few seconds – caught in the vacuum of her mind – Iona could not move. Then she sat up slowly, her eyes wide. "What did you say?"

"I said – she was not your mother. I have wanted her to tell you that for many years. She refused to. She said she had made a promise."

"You're telling me she was not my mother – she never was my mother – and I was ..."

"Wait! Wait, Iona, please! Let me tell you. She had promised. She said that my father had made her promise."

"Who was my mother then? Who was she?"

"I am."

"You …? You can't be! You've never had a child. Mother said. Oh God, what are you saying?"

Iona got up and paced up and down the kitchen.

"Stop, Iona. It's the shock. This is a great shock to you. I will tell you everything if you sit down and listen."

Iona sat down. She was shaking. Maud took an old house cardigan from the hook on the back of the kitchen door and draped it around her daughter, then made her sit quietly while she brewed another cup of tea – 'the medicine for everything', she thought, as she wiped the younger woman's face with a cool, wet cloth, giving her time to adjust. She wanted to put her arms around her, to comfort her, to claim her at last as her own; but she could see this was not the time, and she wondered – uselessly, because it was too late to take back the words now – whether she should have kept this knowledge hidden a little longer.

At last Maude Denby, née Kelly, said, "I want you to listen, Iona. I know you will want to ask me many questions. Later, ask me later. I need to tell you about Sybil and about myself, but – I need you to … ah, let me tell you – in my own way. Will you just listen to me for now?"

"Yes."

And so Maude started.

"You never met your Granddad Kelly, did you? Well, Sybil is very like him. I took after mother, your grandmother. There was a big gap in years between Sybil and me – seven years. She was always cleverer than I was, but as a child I was the pretty one. Father was very proud of Sybil's brains; however, he thought that because she was a rather plain young woman … ah … that she might as he said, 'be left on the shelf'. Then one day when Sybil was twenty-five and I was eighteen, Uriah came into our lives."

"Uriah? My father?"

"Hush, dear. This is difficult enough. Sybil fell in love with him so madly she couldn't sleep and she couldn't eat properly. Mother told me this when she thought Uriah might be looking at me."

"You …? Aunt …?"

"Just listen dear, please. This is so hard. I have not spoken of this for years. Well, Father was determined his Sybil would have Uriah and he … set out to help. Uriah had just arrived here out of his apprenticeship, and he was talking about taking a year in Australia before he started full-time work. Father didn't want that. Oh no! Father knew that if he didn't help Sybil catch Uriah quickly, that trip to Australia would put an end to it. He pointed out the block of land at Kotare, showed him some plans of a work shed to be built near the creek entry, close to the open river – a desirable position for a furniture business, giving cartage access by both water and road. There would also be a new house built, close to the road, for which he said he would 'stake' the young man.

Uriah at twenty three was still gullible. His apprenticeship years had been under a 'live in with a family' contract, and he and Toi had been kept well under the eye of their master trainer. His parents had died when he was a country boy of sixteen. He was their only child.

Well, anyway, my father made sure Uriah saw a lot of Sybil. And Sybil, so crazy in love with him, was always sweet and considerate in his presence. Anyway, they married about the same time Uriah signed up for the land at the Creek."

Maude stopped. She sipped her tea, going cold in the waiting, and looked at Iona.

"I was also in love with a young man – a soldier. He was to ship out to the Boer War. He was so very frightened. I ... we ... I got pregnant."

"With me?"

"Yes. He sailed before I knew ... I was ... and he was killed. My father was so angry with me I thought he was going to beat me. Sybil had just told them she was expecting their first grandchild due a month after mine. Mother was distraught, and I was scared witless. An unmarried girl having a baby was a terrible, terrible sin – an even bigger scandal than it is today and a terrible shame on the family. They sent me away from Sedgely before anyone could see what was happening. They told their friends I had gone away on a musical training year with relatives down the South Island."

"Where did they send you?"

"To a place near Wellington; Mother took me to one of her friends who had come out on the same ship as she had, from Ireland to New Zealand. The friend and her husband had a farm. They looked after me, and I worked for them in return, until … until you were born. I was very happy there and would have stayed with my … with you, living and working to keep us both. They were kind, uncomplicated folk."

Maude sat quietly with her own thoughts, and Iona reached to touch her hand. Maude whispered, "I have always loved you, Iona."

Then she stood up and went to stare out the window. In the silence Iona wiped her own eyes.

"Unfortunately," Maude continued as she turned and leant against the bench, "for both Sybil and I, she miscarried early in her pregnancy. Only mother was with her. No one else knew except Uriah. Then Father had his idea. He went to them and told them what would have to be done. To cut a long story short, Sybil padded herself up, a little bigger each month until she knew I would be nearly full-term. It was before Dr Jenkins came here. The nearest doctor was in Helensville. Sybil never attended a doctor during those months. And mother, carried along by my father's determination, and in her heart not wanting to lose another grandchild, wrote to her friend telling her what was required of her.

"Sybil and Uriah started travelling down the island on my due date – for their supposed holiday. They arrived two days after you were born. The next day they took you from me and travelled to the nearest town with a registry office. Sybil made Uriah fill in the birth certificate naming them as your parents. They brought you back here as if you had been born prematurely on their holiday."

Maude sat back down at the table.

"Isn't that against the law? Didn't they write a lie?" Iona whispered.

"Yes. That's why Sybil would never tell anyone. And I think it was true that she had promised Father she would never tell. Probably Uriah had also. But I hadn't. By the time I got back no one thought to make me promise anything."

"Why didn't you say something then?"

"How could I? At first you were only a wee baby, but you were accepted as their baby. I had no husband. What could I give you? I used to try to watch over you and hope I could help you. I used to think that one day … well."

"So that's why she never liked me?"

"Oh, she did at first, when you were tiny. You replaced the child she had wanted and had lost. Then she fell pregnant with Edward a few months later, and he was her own child. For about three to four years everything went well, and I learnt to be grateful that my shame never touched you or my parents. Sybil didn't want any more children. Edward was a bonny boy. You were a beautiful little girl. People stopped her on the street to gaze at you and cuddle Edward. They were the town's top young family. Kotare Creek House became a gracious home. It had a fine-looking couple and two lovely children. The name of Uriah Anderson-Keyes grew and grew. He was excellent at his trade, and Sybil gloried in success. Her life was perfect."

"So what happened?"

"Uriah loved both of you children as his own. He never discriminated. Sybil could not do that. Edward was hers. You were her sister's child born out of wedlock. She began to favour Edward. She could not help loving him more, and she could not understand why Uriah didn't love Edward more than he loved you. He was always a fair and steady man. It didn't help that you grew so beautiful. You were hauntingly beautiful. Then, as Sybil's jealousy became unbalanced, you began to stay away from the house. Uriah and I could understand why – we both knew what it was like to live with Sybil's barbed tongue. We tried to protect you, but of course we couldn't always be with you. May I have another cup of tea, dear? Tom will be here in half an hour to pick me up."

"Do you have to go?"

"No. but I think you should have tonight away from me to talk with Caleb after the children are asleep – and to get your thoughts sorted."

Maude made the tea while Iona's thoughts floated from this to that as if she was in a dream.

"No one else knows?"

"Not now. Mind you, I sometimes wonder if Dr Jenkins knows anything about it. I wonder if one of them talked about it in a doctor-patient confidence. Maybe not."

"What about Grandma's friend where you stayed near Wellington?"

"As time went by Father made my mother stop writing to her – and then, about seven years ago, we had word she'd died. I'm sorry, Iona. I've wished and wished so many times that things had been different but … Is that the children?"

"Yes. They're wandering up the back path, hungry, probably. I must do the vegetables."

"Here. Let me help you. The children mustn't know."

They looked at each other. Iona gave Maude a fleeting embrace. They were both trembling but made sure they were at the bench peeling potatoes and onions when the children's voices got louder.

Iona whispered, "Thank you for telling me, Aunt …"

"Call me Aunt Maude … or Maude, Iona. It's what you're used to."

"Yes."

Two pair of moist eyes and shaking hands were busy when the children burst through the door.

"Mum, Mum, you've got to come and see it. We've called it Grass Castle. Come on, Mum! Come on, Auntie Maude."

The women smiled.

"Not this time, children," said Maude. She hugged each of her secret grandchildren and walked up the path to wait at the gate.

"I'll phone you tomorrow!" Iona called.

"When you're ready, dear. When you're ready."

After Maude had gone, Iona did everything she would normally have done but in a cloud of not knowing what she was doing. When Caleb came home early she could tell immediately that Maude had been to the garage and told him, and she was grateful for that. At least she didn't have to wade through all she'd just heard. At least Cal knew.

Maude's words kept going round and round in her head. 'It's what you're used to. It's what you're used to.' Like a stuck record stupidly repeating a worthless phrase over and over and over again, it kept her awake all that night.

Chapter Thirty-one

Three days later she managed to get down to the Creek and to pretend nothing had happened.

Edward and Jane had moved into the big house with their children. It was sensible, as the small cottage they'd built on the farm needed extending. It could be sold for removal or used as a sharemilker's cottage or they could even rent it out.

On the old family home's porch Jane, lovely calm Jane, gave her a hug which nearly unravelled Iona's composure. "He's so upset, Iona, and so am I."

And when Edward came in for lunch she could feel his distress.

She went into the hallway by the main bedroom. Last night she'd decided on this, even in the middle of her whirling thoughts. There was a painting on the wall that had been hanging there as long as she could remember. It was of a river scene – a hint of raupo and flax in the left foreground and two parera, native grey ducks, lifting up from the misty river. The common grey of their feathers caught in a sliver of light, turning them into fey, feathered lovers.

"I would like to have this, Teddy. Do you mind?"

"Anything! Anything you want, Sis."

He was so beside himself that she had chosen something to take, she could have cried for him. He would not remember the painting had come originally from the Kelly home. She remembered because she had just started school and come home one day to find Uriah in a smiling mood. His mother-in-law had found the painting at a house sale and bought it especially for him. Over the years she had seen him pause by it now and then, and when she was near it she always felt like smiling. It had hung there so long it left a white rectangle on the wall when Edward lifted it down. An old tear in the wallpaper, with the scrim backing sadly grinning, made them smile.

"Huh," said Edward. "I'll get something to cover it up, perhaps a bigger picture, eh? Come down and visit Dad with me, Sis?"

Iona shut her eyes to think. *I suppose I should, even though I'm tired out.* They walked slowly down to the shed paddock, she on the trodden track, he pushing through the last of the long autumn and the first of the new winter grasses. He had huge feet – made for the land.

The grave had a headstone by now with unpretentious, strong lettering:

URIAH SAMUEL ANDERSON-KEYES 1873–1933
R. I. P.

She hoped he was resting in peace, but more, she hoped he was happy, shiningly happy. *Please God give him joy and lightness of heart.* Surely he's paid – if he had anything to pay for by not making her happy.

Edward broke into her thoughts. "Is there anything you want from his things in the shed?"

They went in. Everything looked a mess. It wasn't the place for her to be at the moment, but it was freezing outside and Teddy wanted to get this done, she could tell. "I don't think there's anything here I really want, Teddy. Cal has so many tools, you know."

"I suppose so."

"Wait." She'd spotted something. "That's the Tilley lamp we used for spearing flounder, isn't it?"

"Oh yes! I speared my foot instead of the fish when I was eight."

They laughed together.

A brother-sister, laugh? Oh God, what a pretence!

"We're deeding these two fields and Dad's shed over to you, Sis."

She was so surprised she couldn't talk for some time, until too loudly, she said, "No, Teddy. Oh no. Don't break her will for me!"

"But it's all ours now, and we want to, Sis. Jane and I want to do this, please."

Sis again! It caught the breath in her throat. Of course, he didn't know. He still thought she was his sister. But Maude had whispered as she left, 'We can't tell anyone. You and I and Caleb, and Tom because he's a lawyer and a kind man. We four know. Perhaps it's not fair to their memory … Let's wait a while. It might hurt Edward at this time.'

Secret whispers of the years, cling like old lichen,
paper thin, tenacious forever.

And finally the concealing phrases once again. 'We have to think of the children.' 'The town would make so much of it.' 'Perhaps when they're older?'

Iona had lived with the truth for a day; however, Edward had no idea they were only cousins.

"I'll give it some thought," she said, to allow them both time before she would most likely refuse the gift. "It won't make any difference to us, will it, Sis? It won't spoil things, will it?"

"No fear, Teddy. Not a chance."

He lifted her off her feet in an unaccustomed display of affection. Then he went off up the paddock, back to work, the rusty old Tilley lamp swinging from his paw, insisting he would clean it up before he brought it in to her.

She stayed on, glad to be alone, wandering around the shed, down to the boat ramp by the tiny beach, then back to the grave, shivering in July's wintry air.

"Loved you – I did – Father Uriah – liar,
brave man, weak man – no blood flows from you
through me.
All those years
Those stony tears
You carried me on shoulders hard and wide.
More the father bones than that young father
dead – on battlefields – of bloody war.
You – you – were father love – all that I knew.
Though I feel nothing
I thank you, kind man,
justice in your soul man."

Then she opened the old box in the corner and took out all the drawings she had done over the years. By the door she found what she wanted – the flax kit Ani had woven for her when she turned eight. That would keep them safe in her home.

Chapter Thirty-two

For the next three months, Iona lived in a disjointed world of her own.

OCTOBER

"Toi Tira's here, Iona."

Uncle Toi?

"We're in the sitting room!" Caleb calls. "I'll make the tea."

She walks in and is enveloped by Toi's strong arms. "Been at Ani's. You heard about Holland?" says Toi.

"Holland?" She can't think who he is talking about.

"Harry Holland, the prime minister. He's dead."

"Dead?" Caleb has come in from the kitchen. He's emptied the teapot, and it's dripping the last of the dregs on the floor.

Shall I say something?

"Ai, Cal. He was at Te Rata's funeral. I only hear he died on Taupiri Mountain."

Caleb looks shocked. "Sad in some ways. He could talk up a storm, could Harry Holland … Oh, there's the kettle." He dashes back to the kitchen and she leaves him to make the tea while Uncle Toi talks himself out.

She knows Cal is sure Coates will benefit; he always insists Gordon Coates is a good Northland farming man who knows his money. Cal has been talking politics a lot lately, which confuses her.

He never used to talk politics in the home, did he?

NOVEMBER-END

The school concert. Miriam and Dan need costumes for *Jack and the Beanstalk*. Jimmy is Jack, that's easy; he'll fit into Dan's bib overalls. Crêpe paper tacked on shirts, pants, old curtains cut up.

"Are you sewing for half the school, Iona? Why doesn't some other mother sew the costumes? It's too much for you, dear."

"I'm fine, Cal."

Must pretend. Yes, just pretend like nothing's wrong.

DECEMBER-IN-THE-MIDDLE

Shellacking the floors on Wednesday - Danny down with bronchitis Thursday. But, oh, how long the nursing nights! Is this aconite doing any good at all? He doesn't like kerosene muslin on his chest. The night so quiet until he coughs - ah, loosening now. 'Keep the bedroom fire going,' doctor said. 'The weather's gone back on itself. Too cold and damp for chesty people.'

Too hot in here by my boy's bed.

Don't clog up the grate, Iona. Ah, Caleb.

"Has he turned the corner, dear?"

"Just. Just now I think."

"Go to bed. You're wet through in this heat. I'll take the dawn watch."

Thank God. So tired, can't think.

CHRISTMAS

"Butter exports are up, dear. That's good for Edward and Seth and Maryanne in Wellsford, eh, Iona?"

Did the prices go up this year? When was that? Can't remember – can't remember.

"Surely the bad times are nearly over?" says Caleb.

Bad times over? When over? That father used to throw me over his shoulder to piggyback me when my little legs got tired – and her, once. Her knee was soft to sit on – warm, her breasts. Did her hands soothe my fevers? What was real? Was it dreaming? No, no, no ... the smell is still of her ... before she went sour.

BOXING DAY

Caleb drops a black-and-white kitten on her knee. It cries for its mother, meowing up at her with wide-open eyes, tiny pink mouth; such a pretty kitten. She automatically cuddles the wee scrap, with its tiny purr, into the folds of her cardigan.

He knows I didn't want another pet after Swan. Dear Swan! Too old, Died. The children cried.
My heart too heavy in its empty space, sweet Swan.

Even so, she strokes the kitten's bones, feeds it milk-soaked bread. It needs her – like everyone else – this bit of life beating in her hands. The children call it 'Scampy' and kneel at her knee. They pat the baby hair with single fingers so as not to hurt the poor mite.

She hears Miriam tell the boys, "It's Mum's kitten. Leave Mum to cuddle it. Just have a little turn."

Even Miriam is looking after me now. What's the matter with me?

THE NEW YEAR

"You know, Iona, I'm not sure about Savage. I think Coates is covering for him. He'd make the better prime minister in my book."

Politics again? What do I say? Not now. He's counting the garage takings. How long will these hard times go on? Look at Maryanne, making singlets out of flour bags for her girls. Apple boxes with scraps of worn-out curtains for cupboards. Poor Maryanne, she's lost a lot of weight. I don't think she's eating properly – feeding the kids first – even on a farm. Once upon a time farmers always had food for their children.

"You all right, love?"

"Yes, Cal."

Mustn't cry! The tears creep down anyway.

"You must forget," he says. "You must forgive."

Yes. Forgive. Ah, my mother Maude – gagged you were – by grandfather of the photos on the wall. Do I hate him? Terrible tyrant, dead and buried before I even knew him and still he ruined my life.

"You have to stop this, Iona."

"Yes, Cal."

She tries. She stops working around the house in the evenings, makes sure she is in the sitting room with Caleb.

To stop her fingers fidgeting she picks up her latest knitting project. Unwinding the used garments her friend gave her is hard work. The wool is crinkly – hard on her hands – and smells of camphor from its last year's storage.

"What are you doing there, love?"

"I'm undoing that knitted skirt and jumper Sue Halliwell gave me."

"Undoing it?"

"Yes. It'll knit up nicely for Miriam."

"Oh. Yes it will. Um – can we not afford new wool, love?"

"Yes, I think so, but I like this wool. It's sturdy. Is that… all right, Caleb?"

"Yes, of course it is, love. I was just wondering. I wanted to make sure you had enough money for things – like new wool, you know?"

"Oh, yes, I see. Yes, there's enough money, but I like the red colour and I have some grey to twist in with – anyway – as well … for the boys' jumpers."

I have to get through all this work, kitty. Have to do it now, see? Ready for next winter; could even do one for Maggie.

"Oh Scamp, leave the wool alone!"

"You don't, um, have to drive yourself so hard, dear."

What? Am I driving myself? But I can't stop – mustn't stop. If I stop …

She looks up at him, her hands stuck in a winding position.

This is not right. Caleb looks so worried. What should I say?

Then, at the very moment Iona is about to speak, her brain shuts off, and in the empty silence that hangs between them, Caleb sighs. "I'll make the tea." He goes out, lonely, to the kitchen.

What will you do? What? If you never get out of this foggy place? What will you do if you stay like this forever, Iona-no-name; Iona Nobody from the muddy Kotare Creek.

"Drink your tea, Iona love," he says. "It's time to go to bed."

Chapter Thirty-three

Caleb didn't know how long they could go on like this. Here it was New Year's Day 1934 and still she seemed to be living in another world. It wasn't that she didn't manage her work. She did. The house and the children ran better than ever, and she had been a good manager before all this strangeness started. He'd mulled it over enough. She needed a holiday.

He approached Paul Sloane first. "Do you think Ani could step in for two weeks, Paul? She's worked here before on the odd day, and she's so good at this kind of work. Do you think she might manage it somehow?"

"I'll ask her, Cal. You never know. How long are you going for?"

"Two weeks. She'll need at least two weeks – three if I can manage it. Can you ask Ani tonight? Sorry to rush you but …"

"I'll ask her tonight, don't worry, Cal. She's Iona's friend after all, and we could do with a bit of extra money."

"Thanks, Paul."

Paul nodded and Caleb walked back to continue the bookwork, hardly able to believe he had set things in motion. "Oh God," he whispered, "give us a hand here, please! Ani would be perfect."

Caleb remembered how Ani Tira and Paul had met at Grandma Kelly's funeral and hit it off at first sight. Everyone at the side-by-side businesses had teased Paul about being shy and slow to propose.

The men knew it was his lost leg that held Paul back – so one day when there was only Paul and Sam Newbold and Caleb in the backyard, Sam had spoken out firmly.

"For God's sake, it's only half a leg you've lost, ya mad coot. Everything else is in place and working, isn't it?"

Not another word was spoken. Caleb and Sam had strolled back to their premises and left Paul to think it over. He proposed the next week.

Iona had been so happy for Paul – and for her long-lost friend. Ani showed no trace of her childhood reticence. Years of working as a shop assistant in Auckland had developed her confidence and given her natural graciousness a chance to be rewarded. When Paul had first introduced her as his girlfriend the two young women were so delighted to meet up again, they laughed and hugged as if they'd never been estranged.

"Oh, Iona, you've no idea how much I've missed you," Ani had cried as they went off out the back of the shop, chattering like two little birds. So when at last Paul plucked up enough courage to propose, Iona had sparkled almost as much as Ani.

These days, however, Iona didn't respond to anyone except the children, and Caleb wondered if even they felt their mother's remoteness.

"Ah, Iona, darling, where have you gone over all this birth stuff? It doesn't matter. It doesn't matter at all," Caleb said to himself as he walked home at the end of that long day of decisions.

He'd done all that Dr Jenkins had recommended. "Stand back and give her time, Caleb. She's trying to get her balance back. She's like a yacht without a keel. Have patience, man. She hasn't been in since her father died. I'll drop in sometime on my rounds."

Thank God Maude had let him speak with Jenkins, who knew anyway, though he wouldn't say who'd told him. Just tapped the side of his nose and said, "Knew years ago, my boy. Though I'd deny it if you ever divulged that piece of information." However, after dropping in to see her, the doctor had made her go back on the iron tonic.

"I think you're still a bit anaemic, girl. Get this made up and make sure you finish it."

Caleb had waited and kept on waiting, always looking for a sign that she was a little better. Now, at last, he could do something that really might help.

Two days later he had his answer.

At half past eight in the morning, Paul had hurried in the back door calling, "We can do it, Caleb!"

And Caleb could have cried with relief as Paul, so excited to be of help, talked on about how Ani's auntie and uncle on a farm up the line were happy to take the Sloane kids for at least a fortnight, maybe more. "Ani says this way we'll all get a holiday. We'll all have a change." And in a quieter tone added, "Ani has been worried about Iona too, you know, Cal."

After so much waiting, Caleb flew into action. Hope had hurtled into his life, and he grabbed it and went with it before it could get away. Everything sprang into his head, all the plans he'd made while waiting, while being patient. He asked Sam Newbold first, and yes, Sam was more than willing to keep an eye out for the Sloanes while Caleb was away. But he had a question for Caleb.

"Before you take off into the wild blue yonder, will you answer me one question, Cal? Is your business healthy?"

"Yes – it's taking time but it is gradually improving, Sam. I'd have preferred not to take time away yet, and it'll be a bit harder with Ani's extra wage. Then there's always hidden expenses when you're on holiday; but Iona needs this break."

"I agree. Get her away from here for a couple of weeks. Three if you like, and I'm sure she'll come right."

"I hope so, Sam."

"You know – I didn't think she was that close to her mother."

"Oh, it's … well, neither did I."

"Grief can take funny turns, Cal."

"Yes. I … think it was the two of them, you know, her father and then … well, you know – they went pretty much one after the other."

"I guess that could do it," Sam agreed.

Privately Sam was having trouble understanding Iona's reaction; she seemed to have completely fallen apart. She was efficient and scrupulously caring of the children – she just didn't seem to be there. It was like talking to a half-ghost. She hardly said a word to anyone these days.

"I'm bloody pleased Cal is doing something about her at last, poor girl," he told Agnes.

"Oh, you men! She hadn't got over that miscarriage, you know, when her father drowned, and that mad mother of hers had them all running around after her for months before she finally died. Give the girl a chance, Sam."

"Hell, Agnes, only last week you were telling me to talk to Cal."

"Well, that was last week and … oh, I'm sorry, Sam. I'm so relieved she's going to get a break away, I wasn't thinking straight."

"Yes, well. I'm damned pleased I didn't have a talk with Caleb. I'd have probably got a poke in the eye the way he's been lately."

"Oh, poor Sammy. Come here and have a cuddle, you gorgeous creature, you."

And so he did. And it proved a very energetic night.

Caleb still had the *Tara*. She'd been a good boat, serving the business well all these years, and she'd provided many a cheap summer holiday up and down the river. Himself? He would have chucked a tent in the Tin Lizzie and done a camping trip by road, but he knew Iona's heart – the river was where she just might come back to him – to them all.

The children were thrilled to bits. Not only was it January school holidays, but they were going to a farm for two weeks. They packed their bags much too soon and nagged their father every minute they could.

"When are we going, Dad?"

"Have they got a horse, Dad?"

"Can I take my new dress, Mum?" This latest from Miriam who had never worn her good dress before this without grumping; was she growing up?

While Iona's soft query was about Maryanne. "Are you sure she can manage ours and hers for that long, Caleb?"

"She's keen to have them, Iona. Thinks her lot will be easier to handle for the last of the holidays. 'They're bad-tempered and bored' is what she actually said. And, ah, I'm giving them some extra cash to feed our lot. Funny how ours have developed huge appetites lately, eh?"

It was the truth. Maryanne had offered to have their three down for a third week if Caleb and Maryanne needed that amount of time away. Seth's temporary share-milking job had turned into a full-time contract from heaven at Wellsford, and he and the owner got on like a house on fire. So when Seth was offered a small share in the farm with more to come in the future, the Wallaces had grabbed it. However, the Depression was taking so long to lift they lived hand to mouth.

Maryanne was thrilled that Iona would be having a decent break. "I'm pleased to help, Cal. She's done so much for me, and I've been worried about her too."

Maude Denby was distraught. She blamed herself. Iona was polite, even concerned, towards Maude. She just never came fully back from wherever she was.

"If she doesn't improve after this holiday, you must promise me, Caleb, to get her to Dr Jenkins. I don't care how much more you tell him. I shouldn't have told her in the first place. Look what it's done to her – promise me, please."

"I promise, Maude. I'll hog tie her and drag her along if I have to," crossing his fingers behind his back because he couldn't tell her Jenkins knew all about the Kelly secret.

Caleb thought it ironic. As the state of farming began to improve and throw a flicker of a financial glow on the business, his private life was steadily deteriorating into a shadowy world, taking the five of them with it. He wished Maude Denby had kept her damned mouth shut. He could understand her concern and her need, living that sort of life for so long, watching her own child being treated in that hurtful, malicious way. Sybil's actions over such a period were more shameful than any of Maude's – but why Maude had thought it necessary to tell Iona after so many years, Caleb couldn't comprehend.

Chapter Thirty-four

The first week and a half their holiday went reasonably well but not as well as Caleb hoped. He thought Iona would have regained some of her old sparkle. In the past she had always responded to beaches, sand and water. Each day he waited for her to suddenly come running from behind a tree or racing up from the water shouting to him to 'come and see, Cal, come and see what I've found,' like the child she'd always been on the river.

After a few days she did stop being so nervy. There were no more mutterings about not having anything to do, and an unworldly calmness came upon her that unnerved him at times. At least she slept well on the boat, and the weather was superb. By the time they'd gone up past Tangiteroria to have another look at McLeod's Pool, the sweet water of the north, they were like dear friends – having a gentle, quiet time together. They were both as brown as berries and healthier than they'd been for years.

Coming back down river at the beginning of their second week, they stayed a night at Tinopai – she'd always liked Tinopai – she thought it 'enchanting' so they stayed on for a few days. But no matter how well she looked, Caleb knew his Iona was still far away.

The next morning they travelled down towards the Kaipara Heads and all hell broke loose. As he steered the old launch into the meeting of the waters at the top of the tide, a wild bear of a sou'westerly came out of nowhere.

He wasn't too worried. He thought it was one of those sudden squalls that would pass over in a flash, and he knew better than to try and turn back. They were already past Mary Catherine Bank and nearing Middle Bank when he saw the second squall tearing towards them across the top of the chop. The wind, like a conjurer's hand, turned it into a westerly.

"Get the coats," he yelled at Iona and saw her struggle to pull the oilskins out from under the cockpit seats. She wriggled into her coat and helped him wrestle into his. He was still struggling when the storm hit – head on – soaking them and sucking the *Tara* into wet isolation.

The boat tried to screw. He held her head on, seeking that place in this beast he sensed might let them through. He had his hands so full he didn't notice Iona until the rain curtain lifted for a split second.

She was up by the mast, her hair plastered down on her skull like grease, her raincoat, riding dark with the dirty green seas, flapped wet and wild against her bare legs.

"I-o-naaa!" he yelled. "Get back here!"

Then he thought, *My God, no. If she tries now, she'll be over the side.*

"No, no-o!" he screamed. "Stay there," and then he realised she couldn't hear him anyway – and another line of squalls hit them, harder than the first.

The boat bucked and battled him every inch of the way across to South Head. In fractions of seconds he saw his wife pelted by rain, saw spray from salt waves lash at her so hard he felt the cut and the sting across his own body. He groaned as each new wave rose like a pale green wall – or curled fine like a giant, silvery shell – before slamming itself on her and on the *Tara*. They motored slowly in under the shelter of the southern cliffs, and every second he watched her lifeless shape whipped flat against the mast, clutching it as if it were a lifeless lover.

As he steered the boat up into peaceful waters the sun found them, and she came back along the gunnels. She looked alive for the first time in months, and he was furious with her – so furious he didn't dare speak. He went for'ard, anchored and stayed a while in the bow, getting his breath under control and letting the quiet water's silence wash over him.

When he went back down to the cockpit she was standing – waiting. She'd changed into dry clothes, her wet hair combed back off her face, rake lines still showing like furrows in soil, at the sides of her head.

"What in the hell were you doing?"

"I know. Just …"

"You could have gone over before my eyes! Dammit, Iona!"

"Don't, Cal. Don't. Not now. I'm going ashore by myself. Please – let me be by myself … for a little while."

He saw her reach for the short lead of the dinghy rope. "It's half-swamped."

"I know. I'll bail as I drift."

Then she was in the dinghy, drifting with the current towards the sandy shore, bailing, ever so slowly. He went into the cabin to get out of his own wet clobber and began to sob. He had not cried since he was twelve years old, and his man's body fought him because it was like bringing up blood from his guts.

When she had the dinghy more or less empty, Iona rowed it slowly towards a stretch of sand a little downriver from Shelly Beach. She walked barefoot, savouring its satin warmth, feeling the grains blanketing the bones under her feet. She saw bunny tails, bunches of them, growing under the remnants of an old pine, and went to pick them – smiling – smiling, as if this was the first time she'd ever seen the soft, furry tails. When she had a rounded bunch she walked back into the sun and sat on a hard, clay rock.

Above and behind her she could feel the huge cliffs straining for the sky, could hear the wind threshing through the tall pines she knew were up there. Away, way in the distance, she could barely hear the breaking surf of the Tasman's westerly sea surf, but she was safe from all those Goliaths. Nothing could touch her here.

She knew she was in 'the time'. The time Uriah and the priest talked about when they said things would get better 'in time'. She knew most of it was over now. She laughed softly, stopping and starting and chattering to herself. Like a child, she played with the toys of the beach, letting sand spill through her fingers. She collected pieces of river-washed shells and a water-carved length of rimu that looked like an old man and took them back to the rock.

No crying now – too long for tears.
Two people lived dead lives, then died – gone, poor
things like smoke that drifts away, never seen again.
Once, when I was small I twisted thoughts
through tear-wet fingers.
Now my eyes are grown – and dry.
My heart is resting in the alpenglow of my own making.
The 'not-mother' and the 'not-father' aged grey – their
fires dried – too soon.
Sour living drank their sap down into the silence of their
sickness.
Now is the time for my goodbye. And now the sound is
me.
The sand is warm and my heart roars.
Iona's free.

She saw the *Tara* – but not Caleb. "I've hurt him." She knew this now; but not before. She rowed back out and said, "I'm sorry, my dear Cal. I'm so sorry."

They sat in the cockpit – not touching. It was a long time for new-free Iona to be still.

In the late afternoon a shoal of sprats appeared beside the boat, swirling and flicking on the surface. Caleb got up and leant on the cabin's roof, his back telling its own story. And still she waited – hoping.

As dusk threatened, three grey ducks whistled low over the launch. Caleb looked up and watched them veer away from the harbour then turn inland to feed for the night.

"I'm moving us upriver. We need to find a suitable landing to tie up for the night." His voice sounded rusty from lack of use.

He bent his large body in through the cabin door and started to crank the motor. It fired on the third turn, as usual, and he came out, turning up onto the narrow side decking in one fluid movement to run nimbly to the bow, where she lost sight of him as he began to pull up the anchor.

He was a big, deliberate man ashore, but on the boat he looked like a dancer, moving quickly – light and lithe – attuned to the river's music, to the boat's needs, and ever aware of tide times and weather influences.

Iona listened to the rasps of the sodden anchor rope being hauled through the fairlead at the bow and to the rhythmic whumps of the rope as he curled and dropped it to coil on the bow, all in the same process. When the metal chain clanked and the anchor crashed aboard, she turned her head away.

"I will not hurry him," she whispered to the channel waters. "I will not make him feel watched," and she hoped some more, even though fear fell heavy on her shoulders. To lose him after she had fully found him would be too much to bear. "The choice must be his," she told a last and lonely duck, and she wiped the tears from her cheeks lest Caleb see them glisten and be further upset before he was ready to speak.

By the time they found a suitable jetty, halfway up the Helensville Creek, the sky had darkened. Caleb tied up and saw to the launch while Iona went into the cabin and prepared their night meal on the kerosene cooker. This had always been their routine, and she hoped their familiar actions might help them both. The yellow cabin light flickered and died. He came down to replace the battery but still did not speak. He seemed to be in a daze. She knew the bondage of that state well and held her tongue.

During their silent meal she felt his eyes rest on her several times and her heart leapt. When he boiled the water and washed the dishes in the enamel bowl out in the stern counter, she dried them, carefully, and carried them into the cabin. She put them away in the racks of their little cupboard, the cutlery into the miniature drawer. Over their last cup of tea she bowed her head, guarding his secret thoughts that floated, as so often hers had floated, out into the night and back again, changing and sorting themselves and making him vulnerable.

Then, when she thought she could stand it no longer, Caleb took the cup from her hands and, placing it on the cockpit seat, drew her up. He cupped her chin with his hand. The warmth of his skin on hers sent her pulses dancing.

"Are you all right, Iona?"

His breath fell gentle on her face, familiar, bringing fresh tears that teetered on her lashes. "I have found where I am at last, Caleb. Can you understand?"

He nodded. "Wait," he said.

Her body trembled so much she had to sit and calm her thoughts, but it was no use. She could see him moving around the cabin. Watched as he made up a bed on the cabin floor between the narrow bunks and take their pillows and blankets from the bunks, exactly as he had on the first night of their honeymoon – over twelve years ago. The new moon already rested its invitation there.

"Come, darling girl," he whispered, his voice low and husky, and he took her hand and led her towards the cabin he had known since a boy and into his life once more.

"Oh, Cal," she whispered through quivering lips. "I thought I'd hurt you too much for this …"

He smiled his crooked smile and held out his arms. She fell into them and out of the darkness of the lost months. He took off his shirt and wiped her wet eyes. "Blow!" he ordered gruffly as he held the shirt tail to her nose.

She giggled and blew then watched him wipe his own eyes and rub his face. She thought - *I do not deserve this lovely man, but, dear God, thank you for my Caleb.*

"Where have you gone now, my darling Iona Annabel McKay?" he teased.

"I'm right beside you, always and ever, and I love you so very much …"

His lips took her into their magic place, and she melted with him until he undressed her slowly, flavouring her and touching her and drawing her into the power of his love in that same wonderful way he had on their first night together as man and wife.

"My darling, my darling," he moaned and lifting himself, covered her as she longed to be covered, and they moved together into the power of their love and into heights they had never reached before.

Chapter Thirty-five

In the morning light they were a little shy with each other, smiling, touching as they passed, eyes holding eyes in that world where only the heart rules.

They took a walk along the creek bank to stretch their legs, talking in whispers, laughing at nothing, and couldn't believe the depth of their ease.

"It's as if all the years and all their secrets and lies have flown away. I feel so light. Lighter than when I was a child and content to be myself."

Iona's eyes were large with wonder.

"Perhaps I should drag you through another storm if this is what they do to you."

"No, thank you," she smiled up at him. "I've been through all sorts of storms in my time, but yesterday's is the last."

"How do you know that?"

"I believe that yesterday something changed in me. I feel as if I've let Sybil and Grandfather Kelly and the things they did – go right out of my life. They were often like a burden, those things, like an unanswered question that never let me rest. Even Maude seems to have faded in my thoughts. I'm glad, now, she told me the truth – you know, about being my real mother. But her words are not hanging over me any longer."

"That's a bit harsh on Maude, isn't it?"

Iona thought for a minute, and then replied, "I don't mean I've wiped her out of my life. I just have a different view of things now. It's like living in a different place. A place where I can be the person I want. On that shelf of sand yesterday I could see my own mistakes and know I've been forgiven."

He could feel her embarrassment yet she continued despite her discomfort.

"So how can I not forgive them?"

He held her to him and gave her time.

All of a sudden she came to life again. "You know what, Cal? I'm throwing out that wretched red wool. Knitting is in second place now. I'm going to do what I've always wanted to do!"

Caleb stared at her in puzzlement.

"What have you always wanted to do, Iona mine?"

"I've always wanted to paint."

"Well, you are a bunch of surprises this morning. What do you want to paint?"

"Oh, special places on the river, the birds I love and the trees they love – things like that. When we get home I'll show you all my funny drawings I did when I was a kid. Father kept them hidden in his shed in a tatty old box so Mother wouldn't go mad."

"You've never told me all this before."

He knew, from Maude's story, why Sybil had wanted to sequester the child, Iona, but to actually do it to such an extent verged on sin, in his mind.

She read his thought and tugged on his hand so he changed the subject.

"Tell you what. We'll buy you what you need in Auckland tomorrow."

"I didn't know we were going to Auckland. Is this a new surprise?"

"Yes. We're spending a week in a flash hotel. Well, we'll think it flash anyway. How do you like that, Mrs McKay?"

Hesitation showed in her eyes. Then she tipped her head and smiled up at him. "I like it very much, but I thought we only had two weeks away."

"Well, Sam said they could manage three if we had a mind for it."

"Oh, I have a mind for it, Mr McKay," she laughed as he hugged her and nuzzled her neck.

They got to Helensville in plenty of time for Caleb to send off two telegrams: one to Sam and one to Maryanne. 'Can you manage another week?'

By lunchtime the replies were waiting. Maryanne's said, 'Of course. Love Maryanne.' Sam's read, 'We can if you can!'

"Cheeky blighter," chuckled Caleb.

Helensville bustled and buzzed, and so did they; cleaning up and making the *Tara* ship-shape took up all the afternoon. Cal ran up to his parents' home and returned with an invitation to dinner that night. Iona breathed a sigh of relief. A bath and hair wash would have enticed her anywhere after two weeks on the boat, and the visit turned out to be surprisingly nice. On their walk back to the wharf Iona remarked how well Ada and Henry seemed.

"I hope they stay that way for a long time. Mum is not as strong as she used to be, and Dad refuses to leave their house. It'll be a worry if she goes first. Can you imagine him living with us?"

Iona patted his arm. "Don't worry, it may never happen, darling." And racing ahead of him, felt his surprise then heard his footsteps running after her.

"Nothing is going to spoil our holiday," she called back. Caleb beat her, as she knew he would, and by the time she reached the boat's berth, there he stood on *Tara*'s deck with his arms out ready to catch her when she jumped.

"I might knock you flat at your age, Caleb McKay."

"Just be gentle with me," he quipped.

As Iona stepped down the four inches into his arms the launch, riding easy on the high tide, softened into the water, and their laughter floated lightly down the river's stream.

"Cal? Are you awake?"

"I am now. What's the time?"

"Seven o'clock. Cal, I don't really like Auckland."

"No?" He sat up. "Oh, I thought all women liked Auckland."

"Sybil liked Auckland. I didn't. Can we go to Devonport instead?"

She looked up at him like an uncertain child.

God, he thought, *what did they do to her?*

"Of course we can," he shouted and leapt out of the bunk thinking, *how? It's overland. We came by boat and I need a car.* But to Iona he ordered, "You'd better get a bag packed then while I go up town and find out how we get to Devonport!"

The next week took off on its own track.

The manager of the Grand Hotel got them a lift with a travelling salesman.

"Be ready in an hour, Cal. These chaps don't muck around."

Suave, sure of himself and a real comedian, the salesman kept them laughing or amazed or just plain interested until he dropped them off at Takapuna, where they found a bus had left only two minutes before.

"There it goes," a young taxi driver pointed to the fat end of a bus chugging off in the distance. "Do you want me to catch you up with it?"

"You're on," grinned Caleb, and before she knew what was happening, Iona had been bundled into the back seat.

"Hold on, lady," the driver told her and stood on the accelerator with gusto.

The ride, fast and bumpy, had Iona hanging on to the sturdy handle above her seat for dear life, while the boyish excitement of her husband and the driver kept her amused, no matter where she found herself catapulted. As she came back down from nearly touching the roof for the third time, Caleb shouted, "There it is! How much do I owe you?"

"Have you got ten bob?"

"Think so."

Two minutes later Iona and Caleb were trundling along side by side in the bus like a respectable married couple. They reached Devonport and had a cup of tea from the thermos Iona had made before starting out.

Cal left her there, sitting on a park bench, minding their suitcases while he went off to find somewhere to stay. He came back waving a key to a bach. A bach that turned out to be a dear little place set slightly back from Duder's Beach. Each morning they woke to the sound of lapping water, and each day they swam. Out of the way of the summer crowds and yet close enough to watch the boats plying the Waitemata Harbour, it captured Iona's heart.

"I think if I ever had to leave the river, I'd like to live here," she Caleb on the last afternoon of their stay.

"I can't see you ever leaving the north, my girl."

"No. But this is such a happy place. It's airy, and it has a lot of activity to watch on the water. Father loved Devonport."

"Ha! I knew you were a daddy's girl, Iona Annabel Anderson-Keyes."

"Why do you call me that?"

"Because the first time I saw you in that creek paddock, where you nearly tripped me up I might add, that's how you said your name. I can still see you now. Such an unusual, pretty, composed little girl you were."

"It's funny, Cal, but I have no memory of that day at all."

"Of course you don't. You were only twelve and much too interested in uncovering your thistle nut to take any notice of a fifteen-year-old boy. Although you did give me the nut – very gracefully, I might add."

Iona laughed. "Well, you were lucky, my man. I seldom gave those away. They took ages to unravel and were quite delicious."

"It was. And so are you," he murmured as he pulled her to him and kissed her yet again.

"Ah," whispered Iona, "it is so easy to be lazy and loving when the children are not around."

Caleb smiled down at her and wrapped her in his long, eager arms.

"But I have to say I am missing them now, and I'm ready to go home."

"There you go. A man can never compete with children. I will tickle you until you forget all about them for the rest of the day," which suited them both immensely.

The journey home by ferry, train and launch flowed over Iona like a friendly stream. To Iona Uriah's laughter seemed to echo back to her over the choppy little Waitemata waves. The Auckland train station held no bothersome memories of her seventeenth birthday all those years ago, and the train journey out of the city showed her changes in the countryside she'd not remembered during her deep mourning and the shocking disorientation period following Maude's revelations.

Caleb judged the rising Northern Wairoa tide to perfection. There on the Port Albert wharf, as they glided in, were her three beautiful children, jumping and waving, while behind them stood the familiar shapes of Marianne and Seth, their own family gathered respectfully around them, 'dear guardian friends'. Iona, swamped with renewal and gratitude, choked back her tears. The children deserved her happiness.

Once they were back out on the main waters again and the children had settled themselves around her, Iona looked to her river and felt such joy.

Instead of the past riding on her shoulders, all she could think of were her friends. Her old friends like Agnes and Sam and Ani and Paul back in Sedgely where the river would soon meet the skyline. And her family, Teddy and June, her nephews and nieces;

And now her mother, Maude – her real mother, who had been there all those years, watching and praying in the background; "Surely, I have a kind and loving mother," she whispered to the vast sky.

To Sybil's dark shadow she nodded. "Poor, sick-minded woman. Go in peace."

And to Uriah's face with its steady, caring lines, she whispered, "Thank you, Father, protector of a little child."

As if in acceptance, the largest, whitest gull flew in and hovered above the boat then swooped, dipped and soared away.

"Home, river my friend; we're coming home."

Epilogue

In the early autumn of that year, Caleb came around the side of the house and stopped. It was peach bottling time. His wife and their three children were stripping the last of the Golden Queens from the trees down the back. They hadn't seen him and he stood quietly at the corner of the house, unable to move.

"Don't put any more in the wheelbarrow," shouted Danny. "You're not supposed to pile them up."

"Weakling Dan! Weakling Dan!" sang Miriam, wagging her head, laughing. "Can't you wheel a full barrow, Danny Boy?"

"It's not that, Miriam. It's just like Mum says – the ones underneath will bruise with the weight if you put too many on top of them."

"Here's one less then!" She picked up a ripe peach from the barrow and bit deep into its flesh."

"You're such a greedy-guts, Miriam McKay! You've eaten so many you'll be sick all night. Mum wants some left to bottle, you know."

"Have it back then," giggled Miriam, and she threw the half-eaten fruit straight at her brother then took off down the orchard with Dan hot on her heels.

Seven-year-old Jimmy hurled himself out of a tree and whooped after them. The back fence wire twanged – twanged – then twanged again, and Caleb heard their shrieks getting fainter and fainter as they raced through the vacant section. 'They'll be heading for the open paddocks,' he thought.

Caleb's eyes swung back to Iona. She sat slightly back on to him, on a rug on the orchard floor, doing something with the fruit spread out before her – sorting, probably, the rotten from the ripe, and there was something about the way she was sitting that took him back to the first sight he ever had of her – on the side of Kotare Creek. She had been not much older than Miriam that day.

Sometimes the pain of his fear would come on him, his fear that someday she might walk away from him again – into the bush along the river – and disappear out of his life, just as she had disappeared into the rye and long grasses when they had first met. Iona couldn't remember that magical day. Caleb could never forget.

He moved back a step. He did not want her to see these deep emotions. His family knew him as a man steeped in self-control. He was a husband and a father of moderate behaviour, who could be forceful sometimes and given to bouts of wry humour at others. Only Iona knew of his feelings – especially for her – and even she did not know their full strength. He had learnt to be careful with his lovely girl.

In the early years he had thought it was because of her first marriage. At times he wished – irrationally, he knew – that Albert Hammond was alive. It was so hard to fight the ghost of a dead man. Later, he realised it was also because of the Kelly family, and her mother – her two mothers.

Iona half turned. She was expecting another baby, and she looked more than beautiful. It was almost too much for him to bear, smelling her fragrance, knowing those months would be a truer tender, a greater wonder. He was about to retrace his steps when she sensed him near.

"Cal?" she called and held out her hand.

He went down into the misty light; her eyes, still the deep purple-blue of the child, shone true and free.

"Iona …?"

She reached up. Her fingers warm as she placed a blushing peach into his rough, work-worn hand.

THE END

And the story continues…

River at War is the story of Miriam, the daughter of Iona, who is now an adolescent, strong minded, resolute and loving, reaching maturity in the troubled times of the Second World War. When war breaks out life in Sedgely changes for everyone. Will Miriam's loved one return? Will her country be safe? Will her work, family and two careers be too much for her young shoulders? It

takes courage to survive the demands of these distressing times.

This is a feisty book that encompasses more than Miriam and her family. It is alive with the throb of friends, their town and their hardships. Raw, gentle, gutsy, it is sprinkled with humour and backboned with courage. New Zealand as it used to be.

Please consider posting a review of this book on Amazon, Goodreads, or any social media, to help other readers to find the author.